TEMPTING THE SCOUNDREL

TEMPTING THE SCOUNDREL

Private Arrangements
#2

Katrina Kendrick

An Aria Book

First published in the UK in 2023 by Head of Zeus,
part of Bloomsbury Publishing Plc

9 7 5 3 1 2 4 6 8

A catalogue record for this book is available from the British Library.

ISBN (PB): 9781837930999
ISBN (E): 9781837930982

Cover design: HoZ / Meg Shepherd & Jessie Price

Typeset by Siliconchips Services Ltd UK

Printed and bound in Great Britain by
CPI Group (UK) Ltd, Croydon CRO 4YY

Head of Zeus
First Floor East
5–8 Hardwick Street
London ECIR 4RG

WWW.HEADOFZEUS.COM

For those who love second chances as much as I do.

PROLOGUE

LONDON, 1868

Four years ago

Tonight was Nicholas Thorne's last heist.

Rumours swirled that the Earl of Kent's mistress had a vast jewellery collection to rival the queen. If those whispers were the slightest bit true, Thorne would have quite a bounty by morning. He'd stolen many jewels, of course – necklaces, bracelets, rings, earrings, even hair combs. Whatever they wore, he lifted with little difficulty at all.

As effortless as breathing. It only took patience.

And Thorne was a patient man. He had cased the townhouse for over a month, but he needn't have taken so long. Few people came and went: the earl himself, his mistress, and her servants. There wasn't a single guard or intimidating footman in sight – the place was unprotected.

Thorne could not imagine such comfort. He'd seen the size of the rock Mrs Cecilia Dunn donned to the theatre a fortnight ago. There was a certain arrogance in wearing a fortune around one's throat, secure in knowing its absence would mean nothing. Her life would not change.

In Thorne's case, it meant freedom. Influence.

Power.

He was taking it one day at a time. One jewel at a time.

Fuck the rich wasn't his life's motto; it meant the difference between living and dying in the streets these aristos shunned and regarded with disgust. The Old Nichol wasn't kind, but it was home. With his stolen fortune, Thorne would seize control of the East End from the man who'd made him into a criminal.

But first, the jewels.

He slipped through the garden and round to the servants' entrance.

The house was quiet, every light extinguished. The servants would be long abed by now. Thorne had memorised their schedules, right down to when the scullery maid laid her weary head down to rest. He wouldn't risk being thrown in gaol on his last night of thieving.

"Last time," he murmured to himself, a reassurance. Last time.

Last. Time.

Thorne pulled the small bundle of tools from his pocket and went to work on the lock. It was so simple he almost scowled. But money and comfort created a false sense of security – he knew that well enough. The woman's neighbours were successful actresses, other mistresses, businessmen, writers, and artists. They had no reason to secure their homes with anything more than a flimsy lock.

Thorne might have ruminated on the unfairness of it once. When he was younger, his low birth occupied his thoughts. Huddled in the cold, dark cellar with Whelan's lads, he convinced himself it was God's punishment. Maybe for all the thieving. Or for the people Whelan made him kill for shelter, food, and protection on the streets.

Later, he'd lie in bed at night and decide the answer was more straightforward: God didn't give a shit about him. He'd have to change his own destiny.

Last. Bloody. Time.

He slipped through the kitchens and headed up the stairs, his steps slow and quiet. Mrs Dunn would not return soon. Earlier in the evening, it took three maids to prepare her for a gathering that would likely last until the sun peeked through the morning fog. As for the Earl of Kent, he was scarce on Sundays.

Thorne had hours; all he needed was minutes.

The bedchamber was redolent with the scent of perfume, something floral that made his nose itch. He picked his way through the various drawers on the dressing table.

The creams alone were worth enough to buy a starving family food for a year. That didn't even get into the cost of this woman's clothes and baubles. The lowest silver spoon could pay what Thorne owed Whelan for protection this month.

Ahh. There we are.

At the back of the drawer, Thorne spied a hidden compartment with a tiny lock. He almost laughed at the absurdity of it. That might keep the servants from slipping a diamond necklace into their pockets, but it wouldn't stop the greenest of thieves. He had the mechanism picked within seconds.

The sight inside made Thorne draw a breath.

Diamonds, rubies, sapphires, and emeralds – thrown in carelessly. As if they were worth less than a secondhand pair of boots. Mrs Dunn was about to regret her negligence. The whole bloody collection would be enough to pay his debts to Whelan – hell, the debts of every lad who owed Whelan blunt.

Money came with power – an end to thieving.

How could he turn down the opportunity? Thorne didn't care about morality; desperate men couldn't afford principles. Not when they answered to a man who demanded payment for services rendered. Not when those services included protection at a steep cost.

No, he had little time for guilt. That was for those with choices.

Thorne stuffed the jewellery into his bag: every diamond necklace, every earring, every sapphire-encrusted hair comb, every bracelet. Even fenced at a fraction of its worth, this was more money than he'd ever seen in his worthless life.

Wait.

Out of the corner of his eye, the shadows shifted. Thorne paused and slowly turned his head.

George Grey, the Earl of Kent, sat in the shadowed recesses of the room. He sipped from a glass of port and watched as his mistress's jewellery disappeared into the cloth bag of a thief.

Thorne lunged for the door, but the earl's voice rang behind him. "I've got the authorities waiting outside for my command, so you might as well stay for a while."

Thorne growled low in his throat, conscious of his purloined haul weighing heavy on his back. "How did you know I'd come?"

The earl smiled into his glass, a cruel twist of lips that spoke of broken hearts and cold revenge. "You've stolen from friends of mine. So I had my mistress wear something expensive enough to tempt you."

"Tell the coppers, then," Thorne said, wheeling around. "Have me arrested."

The other man's eyes glittered in the darkness. "And if I had them sent away? Told them you never showed?"

Thorne's laugh was dry. This man wasn't about to let Thorne walk with a sack full of his woman's jewels out of charity. No, this toff wanted something. They always wanted something.

"What's your favour?" Thorne asked.

"Addington's widow mentioned that when you stole her diamonds, she thought you were a nobleman. But you're Irish?"

Throne returned his stare evenly and offered an icy smile. "Yes," Thorne said, enunciating the word slowly, using the earl's posh accent. "And I can mimic any accent I like, even yours."

The earl laughed. "You're perfect."

Thorne had a decent understanding of toffs, but the vicious delight in Kent's expression surprised him. "For what?"

Kent leaned forward into a ray of moonlight that illuminated his face like a halo of hellfire. "What if I let you keep those jewels and more besides?"

Thorne's eyes narrowed. "I've a mate who'll let you stick your cock in him for a hell of a lot less than that."

"For God's sake, man, I'm not asking about buggery. This is a business proposal."

"Don't make deals with toffs," Thorne said, reaching for the door.

"Not even for one hundred thousand pounds?"

Thorne froze, his hand on the doorknob. His heart stuttered in his chest.

Surely he'd heard wrong.

But no, that devil in the darkness smiled and repeated the impossible sum. "That's right. One hundred thousand pounds. I'll even include the jewellery. All you have to do is pretend to be a nobleman."

Experience had taught Thorne to be suspicious of all aristos. They were a selfish lot – willing to throw a child under the nearest carriage wheel if it benefitted them. Their charity did not come without a price, especially not for men like Thorne.

But for that amount of blunt, he'd consider the game.

"For how long?"

The earl lifted a shoulder and sipped his port. "However long it takes. Three months, let's say."

Thorne chuckled. "I apologise," he said, flawlessly mimicking the earl's accent. "I may sound like a lord, but the act is only intended to last as long as it takes to make off with a lady's valuables." When the earl remained silent in shock, Thorne added, "You like that, eh? I ain't from St James's. You lot have rules I've never even heard of."

"Rules?" Kent tilted his head. "Etiquette, you mean?"

"Sure, start there."

Kent didn't seem worried. "You'll receive lessons. I recently acquired the estate next to mine in a card game. You'll stay there, pretending to be some low-born chancer who inherited a title from a distant relation. Any holes in your performance will be attributed to your low birth. It need only last long enough to make her like you."

This toff was mad, he was. Cracked in the head. A Bedlamite with a posh title and more money than sense. "Who are we talking about?" Thorne asked.

The earl's face hardened. "My wife's bastard. You'll pose as a nobleman, seduce her, and marry her."

This was too much. Thorne rubbed his forehead with the back of a hand. "Not interested. Best of luck with" – he gestured vaguely – "all that."

All that shite.

Thorne had wrenched open the door when the earl spoke again. "It's this or the gaol. And the prison cell doesn't come with one hundred thousand pounds and a sack full of jewels."

He shut the door with a snick. *One hundred thousand pounds. One hundred thousand pounds. Christ.* Thorne thought he'd imagined that part. "Why not marry her off to some aristo with a gamblin' problem? One or two of 'em are bound to be desperate enough to marry a lass born on the wrong side of the blanket."

Kent sneered. "My wife made sure I believed the child was mine before she passed. I only found out about the deceit from her diary."

Brilliant. Thorne had come for jewels, but now he was dealing with family drama. "You're tellin' me your wife's daughter doesn't know about any of this?"

"She'll comprehend after I see her married off to a baseborn man as she deserves. That you're an Irishman and a criminal only adds insult to injury."

Thorne's expression hardened. *Baseborn. Irishman.*

Criminal. Aye, that'd put him lower than shit in the eyes of an aristocrat. He almost felt sorry for the lass; as far as she knew, she was legitimate – and the man she thought was her father planned to marry her off to a confidence artist.

Toffs were a callous lot.

"I suppose it's generous of you to settle one hundred thousand pounds on a bastard rather than tossing her into the street."

Kent didn't indicate he'd heard Thorne's sarcasm. "I wouldn't settle a farthing on the chit, but my wife ensured the money was put in a trust. If Alexandra doesn't marry in the next three years, the fortune is hers by law. I won't let that happen. Do you understand?"

Thorne shrugged. "Don't care."

He wasn't interested. Not about anything other than the money and how to get it.

"Mm." Kent sipped his port. "The girl is staying in Hampshire at present. I'll throw in an extra thousand pounds if you persuade her to elope with you by Michaelmas."

Good God. Thorne couldn't help but rear back in disgust. "That desperate to be rid of her?"

The temperature in the room plummeted at Kent's icy stare. "My wife made me look like a bloody fool. Since she's not alive, I'll do the same to her daughter. Do we have a deal or not?"

Thorne exhaled slowly through his teeth. "For one hundred thousand pounds, I don't care if she looks like a fool. But I'll take some blunt upfront for takin' her off your hands."

Kent's smile was slow, as sharp as cut glass. "I would expect nothing less of a criminal."

1

LONDON

Four years later

Lady Alexandra Grey flung the newspaper aside with a frustrated noise. "Bloody hell," she muttered.

Her brother, Richard, watched the broadsheet flutter to the floor like an injured dove. The startled footman waiting by the breakfast sideboard delicately cleared his throat. Barnes might as well have said, *For the love of God, instruct me on how to respond to this*. Alexandra ought to have commended him on his measured expression; one really only saw it in place for recalcitrant children.

"Hand it here, Barnes," Richard told the footman. "I'd like to read it before she burns this one."

"Don't bother," Alexandra said, angrily buttering her toast. "It's absolute rubbish. Dross. A waste of paper and ink. Who told men they could publish?"

Barnes hesitated, but at Richard's gesture, handed the paper over. Richard took it and murmured a calm dismissal meant to soothe a servant who'd grown accustomed to the mercurial moods of his master's sister. Alexandra had made a recent habit of visiting Richard's townhouse to drink his coffee, break her fast, and destroy his newspapers.

No, no, it wasn't an *intention*. That implied Alexandra found some perverse joy in setting fire to the dull words of mediocre men. Rather, it was their topic of choice over the last few months: her.

Well, and her complete bastard of a husband.

Since her disastrous marriage leaked to London's gossips, she'd had no peace. Everyone knew Nicholas Thorne was her husband.

Lady Alexandra Grey, secretly married to a gaming hell owner. It was the scandal of the year! Why, rumour had it that her husband was a former criminal who blackmailed politicians! He had the distinction of being loathed by *both* Houses of Parliament.

Husband, *bah*. Alexandra tore into her buttered toast. That was too kind a word. Nick was a pestilence. A grotesque, scabby pestilence. Something that ended in agony and suffering. After the sores.

A deep sigh from the other side of the table stirred Alexandra's attention. "What?" she asked, her voice a touch too sharp.

Richard regarded her with that indulgent look that always made her feel like an unruly orphan – or, worse still, a miscreant lunatic. His gaze seemed to say: *You're spending too much time alone, and you're coming undone. Your hair looks like a family of birds has nested in it. I can't believe you married a degenerate from Bethnal Green four years ago – and our cad of a father was the only one who knew.*

If the previous Earl of Kent hadn't unexpectedly died

in the middle of the soup course over three years ago, Alexandra would have considered patricide. This entire stupid mess was his fault.

"Don't look at me like that," Alexandra told her brother. "It's only *The Times*. You don't even enjoy reading it."

"No," Richard admitted, drinking his coffee. "I'm not expecting any unique insight from a Tory newspaper. But I do require some knowledge of their views."

"Yes, well, their current view is that I represent yet another wayward example of traditional values gone awry. They suggested James consider sending me to an asylum once he returns from his honeymoon. There. What else shall I tell you from this lovely Tory newspaper?"

Richard sighed. "Alexandra."

"What?" Alexandra scowled at her brother, who replied with a mere raise of his eyebrow. "I told you not to look at me like that."

"Like what? I'm not looking at you in any particular way." He gave her an innocent shrug and reached for his coffee cup.

"I'm fine," she muttered.

"This is the sixth broadsheet I've saved from you. The other twelve are, sadly, ashes in the fireplace. Now, let me look at this without your input." He shuffled through the pages until he located the one that had sparked her ire. "Ah," he said under his breath.

Anne strolled into the room at that moment, humming a cheerful tune. "Oh, is that *The Times*? May I see it?" Without waiting for a response, she plucked the paper from Richard's hands and studied the page. Her eyes widened, her mouth dropped slightly, and she said, "Ah."

"*Ah?* Why does everyone say *ah?*" Alexandra grumbled, setting down her knife with a clatter. "It's a silly illustration drawn by a man of middling talent."

Anne pursed her lips and settled into her seat. "The drawing is…" She glanced at Richard, as if for assistance.

"Interesting," he finished, hiding his wince behind his hand. "The horns, particularly. It's very, erm, animated."

"It means nothing," Anne smoothed over, eyeing her husband. "They depicted me as a crying mess outside the courthouse. The illustrations are always unflattering."

Anne's father, a prominent member of the Conservative shadow cabinet, had confessed to covering up the crimes of a critical ally in Parliament – and Anne's former fiancé. Anne and Richard blew the lid off their corruption, setting off a parliamentary upheaval.

Stanton Sheffield leaked Alexandra's secret marriage to the papers, hoping to ruin the Grey family's reputation. It nearly worked. In the following months, articles pinned the blame for the political chaos on Anne. Richard paid off and intimidated columnists to print the truth: Anne had come forward against her father at significant personal risk.

Richard's efforts were rewarded. He and Anne received a deluge of invitations to every party, gathering, and ball in Britain. Everyone wanted to know how Anne had coped with living in her father's brutal household.

But as much as Richard had rehabilitated his wife's reputation in the public eye, he couldn't do the same for his sister. Not without exposing the fact that their father engineered her disastrous marriage.

"Even charities are turning me away because they don't

want to be the subject of malicious gossip," Alexandra muttered.

"Oh, dear." Anne winced.

"At least they were perfectly nice about it when they slammed the door in my face," Alexandra added.

"Good God, you need to get out of London," Richard said immediately. He went to the sideboard to gather his wife some breakfast. "Anne and I have an invitation to the Pemberton house party in Yorkshire. Say the word, and we'll take you along."

"I can't."

"Why not? I've heard Yorkshire is stunning in the autumn," Anne said, taking the plate from Richard.

"I have work to do," Alexandra reminded them. "All my sources are here. I'm in the middle of a manuscript."

One that would create even more scandal if it came out, but that was neither here nor there.

"Luckily for you," Richard chimed in, "the Pemberton house party only lasts a fortnight. Your work can survive the hiatus."

Alexandra sighed. "Fine, I'll get straight to the point. Lady Pemberton loathes me. I once called her husband a windbagging idiot." At Richard's raised eyebrow, she continued, "He said that women didn't have the brains or depth to comprehend political affairs. It doesn't help that their cousins, the Astleys, own factories I've criticised for being unsafe for workers, and—" Anne and Richard exchanged a knowing look, which Alexandra caught. "I see you two communicating telepathically in that grotesque way people in love do. Out with it."

"New strategy," Richard proposed. "Is there anyone who doesn't hate you?"

"*Richard*." Anne elbowed him in the side. "What he means is… dear, is there anyone we may call upon? The sooner we have support, the better."

Alexandra put her cup down gently. "I have friends." Her brother and Anne both seemed relieved until Alexandra continued. "But they've asked me to stay away. Being associated with the wife of a gaming hell owner would ruin their marriage prospects."

Richard shifted in his seat. "Thorne is an ally—"

"But only yours," Alexandra said, pushing away from the table. "From what I understand, he's a useful associate to have if you want to threaten someone. He's good for little else." Richard opened his mouth to speak, but she held up a hand. "I have an entire box of the articles he's submitted to the newspapers about my work – none of them complimentary. He might make you a decent ally, but he's a lousy husband."

Her brother let out a breath. "Fair enough."

"Just take care that Nick's not using you, Richard. I've endured too many deceptions to bear another at his hands." She glanced at Anne and gestured at the broadsheet. "May I have that? I'd find it cathartic to watch it go up in flames."

Anne offered the paper to her, studying the caricature with a critical eye. "Well," she said, "at least you seem to have the devil in your thrall, don't you?"

"I should hope so," Alexandra said dryly, "considering he's my husband."

2

The Brimstone was Thorne's pride and joy.

Those in Whitechapel often desired a place to call their own – but few got out from under the boot of a landlord. It was the cold, hard reality of the East End that you were born with nothing, you lived with nothing, and you died with nothing. Possessions were as easy to keep as a fistful of sand. There wasn't a thing you owned that wasn't up for sale to pay the landlord just to ease that boot off your neck for a short while.

That could have been Thorne's fate had it not been for Lady Alexandra Grey's money.

That fortune had helped make him the most powerful man in the East End – in all of London, some claimed.

But Thorne didn't give a shit about the rest of London. He surveyed his club from the balcony of his private wing, watching as rich men spent their money. He used that income to pay his workers. To take care of the people in his streets. To house them, feed them, and put clothes on their backs if needed.

They called him King of the East End. The moniker chafed; monarchs, after all, built fortunes off the exploitation of labourers. Thorne was a republican – an Irishman – but he knew the burden of being responsible for people. He took it seriously.

And all he'd lost to gain this immense fortune was a woman's trust. Some might consider that trifling. What did trust matter compared with security, food, money, power? So much to gain, such a small thing to sacrifice.

Except for one problem: Thorne had been fool enough to fall in love with her.

He thought of Alex too often these days. He heard her name whispered in the dark corners of his club, where members figured he couldn't hear.

Lady Alexandra Grey and Nicholas Thorne. Secret marriage. Gretna Green, four years ago. Can you believe a lady marrying that bastard? Pfft. Not a lady, anyway. She's a bloody suffragette with nice tits and a shrill mouth.

Thorne had taken a lord outside for that last one. Asked which arm he favoured.

And broke it.

"Looks like you could use a drink," a voice interrupted Thorne's thoughts.

He turned to see Leo O'Sullivan, his trusted friend and factotum, standing behind him.

"How can you tell?" Thorne asked, his tone dry.

"Might be because you're scowling at the customers like a fucking gargoyle," Leo replied with a smirk.

There were few people Thorne trusted with his life, but O'Sullivan was one of them. They had grown up together on the streets of the Nichol, stealing and fighting to survive. They had been through hell and back.

O'Sullivan joined Thorne on the balcony. It wasn't just his height and build that caught people's attention. O'Sullivan's face was almost too pretty for a man, his features sharp and striking. It made him seem almost untouchable, intimidating even.

Thorne knew better, though. He knew that pretty faces hid broken people.

"I'm not scowling," Thorne said, leaning against the balcony railing. "I'm watching."

O'Sullivan chuckled, a deep rumble in his chest. "Sure thing, boss."

Thorne gave him a look before turning his attention back to the bustling club below. The sounds of laughter and conversation filled his ears, mingling with the scent of cigar smoke and fine spirits. It was all so familiar, so comforting. The buzz of his business was like a drug, heating his blood and fuelling his ambitions.

Thorne knew he was a ruthless businessman, a cutthroat in a world of cutthroats. But he also knew that he had to be that way if he wanted to survive. In the Nichol, weakness was death.

And Thorne refused to be weak again.

But he'd come a long way from those days. Now, he owned one of the most successful establishments in London, and the city's wealthiest and most powerful men owed him their debts.

But some of those bastards were struggling to pay up.

"Latimer's playing deep again," Thorne grumbled, his annoyance palpable.

"Should I remove him?" O'Sullivan asked, his fists clenching at his sides. "That stupid bastard has the highest number in the books."

Thorne shook his head. "Let him be. If he wants to destroy his life, that's his problem. If he can't pay up, we'll visit his house and take some antiques off his hands."

O'Sullivan snorted. "Assuming they cover what he owes. I've seen that fool get shite deep in a single night."

"Then take the house," Thorne said simply.

Thorne kept a close eye on the hazard tables, scanning the faces of the players for any sign of cheating. Two of the blokes looked nervous, their eyes darting around the room like caged animals. Thorne signalled to one of his employees, a slight raise of one finger, then two, with a nod towards the men of interest.

He didn't need to explain himself. The Brimstone was a well-oiled machine, with every employee loyal to its owner. They knew his every mood, his every gesture, his every need. And Thorne rewarded them generously, paying them wages unheard of in Whitechapel. He supported their families, children, and wives. His protection came without strings attached. Unlike Whelan, he didn't demand that they steal or kill for him.

What did they offer? Respect, that was all. In Whitechapel, respect was worth its weight in gold.

"Shipments come in?" he asked O'Sullivan.

"Whiskey, cards, chips accounted for. Food shipment's late, and Burke's got his dander up. Might want to avoid the kitchens tonight."

Burke, their cook, was known for his temperamental nature, especially regarding his cuisine. He may not have had any formal training, but his dishes were some of the best in London. And he had a reputation to uphold.

Thorne knew the game well. If he wanted the rich and powerful to spend their fortunes every night, he had to provide them with comfort: good food, good drink, proximity to brothels, and a few well-placed bribes to keep the coppers at bay.

"Damn," Thorne muttered. "All right. Get 'em drunk and bring in some ladies from Maxine's. With a woman in their laps, they won't give a shit about eating."

O'Sullivan chuckled. "Anything else?"

Thorne spotted a familiar face in the crowd, one that made him swear and push away from the balcony. "Yeah. Tell Matty I'll break his face if he's late with that food shipment again."

Thorne strode down the public staircase, his gaze sweeping over the hazard tables and the players gathered around them.

People greeted him as he passed, some of his employees, a few members of Parliament and aristos. He didn't consider them his friends, but this was his establishment, and if they treated him with respect, they were welcome to stay. When they forgot it, Thorne knew how to deal with disrespect in his own way.

He was a master of destroying men, both inside and out.

Some of that skill he learned from Richard Grey. Sure, his brother-in-law looked like a gentleman, talked like a gentleman, and played cards with the incompetence of a gentleman, but Thorne knew better. Grey was one of the

most accomplished political schemers Thorne knew. They'd
worked together from time to time when a bill needed to be
whipped. The toffs in Parliament didn't give a damn about
the East End, but they did care about their pockets. That
was where Thorne and Grey came in, whispering in their
ears and making sure the right palms were greased and the
right threats were made.

'Course, at the time, Grey wasn't aware that Thorne was
his brother-in-law. Thorne had been expecting this visit for
a while.

He leaned against the table. "Got something to say to
me, Grey?"

The blond man leaned back in his chair, surveying his
cards. "Just visiting my brother-in-law's establishment," he
replied coolly.

The other aristos at the table looked over in shock, their
eyes widening at the reminder. By now, the entire city knew
of Thorne's marriage to Alexandra Grey. Four years ago,
she had demanded they keep it a secret, and Thorne, still
wracked with guilt over betraying her, had agreed.

Could Thorne blame her? No. She had gone to the altar
thinking she had married a nobleman and left married to a
criminal. He deserved her disgust, had grown used to being
her shameful secret.

Now that their marriage was public, she probably hated
him more.

Thorne clapped Richard on the shoulder and beckoned
with his fingers. "Deal him out, Doyle," he said, then strode
off without another word.

"I was enjoying that game," Richard said, as they walked
down the hallway towards Thorne's private wing.

"You were about to lose one hundred pounds," Thorne shot back.

"Money I could stand to lose for the enjoyment of seeing you this angry at my presence." Richard leaned his shoulder against the wall. "You're positively glowing with indignation."

Thorne whirled on Richard. They were alone in the hallway. It was as good a place as any to have words with his brother-in-law. "You want to lose one hundred quid and line my pockets just to annoy me? Have at it."

Richard's smirk widened. "If you wanted me to do that, you should have left me to the game. I've never been terribly good at whist."

Thorne's lips curled in disdain. "You aristos and money. Wasting it is about the only thing you're good for."

"Nicholas Thorne, criticising another man for having too much money?" Richard barked a laugh. "Now there's hypocrisy if ever I saw it. You're one of the wealthiest bastards in England."

Thorne's eyes were black pools in the firelight. "Having too much coin is one thing, pissing it away is another." He bit out his words, voice low and dangerous. He crossed his arms over his broad chest. "Now, stop wasting my time. Finish it. Hit me in the face."

Richard raised an eyebrow, looking thoroughly bemused. "Are you foxed?"

"If only," Thorne muttered ruefully. "See, I reckon I owe two punches: one for not telling you Alex was my wife, the other for dragging her through this hellish ordeal. So go on, then. Let's get it over with."

Richard took a step back. "Good Lord, man. I'm not

here to beat the shit out of you. I'm here to tell you to see my sister. She's a wreck, Thorne."

Thorne snorted. "She'll be fine. Not having her bastard husband around will make it easier for her."

His brother-in-law pushed away from the wall. "You really are a stupid sod. I hadn't planned to punch you in the face, but perhaps I should."

"Then do it," Thorne declared, extending his arms wide in invitation.

"Listen to me, you stubborn idiot," Richard growled, advancing closer still. "Alexandra refuses to withdraw to the country because of her work, and I can't leave her alone in London. I don't know where my brother is or when he plans to return from his honeymoon."

"Then stay in London until Kent returns. Easy."

Richard ran his fingers roughly through his hair. "My hands are tied," he said quietly – then his expression melted of its former severity. "Anne is with child. She's not showing yet, but she'll enter confinement soon. We're planning to stay in Hampshire until next season."

"My congratulations," he forced the words out, his voice devoid of emotion.

"Go see Alexandra," Richard repeated, tiredly. "Act like a husband, for once."

Deep in Thorn's heart, something ached for what might have been with Alexandra if he'd been more than a bad husband. All the possibilities that had never come to pass, children they would never share, a future thrown away the second she learned his lies.

And now his reputation had sullied her own, ensuring

the scornful glares of society and leaving her isolated from those that once called themselves friends.

"Her maids talk, Grey. I know she's been shunned by those nobs. You might have given her some warning that you'd made an enemy of the most corrupt politician in Parliament."

Richard's expression darkened. "There wasn't time—"

"I know it. I don't blame you for damaging a woman's social connections. They're easy enough to lose if you marry a man born on the wrong side of the blanket and on the wrong street."

Richard whistled. "Look at you. You speak quite prettily when the mood strikes."

"Aye. I learned it from your father."

The other man went quiet. He stared at Thorne with an unnerving astuteness, but then, he had a habit of turning those pretty blue eyes on a person and making them feel like baring their soul.

Thorne just didn't have a soul to bare.

"My sister told me everything," Richard said. "Including your deal with the old earl."

"Yes, I made a deal with the old earl," he said, his voice low and tight. "And yes, I'm no good for Alex."

Their marriage was undeniable proof that Thorne was a deceitful blackguard. There wasn't a person alive who wouldn't empathise with a lass swindled by a man who lied about being a lord.

Richard raised an eyebrow. "You call her Alex?"

"She can be *Lady Alexandra* if you like. I don't give a damn." Thorne brushed past Richard. "If you'll excuse me, I have work to do. Give my regards to your wife."

He turned to leave, eager to escape the suffocating weight of Richard's judgement.

His brother-in-law's words echoed down the corridor. "You've got to speak to her sometime, Thorne."

"Mind your own damn business, Grey," Thorne called back.

The knock came at Thorne's office door during the very early hours of the morning. He had been at his desk, poring over the club's books – a distraction that kept his mind calm.

Words were difficult for him; he found reading a chore. Numbers, on the other hand, made sense. There was no emotional burden connected with the tallying of sums, the ease of arithmetic, the number of wine bottles, spirits, and card packs. For a few moments, he could forget the club, his errant wife, the dagger in his heart that twisted when he remembered making love to her.

Christ, he wanted to be here until morning. Tallying until he was too exhausted to think of Alex.

But someone knocked again.

"Come in," he called, setting down his pen. O'Sullivan appeared in the doorway, his face grim. Thorne braced himself. Bad news always travelled fast in Whitechapel. "What is it?"

O'Sullivan let out a gusty breath. "It's Mary Watkins."

"Flower-seller, aye?" Thorne's expression hardened. "If her brother's returned to beat her again—"

"She's dead," O'Sullivan said, then he swore. "Murdered."

Thorne shoved his chair away from his desk and rose. "Find her brother. Bring him to me."

O'Sullivan shook his head. "I don't think he was involved. You… You need to come see this."

The look on the other man's face was alarming. Thorne and O'Sullivan had grown up in the Nichol – some of the worst streets in the East End. They made the rest look peaceful in comparison. Corpses were a sight more common than blue skies. While there were a thousand ways to die in the East End, murder was a frequent cause. Thorne and O'Sullivan had contributed a few in their day.

That's why Thorne followed O'Sullivan out of the Brimstone without question.

Anyone from outside those streets might have hurried through them. The East End had an atmosphere that repulsed those unused to the overwhelming, burning odour of the coal fire that kept families warm even as it choked them.

But it was home. Even its ugliest, most violent parts were under Thorne's skin, in his blood, marked on his bones.

At the end of an alleyway stood the silhouettes of Casey and McCabe. The two men each raised a hand in greeting, but Thorne didn't return it. He examined the shadowed corpse on the ground; already, the stench had started to waft through the alleyway, mingling with the sharp tang of vomit nearby. Thorne didn't blame whoever had thrown up, not after he saw what happened to Mary.

"Bastard slit 'er throat twice, boss," Casey said. "Fuckin' sweet lass, she was. Christ."

Thorne kneeled beside Mary. "That she was," he murmured, trying to avoid staring at her face. "Casey, McCabe, run to find a constable. Off you go." As the other men left, Thorne looked up at O'Sullivan. "You don't think her brother did this?"

Thorne slipped back into his old accent like a worn pair of leather boots. He'd never be wholly rid of the Irish lilt, courtesy of being raised by a ma from the streets of Dublin. His work with toffs taught him to soften it, but every so often, those dropped letters reminded him of where he came from. Here, the streets, not far from this corpse.

O'Sullivan shook his head, the droplets of rain sliding off his spectacles. He was well accustomed to the weather, having spent his earliest years with his mammy in Cork before her passing. He was sent to London to live with his uncle, who perished six months later after a bad spate of bilious fever. Left alone, like Thorne, he had been forced to rely on his wits to survive in a world where men preyed on desperate lads in search of food and shelter.

"Baily's a fool," O'Sullivan said, "but he values his life enough not to bait you. Whoever did this wanted you to see her." The other man passed Thorne a scrap of paper. "She had this in her hand when the lads found her."

Thorne frowned, holding the folded note up to the lantern O'Sullivan held. "What is it? Page from a book? Mary couldn't read."

"Whoever killed her put it there. You might recognise the book it's from," O'Sullivan said, his eyes meeting Thorne's. "Your wife wrote it."

ᴄᴍ 3 ᴄᴍ

Alexandra stormed into her solicitor's office, slamming the door behind her. "Tell me what I need to do to petition for divorce."

The morning had been a complete shambles. First, another mortifying illustration in the dailies. Then, some insufferable suffragists dared to kick her out of their meeting. And to top it all off, the milliner had given her the coldest reception she had ever received.

Even the damn hats seemed to sneer at her.

Annabel Dawes peered up from her desk, one eyebrow raised, with a habitual stern expression that had been known to make grown men tremble. Alexandra estimated Annabel's age to be somewhere in her early thirties, but it was hard to tell. Her brown skin was as smooth as silk, unmarred by any laugh lines. Alexandra had never even seen her crack a smile. All she knew about Annabel and her brother Benjamin was that they were born to an Indian mother and an English father in Calcutta, and they left India after the Sepoy Mutiny. Their grandfather had raised them, and while he paid for Ben's education, Annabel benefitted from private tutors. But both siblings shared a passion for law.

Though Miss Dawes held the title of *clerk* – women, after all, were barred from practising law – she counselled out of her brother's offices. On paper, Benjamin Dawes was the sole solicitor at B. Dawes, Esq. In truth, his sister ran half his firm and did everything short of litigating cases in court.

Putting down her pen, Miss Dawes leaned back in her chair and regarded Alexandra calmly. "Very well," she said, her accent still carrying the lilt of Urdu. "Reason cited?"

Alexandra paced back and forth on the plush carpet, the thudding of her boots filling the room. "He's a complete scoundrel, a blackguard, and a cad. I loathe him with every fibre of my being."

Miss Dawes raised an elegant eyebrow. "You've just described half the marriages in the *ton*. The court will need more than mere loathing to grant a divorce."

"He married me under false pretences," Alexandra said through gritted teeth.

Miss Dawes sat up straight, her expression intent. "Have you seen the marriage lines? Did he sign under a false name?"

"He signed his real name while I was distracted, damn his eyes," Alexandra admitted. "But surely Mr Dawes can—"

"No," Miss Dawes cut in with a sigh, a strand of black hair escaping her neat chignon. "If your husband contests the petition, he could argue that your four-year marriage constitutes tacit acceptance of the union. Imagine it from the judge's perspective: if you truly felt deceived, you would have sought an annulment as soon as you uncovered Mr Thorne's deceit. But it's been over four years."

Only Mr and Miss Dawes knew of Alexandra's marriage before the gossipmongers got wind of it. For the first two years, any money she earned from publishing belonged to Nick by law. But with the passing of the Married Women's Property Act, Alexandra finally had control of her income.

She paused, her gloved fingers pressing together. "I was devastated, Annabel," she said, her voice barely above a whisper. "I wanted…"

She wanted to forget. To erase the memories of a love that had turned sour with deception.

As if sensing Alexandra's thoughts, Miss Dawes's expression softened. "I understand," she said sympathetically. "But my role here is to advise you on the most likely outcome."

"Then advise me on another option."

Miss Dawes hesitated, choosing her words with care. "Ben could make a case for cruelty."

Something tightened in Alexandra's chest. "But Nick hasn't harmed me. Not in that way."

At least not in a way that would matter to a judge; the law did not recognise betrayal as grounds for cruelty. Broken hearts stayed tucked away, concealed from the outside world – carrying the burden of marriage, always hidden and always aching.

"Mr Thorne holds no goodwill in Parliament," Miss Dawes stated. "He hasn't bothered to deny the rumours circulating about him for years. If you claim he was cruel to you, the public will believe it. *A judge* will believe it, no matter how well Mr Thorne argues in his defence."

The pressure in Alexandra's chest constricted. "But it would be a lie."

"Yes." Miss Dawes leaned forward, her golden eyes fixed on Alexandra's face. "But these cases always come down to public opinion. Spectators will gawp at you from the gallery, and they'll decide whether what you say is true or false. Your entire marriage will become a subject of public debate, no matter how we frame our case. You know that."

Alexandra's legs felt shaky, and as she sank into the chair opposite Miss Dawes, her anger dissipated, leaving only weariness. "I can't do that," she said in a low voice. "I can't lie about him like that."

Nick deserved every ounce of Alexandra's fury. He had earned her loathing and utter contempt for leading her to that anvil. Some days, she couldn't help but remember his smile at the lake, the way he spoke to her, and wondered if it was all just a cruel game to him.

But as much as she hated Nick, she couldn't go into a courtroom and tell such a blatant lie to the public. Not when so many women faced much worse circumstances.

Miss Dawes let out a breath. "All right then. Let's try a different approach. Is there any chance that your husband has been faithful to you during the four years of your separation?"

Alexandra resisted the urge to flinch. Why did it matter so much if Nick had slept with someone else? Why did she torture herself with the thought of him in bed with another woman? And why did that thought hurt so damn much?

"No," she replied, pushing the image out of her mind. It wouldn't do her any good here. "None at all."

"Very well." Miss Dawes began gathering her papers. "We

shall try that option. Take this suggestion as you like, but the process would be more expedient with his cooperation."

"You want me to talk to Nick," Alexandra said flatly.

Miss Dawes put a hand up. "It's a suggestion. If he challenges your case, this will become unpleasant. The gossips will be merciless." She paused for a moment, as if struck by a thought. "Are you planning on publishing another book soon?"

Alexandra's cheeks grew hot. She had told no one about her latest project, the countless hours spent researching and collecting information about shipping routes and illegal smuggling operations. She had been working to expose a member of Parliament for his criminal activities.

"You are," Miss Dawes said, reading the look on Alexandra's face. "And I'm almost afraid to ask, but how will the public react?"

Alexandra bit her lip. "It will cause an uproar."

Miss Dawes muttered a word under her breath, too softly for Alexandra to catch. A curse? No, it couldn't be. Miss Dawes was far too composed for that. "Take my advice as you will," she said, regaining her composure. "Hold off on publishing your manuscript and ask your husband if he's willing to agree to a divorce. Either way, I suggest you make plans to retreat to the country. The public will not be kind."

Alexandra didn't bother telling Miss Dawes that she had already arranged to leave. A ship was waiting for her, one that would take her far away from England.

And far away from the man who had caused her so much hurt.

∽ 4 ∽

The Earl of Kent's domicile on Pall Mall loomed like a monolith as Alexandra mounted the front steps. The house itself was not the problem – it was how hollow and cavernous it had become since her brother, James, and his new wife, Emma, had departed on their extended honeymoon to America. What used to be filled with warmth and mirth was now desolate and alone.

Jeffries, the ancient butler, greeted her with a deep bow. "My lady—"

"I'm only here for a change of clothing, Jeffries," Alexandra interrupted, handing over her gloves. "Send a maid up to my bedchamber. I need to look suitably intimidating when I threaten my husband later this evening."

Alexandra was not about to visit Nick's club wearing a dress spattered with city mud. She needed something that said, *I've come to menace you.*

Would red silk be too much? Too dramatic?

"My lady—"

"And tell Amelia that she's not to touch the papers on my desk. I have them right where I want them."

"But—"

"Spit it out, Jeffries," she prompted, eager to finish so she could begin terrorising a man before her afternoon tea.

Perhaps a pastel pink. One that gave the impression, *I am here for your destruction*. Or blue? Blue always suited her colouring.

The butler straightened. "A gentleman inquired after you at the service door a short time ago."

"Did this gentleman come with a name?" she asked distractedly.

Jeffries hesitated. "He said he was your husband."

Alexandra froze. All thoughts of dresses disappeared from her mind. "I see. Did he happen to leave a message?"

"No, but—"

"So he appeared and vanished, rather like a noxious odour. That does sound like Nicholas. Thank you for telling me, Jeffries. That will be all." The emerald green, then. It gave the impression of wanting to burn his life to the ground. Alexandra started for the stairs, but the butler cleared his throat. "Unless there was something else?"

Her butler shifted on his feet. "The gentleman in question is... still outside, my lady. Across the road. He's requested your presence in the park."

All at once, Alexandra's anger returned. *Fine*. She could make threats of divorce in a mud-spattered dress. It saved her a trip to that monstrosity he called a business. "Very well."

Alexandra snatched the newspaper from the table beside the door and strode out of the house, her heart pounding.

As she crossed to the park, a tall, muscled figure stepped away from a nearby tree and into the sunlight.

Nick.

God almighty, but he still made her breath catch in her throat. A breathtaking combination of sensuality and brutality – eyes that could eviscerate a woman at fifty paces.

Beautiful. His midnight hair tumbled over his brow, picking up glints of sunlight and setting off his chiselled features like divine artistry. The costly overcoat and trousers seemed wrong on him, almost farcical compared to the feral gleam in his eye. An outrageously handsome predator, a dark prince garbed in the finest garments money could buy.

Her money.

Black eyes met hers, unblinking and piercing. Directness was always his weapon of choice, intimidation his method of operation. Alexandra refused to kneel before him.

"The servants' entrance," she said, chin held high. "Terrifying the staff or trying to annoy me?"

Nick lifted a shoulder. "Figured you'd think it more considerate than showing up at the front door."

"Considerate would be not showing up at all," she said dryly.

His black eyes gleamed. "Did that for over four years."

"Try it for another four. Perhaps then I can read my morning broadsheet" – Alexandra launched the paper at his chest – "without us being the featured scandal."

Nick caught the sheet and examined it. His gorgeous grin made Alexandra unspeakably angry. She'd devoted her past four years to wishing him all manner of facial misfortune – warts, boils, spots, baldness – however nothing could mar the beauty of his visage nor penetrate the frozen lump of coal masquerading as his heart.

"I take it you're the witch beating defenceless men in this illustration," he drawled in his Irish brogue, a reminder of their first days together in Hampshire when he'd hidden that part of himself away. Back then, he'd sounded as English as Her Majesty.

The reminder infuriated her.

"Look behind me." She thrust an accusing finger his way. "That's *you*, you absolute cretin of a man."

Nick barked a laugh. "I'm the devil?"

Against her will, Alexandra went motionless. She hadn't seen him laugh since their wedding day.

You're stuck with me now, Nicholas, she'd told him with a smile.

His whisper against her ear, sonorous voice sending heat over her skin. *That sounds like the start of an adventure.*

Alexandra's lips grew thin as the memories returned. What had seemed like an adventure when they married was now revealed to be something else entirely. Her role was little more than a bank account Nick could access in his quest for glory.

How dared he laugh?

She glanced around, noticing curious eyes lingering in their direction. No need for a public show. She latched onto his arm and dragged him further into the shadows of a tree.

"Stop that," she commanded through clenched teeth, not caring if her tone sounded so harsh. "Stop laughing."

But Nick only grinned at her. "It's flattering. We make a pair, eh?"

Gritting her teeth, she spoke slowly: "I don't want us to make a pair. *We. Are. Not. A. Pair.*"

The grin faded from Nick's face, replaced by something else. Guilt, perhaps? "Alex," he breathed quietly.

"No," she snapped, temper flaring again as she tried to remain composed. She couldn't think straight when he used that name – one reserved for the man he'd pretended to be back in Stratfield Saye. "I don't want apologies. You and I will have words, but first, tell me why you've come."

He reached out – to touch her? – but then aborted the motion. "There was a murder last eve in Whitechapel," he said, his voice quiet. "Her corpse came with a message for me."

Why was he telling her this? "What was the message?"

Nick's eyes met hers. "It was a page from one of your books."

Alexandra shuddered as his words sliced through the air with deadly precision. His face was no longer alight with mirth, instead replaced by a stony expression that sent chills running down her spine. The murder must have been truly horrifying for Nick to be so serious. She knew from her work in the East End that death was all too common in those parts.

"Who was the woman? Did you know her name?"

Nick nodded solemnly. "Mary Watkins. A flower-seller."

"Yes." Her voice trembled. "And a former maid for Sir Reginald Seymour."

Nick's gaze sharpened. "You knew her?"

"She was one of my informants. Sir Reginald has been illegally smuggling opals and workers to his mines under the pretence of essential import and export shipments on the Australia route. Do you think Sir Reginald found out, somehow? About Mary speaking to me?"

Nick seemed to contemplate this for a moment before replying. "Maybe. Or that she was seen with you, and she's one of mine."

"One of yours?"

"Under my protection," he said. "Her brother had a habit of beating her. She came to me once sporting a shiner and cradling a bad arm, so I dealt with him."

"Dealt with him?" Were the rumours about him true, then?

He didn't pretend to mistake her meaning. "Did I kill him? No. I stuck a finely aimed boot up his arse and promised, in no uncertain terms, that I'd do worse if he hurt her again."

The man he had pretended to be in Stratfield Saye was gentle, a former schoolmaster. Looking at him now, Alexandra wondered how she had been stupid enough to believe such lies. The creature standing before her now had been forged on the anvil of deceit. His animal grace was barely contained beneath the cloak of civility.

Panthers, after all, were beautiful until they ripped your throat out.

"Good," she said, surprising herself. "I'm glad she… could count on you."

I couldn't.

Nick took her by the shoulders, and his touch startled her into stillness. When he spoke, his voice was both grim and urgent. "I've a lot of enemies, Alex. Now that our marriage is public, word gets around the East End. You understand?"

"You think this person will come for me."

"Yes." He nodded toward the silent mansion behind

them. "I've instructed one of my men to keep watch on you tonight. If you leave the house, take a footman with you and don't stay out after dark. My man will follow to keep you safe."

Why should he care? They were only married in name, bound together by his greed and her naïveté. They had no children or fond memories – only lies that snatched away every moment of happiness.

Alexandra lifted her chin. "What a strange thief you are to care for the safety of a mark you once swindled."

Nick's grip tightened. "I made a mistake letting you go four years ago, thinking you were just a mark to me."

A noise escaped her lips without permission. How could she trust him now? When had Nick ever been honest with her? She couldn't think of a single instance, not even one.

Divorce, she thought. *We'll have words about that another time.*

"Enough." She yanked herself from his grasp and stepped back. "I'll do as you ask."

Nick stared at his hands as if recalling the feel of her skin against them. He was quiet for a moment before saying softly, "Come to me if you need anything. No matter the hour."

Anger flared in her like a lit fuse, burning away any other emotion. "There was a time when I would have sought your help without being asked."

∽ 5 ∽

STRATFIELD SAYE, HAMPSHIRE

Four years ago

"Mr Marlowe," Alexandra said impatiently, "I have the money for this book. Do you want to take it or not?"

The bookseller's expression was stubborn but firm. She had been here before, the same argument every time. The old curmudgeon would not be moved, not by money nor reason, and certainly not by her exasperation.

Marlowe's hands closed about the book she'd chosen with such care and determination – a choice he felt was inappropriate. Really, she had already had one overbearing lout of a father. The last thing she needed was another.

Mr Marlowe was ancient; he ought to have passed the shop to his son, but that man had all the wits of an addled squirrel. It didn't help that Marlowe's decrepit bookshop was the only one in the entire village of Stratfield Saye.

Marlowe plucked the book from her hands. "I can't sell it to you," he said sourly. "I shall sell you the Acton Bell, but not this one."

Alexandra snatched it back and bristled. "Then why is it even here if you won't sell it?"

"Adam put in the order to the stockist," Mr Marlowe grumbled.

Ah, the drunk son.

"Well, that's hardly my problem, is it?" The bell over the shop door gave a jingle, but Alexandra ignored the new arrival. "*This* book was on your shelves, so *this* is the one I want."

Marlowe smiled over Alexandra's shoulder at the customer, with a politeness he'd never afforded her. "Good morning, sir. Anything you need, give a shout." Then, in a hiss that only she could hear: "It's not suitable for young ladies. Filth and depravity."

Alexandra held it out of his reach. "Why, Mr Marlowe, I ought to tell you that only makes me more determined to have this. I have a personal interest in depraved literature. Name your price."

The bookseller's lips flattened as he crossed his arms. "No."

"Not even for roof repairs?" She raised an eyebrow, knowing full well how desperately he needed them. "Twofold? Three?"

Mr Marlowe hesitated. "My lady—"

"Might I offer some assistance?" Alexandra froze at the velvet timbre that caressed her spine like a lover's touch.

Slowly, she turned to meet the source of that voice. And there he stood, a vision too beautiful for words. Every feature seemed crafted for perfection – strong jaw, high cheekbones, hair black and glossy as polished obsidian. Yet it was his gaze that held her captivated; there was no mistaking the bold admiration in those dark eyes.

But Alexandra had grown accustomed to male attentions. She'd taken after her mother, and the way his gaze drifted over her figure said he found her appealing.

Men usually admired her before she spoke. She doubted this one would be any different.

She lifted her chin, an unspoken dare. "Unless you can persuade Mr Marlowe to take my legal tender, then no. You cannot offer assistance."

The words barely left her lips before Marlowe interjected. "Sir, this book is not appropriate reading material for a lady. As I have explained to *this one*." He glared at Alexandra.

She almost rolled her eyes. *This one. Bah!*

The stranger gestured to the book. "May I?" She complied, noticing then how dark his eyes were. They were as deep and black as pools of ink. "*Pandora's Box*," he murmured, returning it to her with a raised eyebrow. "Mythology?"

The bookseller gave a choking cough.

Alexandra's smile grew slow and wicked. "No, no," she said. "Clever euphemism for another box."

His surprise was fleeting, replaced by a soft laugh as lovely as his voice. Something warmed within Alexandra. Why, he was amused!

The bookseller's face had gone an impressive shade of red. "Get out!" he squawked, pointing wildly toward the door. "Get out of my shop!"

"Very well," Alexandra replied calmly, hiding her disappointment behind politeness. She'd have to resort to subterfuge if she wanted the book now. "Then I'll take the Acton Bell" – she began scooping up her things before anyone could object – "and leave you with money for the trouble. Thank you very much indeed, Mr Marlowe. And to you, sir," she told the beautiful man, flashing a dazzling smile. "Good day, gentlemen."

Alexandra hurried out of the shop and strode down the road at a decent clip. The hills of Hampshire spanned before her in a stunning vista, but there was no time for admiring the view. She had to get away fast to keep her precious cargo.

"Miss!"

Damn.

Alexandra walked faster.

"*Miss!*" The man from the bookshop caught up with her in no time flat. "Miss, you forgot your hat."

"Oh." Thank goodness. She took it from him without breaking her stride. "I'm sorry, but I must keep walking. Fast."

The bookshop man kept pace with ease, eyes twinkling with amusement. "Fleeing someone?"

"You could say that." Alexandra fumbled inside her dress and held aloft her rare volume of vulgar literature destined for some soused son's hands.

Bookshop Man threw back his head with a laugh. "You stole that book?"

"Shhh!" She glanced around, relieved to find no one about. "I paid Mr Marlowe extra in coin. And I have merely taken it off his shelves before his son, who is always drunk, discovered it was a naughty book and stole it to do…" She glanced at him. She was being far too familiar with a man whose name she did not yet know. "To do whatever it is men do in private," she muttered.

"I see," he said, smiling knowingly. "It was a kindness, then."

"Yes." She would take excellent care of this book. It would grace the shelf with all her other offensive literature.

"An act of benevolence, saving naughty books from drunken sons."

What manner of man was this? He unnerved her with his attentiveness. She'd expected him to be gone by now, yet instead, he seemed almost… intrigued by her? No, no. It must have been her imagination.

But she was aware of his gaze, hot upon her skin. As intimate as fingertips caressing the nape of her neck.

Alexandra stared at him in astonishment, which only gave him cause to smile – a beautiful smile, both devilish and sublime.

"What?" he remarked, their gazes still tangled together.

Alexandra tried not to blush as she maintained a quick clip. The road was far enough from the shop for them to take their time now, but his presence threatened her composure.

"I thought I knew everyone in Stratfield Saye," she said, as if she had been trying to place him.

"I only just moved last month. Nicholas Spencer, at your service." He sketched an elegant bow.

Ah, so this was the infamous Lord Locke. She'd heard all about him from her father's house staff, who were all abuzz with "tall stranger" gossip. "So you're the new Lord Locke. I'm Alexandra Grey, your neighbour at Roseburn. My maids were saying all sorts of things about you."

Something flickered across his face, too fast for her to make out before it vanished altogether. "Anything noteworthy?"

"The maids said you were handsome as sin." And they weren't lying, either.

A wry smile curved one corner of his mouth. "Is that so?"

"Oh, yes," she said. Her father's staff had claimed he was a former schoolmaster, but peers of the realm weren't usually schoolteachers, and he did not seem like the kind of man who spent time in a classroom. His figure was, frankly, as strapping as a labourer's. "Were you really a schoolmaster?"

He tilted his head, his expression strangely sombre. "What were you expecting?"

She gave an apologetic smile. "A dusty old curmudgeon with spectacles and a grim expression?"

He laughed, and Alexandra's heart felt a little lighter.

Thorne's manners had become polished over the month spent practising with tutors. He'd learned deportment. His toff's accent no longer slipped; he'd learned to maintain it from sunrise to the moment his head hit the pillow at night. He'd excelled at mimicking the behaviour of a gentleman with only the occasional mistake.

Day in and day out, he played the role of Nicholas Spencer, a schoolmaster who inherited a barony from a distant cousin who died childless. Thorne became so self-assured in his performance that he followed Lady Alexandra into the bookshop with a jolly spring in his step.

So effortless, he had thought. His target was a sheltered debutante with all the awareness and life experience of a caged songbird.

A future spinster, her father had called her. *An arrogant little shrew who irritates every man who speaks to her.*

You'll have your work cut out for you. Don't waste my time, Mr Thorne.

Thorne half expected some severe, disapproving woman with a permanent scowl. But this woman was nothing like what he had expected. God almighty, the earl had failed to mention his daughter was a stunner. And not just lovely – confident, quick-witted.

And a damn fine thief.

Sure, she was no seductress, no accomplished flirt. She didn't hide the fact that she liked the look of him. But rather than blush, she'd been brazen when handing over that book.

Pandora's Box. He almost laughed. No, she wasn't a woman who wanted a husband who'd force her to subject herself, to make herself smaller. No wonder she'd found no one suitable among the arrogant toffs in London.

She needed a man who could fight fire with fire.

"So, are you misrepresenting yourself?"

They were almost at the edge of the village now. Lady Alexandra tipped back her head, and the sunlight limned her hair into a molten halo. A creature of light, she was. And he was the bastard about to dim it.

Then he realised what she'd just asked. "Sorry?"

She smiled as if she knew he was admiring her. "Misrepresenting yourself. Are you a dusty, curmudgeonly schoolmaster with the look of a rogue, or a rogue who plays the part of a dusty, curmudgeonly schoolmaster?"

Too clever by half, this one. "What do you think?"

Lady Alexandra toyed with her hat. "You did not look appalled by the real meaning of the book's title."

"And so?"

"You are a rogue." She spoke with absolute certainty.

A chuckle rolled from deep in his chest. "Just moments ago, you seemed more appalled by me being a schoolmaster."

"Oh, I am. Rogues, I can handle." She waved the hat as if to punctuate the point. "Schoolmasters who *look* like rogues... Now that, Lord Locke, makes you dangerous."

Now they were getting somewhere. "Nicholas," he reminded her. "Or Nick, if that suits your fancy."

"Now, now," she admonished him with a sly grin. "We haven't even been introduced. And you let me call you dangerous without protest. I find that suspicious."

If Thorne wasn't an accomplished confidence artist, she might have rattled him now. But this was all part of the seduction game – flirt first, then move in for the kill. Thorne knew this well. He had studied Lady Alexandra extensively from the broadsheets her father provided; while he may not have been the fastest reader, he understood why she instilled fear in those high society nobs.

They didn't understand her, and men feared what they didn't understand.

"You didn't seem appalled by the book's title, either," Thorne said.

At the edge of the village, they came to a split in the road where they would go in different directions. She to the Earl of Kent's estate, and he, to a property that did not belong to Baron Locke at all. Baron Locke was a dead title, a role meant only to last three months – the exact length of time Thorne needed to swindle her out of every pound and shilling in her trust.

Lady Alexandra paused, giving him a mischievous smile. "And so?" she asked, echoing his earlier words.

Thorne suppressed any flicker of empathy he might have felt for his mark. He couldn't afford distractions or attachments when there was deceit to be done. "You're a lady rogue," he replied smoothly.

She laughed lightly at his words. "Perhaps I am," she murmured. Then she started down the road, away from Thorne. She looked over her shoulder and called out, "Lord Locke?"

"Yes?" he called back.

"In true wicked fashion," she said, her words floating back to him on the breeze, "I'll dispense with the formalities. I shall call you Nick if you call me Alex."

Thorne watched her go, his eyes tracing her every step until she vanished around a bend in the road. And when she left, she took all the light with her.

∽ 6 ∽

LONDON

Four years later

Alexandra woke to a man holding a pistol to her head. "Get up," the man said in a low, menacing voice. "All nice and easy like. And if you make a sound, I'll blow your brains out."

Alexandra's heart pounded in her chest, her breaths shallow and ragged. She nodded slowly, her nails biting into the soft fabric of the quilt as the cold metal of the weapon pressed against her temple. The intruder hovered over her, his face obscured by the shadows, but the noxious stench of cigar smoke and whiskey clung to him like a second skin.

With a shaky hand, Alexandra eased herself off the bed, her limbs trembling as she stood.

Don't show weakness. Don't let him see you're afraid.

The faint luminescence from the window cast eerie shadows across the assailant's face. He loomed tall and gaunt, with sharp cheekbones that carved deep crevices across his visage. The colour of his eyes remained indiscernible, but

Alexandra felt their weight upon her, assessing her form like a prized mare at auction.

Alexandra tried to conceal her shivering, the thin night rail she wore a liability in her current predicament. It was useless, flimsy, covering little, and unsuitable for escape. He would capture her before she even had a chance to sound the alarm.

Where was the guard Nick had promised? Had he forsaken her over petty squabbles and biting words? Worse yet, her large brothers were absent, and her loyal servants would be powerless against a man wielding a pistol. Alexandra had never felt so isolated, so completely alone.

Her screams would go unheard in this isolated chamber.

The interloper emitted a gruff noise, the weapon still clutched in his grip. "Should've known Thorne's wife would be a beauty. I'd tear off that scrap of silk myself if I hadn't been instructed otherwise."

Alexandra froze, too frightened to move lest he change his mind. "Instructed by whom?"

"I ain't paid to disclose that kind of information. I was paid to eliminate the shadow lurking by your doorstep and deliver you to my employer. I took care of your man in the garden, and here we are. Move at a leisurely pace."

Dear God, he had murdered Nick's hired guard. The thought made Alexandra's knees buckle, but she steadied herself. "What if I offered you more to let me go? No repercussions, no informing the authorities. Just a swift payment in exchange for your departure."

His eyes gleamed in the shadows, assessing her proposal. And why not? He was a mercenary, a man with payment attached to his services. Men like him were easily swayed by money and greed. "How much?" he inquired.

"How much did they pay you to bring me in?"

A sinister grin crept across the intruder's face. "Ten quid to deliver you alive."

Alexandra's breath caught in her throat. That was a significant sum of money. "And if I were dead?"

"Less than a tenner, I reckon. The bloke hiring me probably wants to finish the job himself."

But why? Alexandra was itching to ask again for the name of the person who had hired him, but she focused on her aim: to convince him, to divert his attention. She had prepared for this, having ventured into the East End numerous times. Other women had taught her the art of survival.

Alexandra drew in a deep breath. "I'll give you thirty quid to leave this house. Thirty pounds, paid in notes. Right now."

He paused, tilting his head as he mulled over her proposal. Refusing such a generous sum would be sheer madness. Her thoughts were a constant prayer: *Please say yes. Just say yes*.

The man started to lower his pistol, but then lifted it again. "Can't. He'll find me. He'll—"

"Thirty pounds is more than enough to escape," Alexandra gently reasoned. "You can run wherever you like. Start anew."

The intruder licked his lips. *Yes, keep talking*. It wouldn't be long now. Alexandra knew that this man would turn on her. Mercenaries had no sense of honour, and he would likely kill her for the smallest gain. No one was coming to her aid.

She had to rely on herself to survive.

"Show me," he demanded.

Good. Stay calm.

Alexandra approached her dressing table and retrieved the key from its secret compartment. The top held stacks of letters and documents she used for her essays and books. They were reminders that she still had work to do.

Beneath the letters lay the item she sought: a small, intricately carved knife.

She had commissioned the knife herself, intending to use it as protection in the slums of London. Her contacts lived in dangerous areas of the city, where it was unsafe for a lone woman to venture out. Those women had advised her to carry a weapon.

And they had taught her how to wield it.

Alexandra felt the cold metal of the blade against her skin, the weight of it reminding her of its purpose. She shifted the papers on her dressing table, the rustling almost deafening in the room's silence. The intruder shifted his weight from foot to foot, his impatience palpable.

"Hurry the fuck up," he growled.

"Of course," she murmured, plucking out the small wad of notes she kept for paying her informants. "Here you are."

Thirty pounds. The sum seemed to have eluded the man for the better part of his life. And Alexandra could almost hear the click of the gears turning in his head: he was a hired killer, and thirty pounds was a small fortune to this man – her life was worth nothing to him.

Thirty pounds was more than ten, and he wouldn't have to trouble himself with keeping her alive to earn it.

"Give it here," he said, his voice rough and impatient, his fingers snapping like a predator's jaws.

He lowered the pistol and reached for the wad of notes.

She struck swiftly, driving the blade deep into the intruder's shoulder. A guttural howl escaped his lips, and his pistol clattered to the floor. Alexandra kicked it away, and as the weapon rolled beneath the bed, she held the slick, bloody knife aloft, ready for another strike.

But the man was quicker than she had expected. He seized her hair from behind with a fierce grip and hurled her to the floor. Pain seared through her body as Alexandra gasped for air.

"I'll take your blunt and leave you dead, you little bitch," he hissed, his fist raised high.

Not today. With fierce determination, Alexandra lunged forward, plunging the blade into her attacker's gut. His expression was one of surprise as he crumpled to the floor.

Oh, God.

"You—" He choked. "Y-you—"

His breathing was ragged, and he stared up at her as the blood pooled around him. His last words were an incoherent garble.

Then, nothing. His eyes gazed up at the ceiling, sightless.

Alexandra had killed a man.

She pressed a hand to her mouth. What could she do? Call the servants? Tell someone to find a constable? They'd ask questions about the dead man in her garden. They'd dig into that murder in Whitechapel. Had Nick even informed the police of Mary Watkins' death?

Nick.

Come to me if you need anything, he'd told her. *No matter the hour.*

Nicholas Thorne was the only man who could help her now. Alexandra couldn't even remember putting on her boots and cloak as she fled Kent House, her mind consumed with a single thought: to reach Thorne at all costs. She hurried down the pavement, her feet pounding the cobblestones as she hailed a passing hack.

"Take me to the Brimstone in Whitechapel," she commanded, barely giving the driver a chance to protest.

"The Brimstone ain't no place for a lady," the driver grumbled, eyeing her warily. "I don't know if I—"

"If I wanted to hear lectures on appropriate places for women, sir," Alexandra cut him off icily, "I'd listen to the imbeciles in Parliament. Now drive me to the Brimstone, and there's a sovereign in it for you if you shut the bloody hell up."

The driver shut the bloody hell up.

The world around Alexandra blurred by in a frenzied rush. The orderly streets of Westminster faded into the grimy, ash-covered tenements of the East End, the looming shadow of the Brimstone ever-present on the horizon.

Safety? The word echoed in her mind like a mocking refrain, reminding her she was far from it. The past hour's events had left her rattled and unhinged, her breathing ragged and uneven as she clutched her cloak close to her body. The memory of the man she had killed – his face contorted in agony, his blood staining her hands – repeatedly played in her mind, threatening to unravel her completely.

Thorne's wife, he'd called her.

No, the Brimstone would not offer safety. Going there was simply necessary.

The lights of the club were visible up the road. Alexandra hated this place. Hated everything it represented: a gambling den to line the pockets of the man who had deceived her.

And now – Alexandra held back a bitter laugh at the thought – she was here for his help.

"Around the back," she told the driver.

The driver gave a grumble but complied. He was not about to risk losing his sovereign.

The hack rolled to a stop at the back entrance. Alexandra tossed the coin to the driver, hoping he wouldn't notice the blood until after he'd left – not that it would make a difference, she suspected. Blood-covered money was as good as any.

Alexandra slipped out of the hack and into the alley, the stink of smoke and urine hitting her like a physical blow. The door to the club was unmarked, but she knew it well.

Alexandra knocked. She didn't know who she expected to answer, but the man before her didn't appear to be a lawless type. He was built like Nick – broad-shouldered and heavily muscled – but with a face that looked like it belonged in a gentleman's club. His sharp, patrician features were a striking contrast to his piercing, whiskey-coloured eyes, which glinted with an intensity that made her uneasy. Intimidating, except for the glasses perched on his nose, which softened the impact.

"Are you from Maxine's?" he asked, eyeing Alexandra up and down. Before she could answer, he gestured to the street behind her. "You ought to go around the front. You can greet the gentlemen there."

Maxine's was a high-class brothel that catered to the wealthy patrons who frequented Nick's club. Alexandra had once penned an essay on the establishment and the women who worked there, and she knew that none of them would ever dream of showing up at someone's doorstep looking as dishevelled and unkempt as she did. It wasn't good for business.

"I'm here to see Mr Thorne," Alexandra declared, her patience waning as she fought exhaustion. The night had been brutal, with one man dead in her bedroom and another in her garden – all because she was married to a deceitful blackguard with a penchant for crime. "Is he in?"

The doorman's gaze narrowed. "If it's more coin you're after, Thorne doesn't bed the ladies from Maxine's. Go to the front—"

Alexandra cut him off with a sharp retort. "No. Now, get out of my way."

She stormed past the towering figure, done with playing nice. The staff in the hallway gawped at her, surprised to see a bedraggled and enraged woman make it past the door guard.

But when a hand closed around her arm, Alexandra whirled to face the giant. "I suggest you take your hand off me, unless you want to lose it," she spat, her eyes flashing with fury. "He might own this place, but my money bought it."

Alexandra strode down the hallway, her steps purposeful and quick. The hulking doorman trailed behind her, calling her *Mrs Thorne* instead of *Lady Alexandra*, which only snapped her already fraying patience.

"Stop talking," she hissed, her temper at its breaking point. "Just tell me where he is."

The giant grunted, pointing towards a closed door. Without a second thought, Alexandra barged inside, slamming the door in his face.

There sat Nick, surrounded by mountains of books and

papers. She had never seen him so engrossed in his work before – rumpled shirtsleeves and ink-stained fingers made him look even more devilishly handsome.

But Alexandra's fists clenched at her sides. How dare he sit there looking calm and collected when her life was falling apart? How dare he bring such chaos into her home?

"I told you not to disturb me, O'Sullivan," he grumbled, still not looking up from his work.

"I would have appreciated the same courtesy," she spat back, her voice cutting across the room like a razor-sharp knife. "But it seems we're both disappointed, aren't we?"

Nick's head jerked up at the sound of her voice. "Alex? What's happened?"

The sound of his concern did something to her. All the careful composure she had held onto for dear life shattered into a million pieces. Without warning, Alexandra sank onto the plush carpet, her breathing ragged and uneven. Holding out her blood-soaked hands, she met Nick's gaze with pleading eyes.

"You said to come to you if I ever needed anything," she whispered, her voice cracking with emotion. "I need you now, Nick."

7

Thorne rose from his chair and approached Alexandra slowly, his movements measured and cautious. It went against every instinct – *Every. Fucking. Instinct* – not to seize her and hold on. Never let her go.

But he didn't want to frighten her.

"Are you hurt?" he asked calmly, his voice belying the chaos inside his mind.

So much blood. *So much blood*. Thorne sank to his knees beside his wife, and she let him reach for her without protest.

"I don't think so," she whispered, her voice barely more than a whisper.

"Whose blood is this? Did you recognise who it was?" he asked as he unbuttoned the heavy cloak. Then he eased the garment off her shoulders. When he saw what was beneath, a breath exploded out of him. She had come in her night rail – white cotton, blood everywhere.

Alexandra could only shake her head weakly, her eyes

unfocused and far away. "No," she murmured, her voice trembling with fear. "No."

"*Shhhh*. Come here." Thorne held her against him. He didn't care if blood ruined his clothes. He needed to touch her, reassure himself she was still alive. "Can you tell me what happened?"

Alexandra's breaths came in swift gulps. "He said he'd murdered the man you hired to protect me, and I didn't... I wasn't sure what else to do. I killed him, Nick. *I killed him.*"

Thorne held her tighter, his heart aching with guilt and responsibility. He had been fifteen when he first took a life, but each subsequent murder had darkened his soul until he felt like there was nothing left unsullied.

But if there was, it was the part of his soul that loved Alex.

And he was supposed to protect her.

Thorne clenched his fists, his guilt and anger warring within him. "You're sure he didn't hurt you?"

"I don't know," she whispered.

"Tell me where, love," he said, trying to keep his voice soft. His fingernails dug violently into his palm, desperate to keep his composure. He couldn't afford to lose control, not now. "Where did you leave him?"

She buried her face in his neck, and he bit back a sound in his throat. Christ, she hadn't been this close to him since... since the night of their wedding. That had been the last time she had trusted him to hold her like this.

Four years ago.

"My bedchamber," she whispered, her words muffled by his shirt. Thorne jerked in surprise, but she only clung to him tighter. "He was going to take me somewhere, but I don't know where. I'm sorry about your man's death. I'm so sorry, Nick."

"Shh," Thorne murmured again, his hand stroking her cheek. He helped her into a nearby leather chair, but she grasped his shirt, refusing to let him go. "Give me a moment, sweetheart," he said, his voice rough with emotion. "I'm not going anywhere, all right?"

Alexandra nodded, and Thorne rang the service bell for O'Sullivan. Within moments, the factotum appeared at the door, raising an eyebrow at the sight of Alexandra in Thorne's chair.

"Taking the night off?" O'Sullivan asked, his tone laced with amusement.

Thorne ignored the question, his mind already focused on the next steps. "I'm going to need a clean-up," he said, his voice clipped and commanding. "The Earl of Kent's residence in St James's. Two bodies – and have the lads do a sweep. I want to know if anyone's hanging around who shouldn't be. Tell 'em to be quick and quiet, then take the corpses to the docks. Stage a scene, call the coppers. Pay them not to ask questions."

O'Sullivan's expression turned serious. "O'Malley? He was watching her, wasn't he?"

Alexandra made a soft sound, and Thorne reached over to take her hand. "It's all right, love," he murmured. Then, to O'Sullivan: "Have Samuel tell O'Malley's widow the news. Make sure she knows she'll be taken care of."

"Damn," O'Sullivan muttered, his emotions briefly getting the better of him before he straightened, all business. He was used to cleaning up messes; it had been his job since they were lads.

"And Mrs Thorne? Would she like anything?"

Thorne answered for her. "A bath, please. And some of our best brandy. Send it up to my suite."

Once they were alone, Alex murmured, "I don't like brandy."

"You don't have to like it to need it." He swiftly fastened her cloak to conceal her night dress. The last thing he needed was a maid seeing her like this. He helped her to her feet, but her legs were unsteady, and she swayed against him. "I'm going to carry you to my suite, all right?"

There was a moment's hesitation, and then she gave a slight nod.

Thorne swung her into his arms. She was so light and delicate, her forehead resting against his shoulder with an exhausted sigh that made him want to grip her tighter. Never let her go.

The thought curled through his chest like smoke, filling him with unexpected warmth. He swallowed hard and strode ahead into the dimly lit hallway.

"You tired?" he asked.

Her voice trembled when she spoke. "No."

"You telling the truth?"

"Maybe."

Gentle as a summer breeze, he ran his hand along her shoulder blade and then tilted his head to speak softly near her ear. "You afraid of sleeping?"

She didn't answer, and for a moment, he wondered if she'd already passed out. But when he looked, he found Alex staring up at him with an expression full of uncertainty. Aye, she was afraid.

"What if I told you I'll stay by your side tonight?" he asked. "Keep watch?"

"I don't believe your promises."

Nick stopped himself from flinching. He deserved that one. "Then I won't promise. You know my reputation?" The flicker across her face indicated she did. "Then I'll put out the word. Anyone else tries to hurt you, their life is mine."

Either she heard the conviction in his voice, or she was too weary of arguing. By the time they reached his suite, she was already asleep.

Thorne held her on the chaise as the maids filled the copper tub in the mosaic water closet and set out a decanter of brandy. He stroked her cheek, careful not to mar her skin with the blood that transferred from her clothes to his hands.

He wasn't sure why – she could clean it off, and he ought to have grown accustomed to sullying her by now – but this single act seemed important. Even while masquerading as Nicholas Spencer, he had never felt clean enough to touch her. Didn't matter how often he bathed or how well he scrubbed. It wasn't good enough.

He wasn't good enough.

Smart clothes and a fake accent couldn't change a man's past or make up for everything he'd done wrong.

When the maids finished, Thorne dismissed them and gently shook his wife. "Alex. Wake up, sweetheart."

She opened those blue, blue eyes of hers, and Thorne felt as if he'd been struck with something heavy. He forgot what it had been like to hold her close, to meet her gaze directly. He forgot how easily she could disarm him.

"Nick," she whispered.

Thorne longed to close the space between them. It was only a mere breath. So why did it seem as vast as an ocean?

Haven't you already hurt her enough? Look at what you've done.

His thumb was on her cheek. He'd smeared blood across it.

Thorne jerked away from her. "Your bath is ready."

Alexandra rose from the chaise, lifted her chin, and unfastened the clasp of her cloak. Thorne couldn't help but notice the slight tremble in her hands as she removed the garment.

Thorne politely turned his back. It was a vulnerable moment, one he had no right to witness. Such intimacies were reserved for actual husbands, not ones who made marriage vows under false pretences.

"Shall I ring for a maid?" he offered, trying to keep his tone neutral.

"No." Her voice was deceptively soft. "You don't need to avert your gaze to preserve my modesty. I doubt there's anything left for me to hide from you."

Longing and regret twisted Thorne's heart at her words. The memory of their past intimacy flooded his mind, the feel of her body entwined with his, her touch igniting every part of his body. He still dreamed of her at night, her legs wrapped around his hips as he slid inside her. He'd brought himself to completion for years based on the few moments of intimacy they'd shared – a laughably inadequate pleasure by comparison. His imagination was paltry.

But he wasn't a bloody saint, either.

Thorne turned. *You're a fool, Nick Thorne. The biggest damned fool. A pathetic piece of shit.*

"There," she said lightly, her eyes meeting his. "What did I tell you? Nothing you haven't seen before."

He was glad she couldn't hear the insults he hurled at himself – *berk, stupid, imbecile. You let her leave four years ago? She still thinks she's your mark?* – because he was trying not to focus on his wife's luscious curves as she tossed her night rail to the floor. He couldn't decide whether to be grateful when she slid into the bathtub and hid from his desperate stare.

Alex's hiss of pain snapped Thorne out of his self-loathing. "What is it?" he asked.

She showed him the scrape along her elbow – something a rug might have caused. A wound she must have got while defending herself.

A haze of calm rage descended over him. Now was the opportunity to take stock of her injuries and count each one. Find the bastard who'd hired her assailant.

Make him pay.

He kneeled beside the tub to get a better look. "Any others?"

Calm. Keep your voice calm. Don't frighten her.

"Yes." She inspected her other elbow and found a few scrapes there as well. "But nothing serious."

"Let me see." She extended her arm, and Thorne gently ran his fingers down her skin. There were more cuts, some blossoming bruises on her wrists. He was glad she had killed the man who came after her; otherwise, he would have knifed the bastard himself. "I'll have one of the lads send for the doctor."

"Perhaps they could send a message to your doorman instead?" She gave a rueful smile. "I ought to apologise for being rude to him."

Thorne snorted in amusement at her suggestion. "O'Sullivan? Aristos try to punch him in the face on a nightly basis. A little rudeness is an improvement." His fingers traced the faint outline of another forming bruise on her shoulder. "My messenger's time would be better spent retrieving the doctor."

"Don't bother him tonight."

"You're my wife, and I pay his salary."

"*Nick.*"

"*Alex.*"

When Thorne moved to stand, she clamped her hand firmly around his wrist. "You won't take that doctor away from patients in need. I've dealt with worse." When he hesitated, she released his wrist and made some amused noise. "What would the people of Whitechapel think to see the King of the East End fussing over a woman?"

The corner of Thorne's mouth twitched upwards. "That I'd finally taken the advice of some grannies and found myself a wife to fuss over?" He could almost hear their cackling.

"Is that what the grannies have been saying?" Alexandra murmured, head bowed as she reached for a cake of soap. The sight of it being dragged across her skin made something tug deep in Thorne's chest; his lips fondly recalled the sensation of that same spot on her arm. "And what did you tell them?"

Thorne's smile was small. "Told them I already found the one I wanted. Ruined my chances with her."

What else could he tell her? That he desired no one else?

No, there hadn't been another woman. There never would be another woman. It was just her.

Always her.

As she tightened her grip on the soap, Thorne braced himself for her next question. "And what did they advise?" she asked, her voice edged with bitterness.

He leaned against the tub, propping his chin in his hand. "Told me to find a new woman or learn how to grovel."

Alexandra's lips tightened in a gesture of disdain. "You had four years to learn, and you know where to find me. Did you need more lessons, or were you looking for another rich woman to swindle?"

Thorne couldn't bring himself to tell her. He'd come to her doorstep, again and again over the years – only to find every apology inadequate, every gesture of remorse falling short. *Sorry* wasn't good enough. Flowers? Pathetic. Everything left him tongue-tied and useless.

The sight of her, successful and content in her work, had only deepened his sense of inadequacy. What purpose could he serve in her life besides as a painful reminder of her father's betrayal?

And so he had returned to the Brimstone – this building her fortune had created – and stopped scheming. What made him think he could ever deserve her?

Thorne met her gaze. "Did you want me on your doorstep, Alex? Should I have gone on my knees and apologised? Would that have been enough after what I did?"

"Does it matter? On your knees or on your feet, you didn't even try." Alex gave a dry laugh. "Perhaps it wouldn't have mattered. You're not Lord Locke. The man at my door apologising would have been a stranger to me."

The blade in Thorne's chest twisted. "Then I should have introduced myself. I'm Nicholas Thorne. And I'm so very sorry."

Alex shut her eyes hard. "The man who came into my bedchamber – do you know what he called me while he pointed the pistol at my head?"

"What?" Thorne asked, dreading the answer.

"*Thorne's wife.* I didn't ask for that name, Nick. I didn't ask for any of this. Being foolish enough to believe a man's lies shouldn't come with a death sentence." She made some soft noise. "Just leave the brandy and get out, Nick. I can't stand the sight of you."

8

STRATFIELD SAYE, HAMPSHIRE

Four years ago

Alexandra fanned herself with her hat as she strolled along the country path.

It was the type of day that would make the devil himself sweat. The sky above was as blue as a robin's egg, cloudless, allowing the sun to bask the land in its merciless rays. If Alexandra had any sense, she would have been lounging in the shade of Roseburn's gazebo. But no, the village matrons had summoned her to deliver a basket to the Stone family at the opposite end of Fair Oak Green.

By the time Alexandra reached the sanctuary of her father's estate, her wool dress was as useful as a ballgown on a battlefield. The feathers on her stylish hat drooped like a dejected lover.

Alexandra took in the breathtaking view as she trudged up the path towards Stratfield Lake, at the southern edge of Roseburn's land. The water shimmered like diamond facets, stretching for acres into the woodland. She hadn't been here in years, but the water's allure was irresistible, and for a moment, she forgot the searing heat.

Alexandra lowered her hat. No one was about. If she swam, who would see her? Who would—

Boots crunched along the path behind her. Alexandra was surprised to see Nicholas Spencer sauntering down the trail with lazy confidence in each step, as if he didn't mind the heat. He had tossed his jacket over a shoulder, and his shirt was open at the collar, exposing a tantalising sliver of golden skin. Alexandra couldn't help but stare, for she'd never seen a man so... undone.

Why, he wasn't even wearing a hat.

"Good afternoon," Alexandra said, hoping she had imagined the squeak in her voice. Her heart was somewhere near her throat. "Fine weather today, isn't it?"

If Nicholas noticed her staring at him like a besotted fool, he made no sign of it. Instead, he flashed her a smile so blinding, Alexandra had to look away for a moment.

"I would say so," he said, his voice as warm as the sun on her skin.

His eyes were difficult to meet directly. They were too astute; he might uncover all of Alexandra's secrets. Like how often he'd occupied her thoughts lately; she had been foolish enough to risk loitering outside Marlowe's, hoping he'd reappear.

Three days ago, she considered making a ludicrous excuse to visit his property and knock on his door. *Have you possibly seen Mrs Langly's dog, an adorable corgi by the name of Linnet?* Of course, he might suspect a thing or two when said corgi failed to show up – being a figment of her imagination. She finally recognised her feelings as the dreadful disease of *infatuation*. And with that came a sudden awareness of Nick's first impression of her.

He'd caught her stealing a book.

He'd caught her stealing *a naughty book called Pandora's Box*.

Oh God, how she longed to have that lake swallow her whole. "I must go," she blurted, backing away. *Flee. I must flee. I must find my dignity at the bottom of the lake.* "Enjoy your walk, Lord Locke."

"Nicholas," he said. "Nick. Remember?"

As he reminded her of their agreement, a spark of electricity coursed through Alexandra's veins. *Nicholas.* She loved the sound of his name, the way it flowed off her tongue, and the shortened version that felt like a secret confession. "Nick," she repeated, eager to leave before she said something stupid and ruined everything. "Try the walk around the lake. It's lovely at this time of day."

But Nick wasn't ready to let her go so quickly. His voice dripped with amusement as he called out, "What if I preferred your company?"

Alexandra paused at the unfamiliar words. She thought she understood men, but *this* one eluded her. "Do you?" she asked, barely daring to believe it.

He shoved his hands in his pockets. How at ease he looked, so elegant. "You seem surprised," he remarked, his brow furrowing in confusion.

Had she become so jaded? Had she internalised every insult from her peers and even her father – the future old maid, the bitch, the frigid shrew – to where she believed her company was a burden? It saddened her to realise how much she valued his opinion.

She *wanted* Nick to like her.

She wanted him to be different.

But a thought occurred to her. "You're new to Stratfield Saye. I suppose you've had little time to make friends."

"That's true," he replied. And she felt a twinge of disappointment until he continued, "But I did meet someone at a bookshop five days ago, and I can't stop thinking about her."

Alexandra forgot about the heat and the lake and everything else around them. All she could feel was the rapid beating of her heart. "You must be starved for companionship if you'll look for it with a book thief."

His smile was devastating. "Perhaps I have a soft heart for thieves." He motioned with a hand. "Walk with me?"

This time, she agreed, and they strolled in comfortable silence along the path. The trail led them through a copse of trees where the sunlight filtered through the leaves, casting dappled shadows on the mossy ground. The water of the lake lapped gently at the shore beside them.

"Why did you seem surprised when I asked for your company?" he inquired.

Alexandra released a measured breath. "I worried I had once again offended propriety," she said with a hint of self-deprecation. "You might say it's a habit of mine. People know me as quite the improper shrew."

Nick swatted away a branch that hung in their path. "Mystery solved, then. What vile deeds have you committed?" he asked, his tone teasing. "Set fire to any buildings recently?"

She laughed at the absurdity. "No."

"Never stolen anything other than books? Not even so much as a tart?"

"Not one," she replied.

"Then what heinous crime did you commit to be labelled such a wicked wench? Did you dare step outdoors without your gloves?"

She made an indignant noise. "I talk about politics in public."

His surprised laugh warmed her. "Good God, politics? Whatever could be more scandalous!" He gasped theatrically.

Alexandra stepped closer to him, heart racing with excitement. "It seems I've reignited the age-old debate of whether women should be enfranchised," she said, fixing him with an expectant look. "What is your opinion on the matter, sir? Do you believe women should vote?"

Nick put a hand to his chest. "Every single election."

Encouraged by his answer, Alexandra continued, "What about allowing women to sit in the House of Commons? Do you believe they have a place there?"

He chuckled. "If there are ladies brave enough to shout at the opposition, why not?"

Alexandra inhaled sharply, her confidence buoyed by his support. "Do you find it acceptable that I want to work, despite being the daughter of a peer?"

Nick paused, tilting his head a fraction as something almost like astonishment rippled across his features. "Yes," he said softly, almost reverently. And then he spoke with an intensity that took Alexandra by surprise: "What work?"

Would he judge her? Would this be what turned him away? Talking about her future often made even the most progressive men uncomfortable. After all, supporting a woman's aspirations and considering her worthy of courtship were two different things. Aristocratic wives simply did not engage in work; it was too vulgar for their station.

But Alexandra refused to be silenced. She would not cower or allow any man to make her feel small.

She didn't believe that work was beneath her.

She picked up a stone from the shore of the lake, running her thumb over its surface. "Have you ever read Mary Wollstonecraft? She passed away seventy years ago, but her writing is still relevant today. Women are still fighting for access to education. London University just allowed nine women to matriculate this year. And you know what I keep thinking?"

He looked so patient and attentive, as if holding his breath in anticipation of what she would say next. "Tell me," he urged.

Alexandra gave a bitter laugh as she hurled the rock across the water. It skipped three times before vanishing beneath the surface. "It's 1868, and women are still fighting for even a fraction of the rights that men have enjoyed for centuries. Every small step forward is met with powerful men patting themselves on the back and taking credit. As if rights were a mere trinket bestowed on a whim, while the people with the most influence, from the House of Lords to the smallest parish council, are men who look exactly like them." She lifted her chin and looked him in the eye. "You asked me what kind of work I wanted to do. What if I said I wanted to write about social reforms? About those society has silenced because it values wealthy men's opinions over everyone else's? What if, one day, I wanted to buy a printing press and give people their own voice?"

She heard him exhale slowly. Nick stepped closer, his gaze never leaving hers. He wore a strange expression, intense and almost feverish – not just because of the heat. Alexandra realised with wonder that he liked what she had said. He looked as if he wanted to pull her close and kiss her passionately.

And if he did, she would let him.

"I'd ask what sort of desk I ought to purchase for you," he said. "A woman who does such work needs a good desk."

Her heart kicked in her chest, and she smiled. "I would say that I shouldn't accept a gift from you. But I may make an exception for a very large, very solid mahogany desk with many hidden compartments."

"Compartments for pens, ink, sweets, and secrets," Nick said with a grin. "Done."

He adored her.

Nick almost laughed at the absurdity of it – some joke the devil would enjoy. Here he was, lying to her, making her think he was some English lord, using a fake accent. Dressed in these smart clothes he'd bought just for the occasion. He had his coat off because it was too damned hot and twill itched.

And he adored his mark.

Nick couldn't help but admire how Alexandra's hair caught the sunlight, illuminating the fire in her eyes. "What about you?" she asked, tossing another rock into the lake. "How did you earn your reputation?"

"Well. I was no angel as a child, that's for sure. Always in trouble for one thing or another."

"And now you're a schoolmaster?" she asked with amusement.

After crafting thousands of lies during his worthless life, this one chafed. Schoolmaster. What had he been thinking?

He laughed, the sound feeling foreign in his throat. "I'll let you into a secret," he said, loathing himself. She deserved better than this. "Schoolmasters need a bit of wickedness to deal with their wicked children."

Alexandra quirked an eyebrow, her expression telling him she didn't believe a word. "My governess would call that absolute nonsense."

He grinned despite himself. Damn, but she was gorgeous when she got feisty. "Were you a good girl for your governess, then?"

The corners of her mouth lifted in a mischievous smirk, and Thorne felt like he'd been pulled beneath the waves.

"I drove her mad," she said with relish.

That's my girl, he thought before he caught himself.

"There, you see?" he asked, a bit unsteady now.

Alexandra didn't notice, thank God. She fanned her face with her hat. Sweat was beading on her brow. "I sense your reputation comes from saying things you shouldn't, just as mine does."

"Well," Nick murmured as his gaze drifted over her beautiful features, "what can I say? You and I must be scoundrels at heart."

Alexandra's breath caught in her throat, giving Thorne a rush of satisfaction. She was as affected by him as he was by her. But then she averted her eyes and regained her composure. "Would you mind if we paused?" she asked softly. "I'm feeling faint from the heat."

As she perched on a nearby rock, Thorne stood on the shore. He had never seen water so clear, as if it were made of glass. Life in Stratfield Saye made him uneasy, the comfort and cleanliness. Constant reminders of what he'd left behind and what he needed to get back to fixing. Would he ever have an opportunity like this again? Clean lake, clear sky? Beautiful lady in the countryside? Walking without purpose?

The time to do these things was a privilege of the wealthy. Safety, too.

Soon enough, Thorne would return to the grime and chaos of city life. The air would be hazy with smoke, and the rural scenes would be supplanted with dilapidated edifices. The fetid Thames would replace the lake view.

He had to make the most of this last chance before it vanished. Throwing his coat to the grass beneath his feet, he began unfastening his waistcoat.

"What are you doing?" Alexandra asked. Her stare lingered on Thorne's body for a moment longer than necessary before she glanced around, as if someone might see them.

Thorne grinned. "It's hot. We're near a lake." He gestured around them. "I assume you can put two and two together."

"Well, yes, but… We can't."

"Oh, but we *can*." He winked. "Scoundrels at heart, remember?"

Alexandra laughed. "You're incorrigible."

"Yes, I am."

"You're not a gentleman."

"Thought we made that clear."

"And it's so hot I think I'm going to melt." Alexandra threw her hat aside in exasperation and began tugging off her gloves with her teeth. "I hate you right now."

"I think you like me."

Alexandra made a face. "Turn your back, if you please."

Thorne turned away from her, unlacing his boots with deft fingers while she shed her clothing behind him. He imagined what it would look like – her petite form naked and wet against the backdrop of rolling hillsides. The texture of her skin beneath his tongue and lips. He almost let out a rueful laugh. She considered him safe.

She ought to remember that the devil was once considered the Lord's most beautiful angel.

A splash broke through his reverie. "Nick!" she called. "You're dawdling."

Thorne removed his boots and rolled up his trousers. When he turned to look at her, his heart skipped a beat. She swam with long, graceful strokes, the white of her undergarment trailing behind her. She was the most beautiful thing he had ever seen, like a luminous sea maiden luring sailors to their doom.

Now he understood why they took their chances with the sea. He was tempted to swim out to the middle of the lake and let the fates decide whether he lived or died.

Alex tilted her head. "You look pensive. What are you thinking?"

Thorne waded into the lake until the water reached his knees. "I've a confession to make."

Alexandra swam closer, her curiosity piqued. "I love confessions. Is it something terrible?"

Thorne smirked. "It's horrifying. It may shock you."

At that, Alexandra turned onto her back and floated, her chest rising above the waterline until he saw the dusky shadow of her pert nipples. Thorne bit back a groan. She was going to be the death of him.

"Shock me? I'm afraid that moment passed when your jacket hit the grass," she said with a sly smile.

Thorne chuckled, trying to hide his attraction to her. "I kept my shirt and trousers," he pointed out.

"You're stalling. Tell me, Nick."

"I can't swim."

"*Whaaaaat?*" She paddled closer. "I'm not shocked. I'm *horrified*. Where did you grow up?"

Thorne wished he could tell her the truth. Of the poverty and squalor of the rookeries, that the people of Whitechapel were not blessed with a place or time to float and swim without worry. The closest body of water was the Thames, and that foul river might as well have been the city's lavatory. And the water in the East End was just as bad; the Bethnal Green vestry was filled with corrupt bastards who didn't live in the district and didn't give a damn about sanitation. Diseases spread quickly when your water made you sick. Worse, the cramped quarters and close tenements housed dozens of people in single rooms. Whole families died together.

But he couldn't tell her these things. Nicholas Spencer hadn't been raised in London. So Thorne gave the first place that came to mind, somewhere far away where a man like Nicholas Spencer might flourish.

"Southwold," he said simply.

"Southwold?" Alex raised an eyebrow. "Really."

"Of course." What the bloody hell was wrong with Southwold? People lived there, didn't they? And presumably had plenty of small Southwoldians to teach.

Alex chuckled. "And that's worse, you know. You lived by the sea and can't even swim."

"I was too busy teaching," he lied through gritted teeth. The life he'd fabricated for Nicholas Spencer was like a poorly fitting suit. Made for someone else, someone with means.

"Then tell me, Lord Locke," she said, perching on a nearby boulder. "What was your life like in Southwold? Do you have a wife?"

"I don't," he said, settling on a rock at the lake's edge. He soaked his feet in the cool water.

"No? You must have been a devoted schoolmaster, then. Do you miss it?"

Thorne bristled at deceiving her. He couldn't bear the thought of wooing her with lies. So instead of answering her question, he offered a sliver of truth. "I miss my friends most, I suppose."

A reminder of the people he'd fail if he didn't marry this woman: Whelan's lads. O'Sullivan, who'd never been the same since Whelan sold him to an aristocrat years ago. Callahan, who Whelan used for his most heinous crimes. All the lads who'd lived and died in the cramped cellar below the streets of the Nichol. And the people who owed Whelan debt for protection, who didn't have the means to pay every month. They were forced to do Whelan's bidding or die.

"I'm sorry," Alex said softly. "It must be hard to go from having friends to being alone."

But Thorne couldn't dwell on the past. "Are we not friends?" he asked, trying to lighten the mood.

Their gazes locked, and Thorne could feel his heart pounding in his chest. Alex's cheeks flushed, and she turned away. "We are," she said, drifting onto her back. "Next time we meet, bring a swimming costume. Friends ought to teach each other how to swim."

9

LONDON

Four years later

Alexandra's entire skull was pounding.

"Ye think she's dead?"

"I think she's pretty."

"I think she's dead."

"She's not dead, ninny. Her eyelashes are fluttering. *Are ye dead, miss?*"

Alexandra peeled open her lids and was immediately assaulted by the searing light. Bloody hell, what had she done? Ah, yes. She vaguely recalled drowning her sorrows with a bottle of brandy somewhere between the ungodly hours of one and three in the morning. Now, she felt like she'd been trampled by a team of wild horses and left to die.

"Ugh," she groaned. "I'd rather be dead."

"Crikey, she don't sound like no proper lady," a voice whispered. "Thought them toffs spoke all posh and flowery, like them poems Mrs Ainsley forces us to learn."

Alexandra squinted at the two little girls with identical red hair and matching freckles. They couldn't have been more than seven years old, but their stares were as sharp as any gossiping matron's. One was dressed in green, the other in blue – a choice undoubtedly intended to tell them apart.

As she adjusted to the light, she took in her surroundings. The room was ornate, with sparkling chandeliers and blue wallpaper adorned with blooming flowers. The window framed an unfamiliar view of crowded buildings and endless rooftops. She slept in a strange bed, a towering behemoth of a four-poster with silky sheets fit for royalty. It could have held a family of elephants.

"Where am I?" she asked, trying to clear the cobwebs from her mind. She would never drink again.

Never, ever.

She couldn't even recall leaving the bathtub. Did Nick carry her out? Tuck her in? At least her pounding headache distracted her from the mortification of passing out in a bathtub stark naked after downing too much brandy in her estranged husband's gambling den.

The girl in the green dress spoke first. "Yer in the room next to Mr Thorne's," she said, bouncing on the bed beside Alexandra. "Are ye a real lady? We heard ye was a lady, but ye don't talk like one and ye haven't looked down yer nose at me yet."

These children only added to her confusion. Who did they belong to? Why were they here?

A thought occurred to her. Oh, dear God, had Nick sired children without telling her? She was going to *kill* him.

Be sensible, she reminded herself. It wasn't *their* fault that their father was an absolute cad.

"Why would I look down on you?" Alexandra asked the little girl as she struggled to regain her bearings.

The pounding in her head intensified as she sat up, but she pushed through it. She needed answers. She had to find Nick. Alexandra lifted the covers, relieved to find she was wearing—

Wait a moment. This wasn't her nightgown.

Was she wearing his mistress's clothes?

She gritted her teeth, plotting her revenge. A sharp knife between his shoulder blades would do the trick.

The little girl in the green dress appeared hesitant now. "Toffs don't look at us nice on the streets," she stuttered, her brow furrowing in confusion.

"Because they're snobs," Blue Dress interjected, with a tone of authority that belied her young age.

Upon closer inspection, Alexandra realised Blue Dress was older, maybe nine years old. She only appeared younger because of her small stature. Malnourishment had robbed her of height and weight, like many children in the East End.

Nick wasn't feeding his children properly?

Never mind the weapon. Alexandra was going to set Nick on fire, *then* shoot him.

The younger girl curled beside Alexandra and propped her chin atop her knees. "Thought ye was dead, but Dot kept insistin' ye wasn't."

Dot rolled her eyes. "And she's not, is she?" To Alexandra: "What's yer name, lady?"

"Alexandra," she said, still confused. If not Nick's, these children had to belong to *someone* here. Why else would two little girls be loitering in the private suite of a gaming hell? "And who might you both be?"

"Two naughty children who picked the locks again and are about to be late for school," a voice drawled.

Alexandra looked over to see Nick leaning against the doorframe, watching the girls with an amused expression.

"Is she really a lady, Mr Thorne?" Dot gave the bed a jostle. "She's ever so pretty. She got skin like milk, she does."

Nick's black eyes locked with Alexandra's. "Lady, she is. And, aye, very pretty."

The force of his heated stare ripped away the years between them. For a moment, it was like nothing had changed; he still held sway over her heart and her body. His presence filled her with a forbidden longing, igniting a fire that she'd tried desperately to put out since she'd left Stratfield Saye. But this time would be different. If it took every ounce of strength she possessed, Alexandra would cut him from her life for good.

Blue Dress touched her wrist. "Why she got bruises? Like 'andprints, them. Looks like me ma's did after spendin' a night with a man."

Nick clenched his jaw and pushed off the doorframe. "Dot, Lottie, time to go. O'Sullivan's going to take you to school, and I don't want to hear any complaining, either. Lottie—" He let out a breath. "Lottie, sweetheart, where are your boots?"

Dot ran to Nick, who clasped her hand. "She lost 'em, Mr Thorne."

"I didn't lose 'em," Lottie said, slowly getting off the bed. "Gave 'em to a girl what just came into the orphanage. She didn't have any boots."

"And now you don't have any," Nick said. He shook his head. "Go find O'Sullivan and have him fetch a pair for you from Mrs Ainsley's. Then it's straight to school, all right? Off you go."

"Bye, lady!" Both girls disappeared out the door.

As the patter of their footsteps disappeared down the hall, Nick cleared his throat. "How're you feeling?"

"Like I'm being stabbed through the skull," Alexandra said.

Nick's smile was slight. "I'd expect so. Didn't think a woman so small could consume that much brandy in a single evening. Want anything for your bad head?"

"No. I'll use the pain as a lesson never to drink again."

Alexandra twisted in the crimson sheets, her skin ashen against the deep scarlet fabric. The morning light cast her bruises into stark relief, especially the five-finger marks above her elbow.

"Any other bruises?" Nick's tone was casual, but Alexandra could see the smouldering anger in his countenance.

"A few." His unrelenting gaze forced her to continue, "But they appear worse than they feel."

Nick took a step closer, and Alexandra felt her body seized by his authoritative presence – as if he controlled the very air around him, constricting it until it became impossible to breathe. He focused on her contusions, inspecting them with an unsettling intensity. It was as if he was committing the details of each mark to memory, imagining the force behind every strike, the viciousness of each blow. This was not Nicholas Spencer, the Southwold schoolteacher. This man reigned over London's East End with an iron fist, his reputation for violence as infamous as a general on a battlefield soaked in blood.

He turned and picked up some folded clothes from the wing chair. "Here." He set the bundle beside her. "Thought you might like something to wear that wasn't a nightgown."

The shades were more sombre than she usually wore: grey, brown, and black. The corset was the only item with a touch of colour, and the pretty rosebuds on the undergarment unsettled her. Had he unlaced the stays while taking it off another woman? Had he admired the shape of her in it?

"Is it from the same place you found this nightgown?" She touched the silk fabric. It was well made, if a bit frayed. "From your mistress?"

"Mistress?" He lifted his lashes. "Is that where you think it came from?"

His gaze lingered on her like an obsidian blade. Cold and sharp yet born of heat. A perfect weapon; brittle, but the edge cut easily through flesh. If he wanted, he could wield his eyes like a weapon.

Alexandra refused to be cowed by this man's attempt to intimidate her. She stood her ground, her spine stiffening with courage. "I have no expectations. It's been four years."

Before she could react, Nick moved swiftly, pinning her to the bed with his arms on either side of her. His lips hovered just inches from hers, his voice a low purr. "Aye, four long years. And I've about worn out my hand, but I haven't touched another woman since you left my bed."

Alexandra's body betrayed her with a shiver. She couldn't help but wonder if he was telling the truth or spinning more lies. Had he really spent four years pining for her, or was this just another manipulation?

She shook her head, banishing the thought. She knew what kind of man Nick was – a master of deception who had destroyed her life with his charm and falsehoods.

But she was no easy mark, not anymore.

Fury coursed through Alexandra's veins as she pushed against Nick's chest, only to be met with an immovable wall of muscle. "You have no reason to lie to me anymore," she said. "You already have my money."

Nick's lips curled into a sly smile. "I suppose it's hard to believe that a man like me could remain faithful to his wife," he drawled. "But then again, I wonder if she could say the same."

As far as Alexandra was concerned, a thousand lovers couldn't erase the memory of Nick's body pressed against hers, his cock buried deep inside her. She could still feel the heat of his kisses trailing down her hips, settling between her thighs. The ache of his betrayal had not lessened, even after four years.

Her lips pressed together in a thin line. "That wife might wonder if her husband has any right to demand fidelity when he began the marriage under false pretences."

Nick's stare burned into hers, unrelenting. "Have you a lover, Alex?"

Alexandra couldn't resist the thrill of cruelty as she asked, "And if I do?" Let Nick be hurt. Let him wonder. He'd done worse. "Would you maim the hand he touched me with? Kill him for giving me what you couldn't?" She rested her hand against the nape of his neck and whispered, as cold as an ice storm, "Will you punish me for welcoming another man between my thighs?"

Nick jerked away from her. "Learned a thing or two from those heartless nobs, did you?"

"On the contrary. I learned everything I needed from you."

He gave a rueful laugh. "Ruthless, I am. But my enduring regret is lowering myself so far in your esteem that you believe I'd punish you, or anyone else, for my mistake."

How could she trust his words? He had hurt her so deeply that even after four years, the wound still bled. He wore the face of the man she loved, but he was not Lord Locke. Lord Locke didn't exist. "Perhaps there is no man in my life. After all, how could I trust them after you?"

His expression constricted slightly, as if he held back his pain at her words. "Then that ought to be my enduring regret."

"Enough." Alexandra had no desire to feel sorry for him. She gestured towards the door, steering the conversation to a more neutral topic. "If those children aren't yours, then whose are they?"

If anything, his expression became more guarded. "Dot and Lottie's mam died in a building collapse in the Nichol eight months ago. Don't know who their da was."

"And they live here? At the Brimstone?"

Nick hesitated. "The orphanage nearby."

He was fidgeting. It was a stark departure from his usual calm and collected demeanour, and it set her on alert. Nick was a man who never appeared uncertain or out of control. That he was acting so strangely only made her more suspicious.

It was a reminder that there was so much about his life that she had yet to discover, so many secrets that she had only pieced together through her work. He was a mosaic with a thousand missing pieces.

Frustrated, Alexandra asked, "But why do they come *here*, then?"

"Reckon they fancied having a sweet roll from the kitchens," he said, expression nonchalant. "The orphanage takes care of their needs, but most have never had full bellies and regular meals. They take it where they can. They know I'll give it to them since I own the—" He broke off abruptly, looking away.

A missing piece of the mosaic that was Nick's life fell into place.

"You own the orphanage?" Alexandra could barely conceal her astonishment.

Nick shrugged. "Few of them. Makes it easier to hire managers who treat the children well, put meals in their bellies, and don't sell them off for toffs to abuse."

It was easier if she believed the broadsheets written by those who did not know him. They called him an Irish upstart with suspected Fenian sympathies. One who used violent methods to claw his way from an impoverished nobody to someone who commanded an East End empire.

His reputation sold newspapers. Members of Parliament deemed him too dangerous, even as they spent money at his gambling den.

And he was the man who had crushed her heart beneath the heel of his boot.

When her work took her to the East End, Alexandra couldn't help but ask after her estranged husband. She heard stories from working girls and miscreants outside gin palaces alike, stories of his fairness and generosity. They spoke of the high wages he paid his staff, of the families he took responsibility for. Alexandra would take these notes to bed and read them over, the tightness in her chest a constant reminder that Nicholas Thorne was capable of caring for others. And he still conspired with her father to destroy her.

"And what about their school fees?"

"It's a small price to pay," he replied vaguely. "It gets them off the streets."

"But *you're* paying it, aren't you?" she pressed.

Nick's expression was inscrutable. "Does it matter who pays it, so long as it gets done?" At Alexandra's long silence, he gave a dry laugh. "If you're worried about mistaking me for a good man, don't bother," he said. "I care for what's mine. No more, no less."

Something in her bristled at that. Nick was giving her permission to hate him, was he? "How kind of you to remind me," she murmured, rising from the bed. She held the dress against her. While a touch too big in the bosom, it was close everywhere else.

Nick spoke from directly behind her. "Mrs Ainsley, the manager of the orphanage where Dot and Lottie stay, offered the dress when she'd heard you came in your nightclothes. The lads didn't have time to go through your wardrobe before the servants woke. They had other tasks."

Yes, focusing on who had hired her abductor and killed Mary Watkins was easier. The sooner they solved that matter, the sooner she could bring up the subject of divorce. Then she could board a ship and travel to all the places she had only read about in guidebooks: Italy, France, Greece, New York. Anywhere.

Anywhere far away from him.

"You don't mean to involve the police?"

"They're involved." At her raised eyebrow, he gave a

rueful smile. "Suppose it doesn't shock you that I've got a few of London's finest in my pocket."

"The only thing that would shock me, Nicholas Thorne," she said, "is if it were only a few. Did anyone recognise the man in my bedchamber?"

"No," he replied, his tone clipped. "Men who kill or abduct for money are worth more if they're not recognisable." She caught his look as she reached for the top button of her nightgown. "Listen, O'Sullivan and the lads cleaned up your room. Had to take a carpet or two, on account of the bloodstains. We'll stop by St James's to pick up a few things, but you're not staying there."

Alexandra shrugged. "Fine."

"Now why do I get the sense that doesn't mean you agree with me?"

"Because I don't. You want me to stay here in your gambling den." She twisted to reach for the back of the nightgown, but Mrs Ainsley must have needed help with this dress.

Nick nudged her hands out of the way and undid each button with ease. "Aye, I want you to stay here in my gambling den."

Alexandra tossed the nightgown to the floor. "Not interested."

Nick gave a slow exhale of appreciation. No, he was not entirely immune to her. He was a deceitful blackguard, a crook, downright immoral, but he couldn't hide his desire. A well of want hidden beneath a gruff exterior. It was the only truth between them.

Her words must have finally made their mark. "Wait, what the hell do you mean, not interested?"

"I'm not staying here with you," she responded coolly, slipping into a chemise, drawers, and corset. "Lace me."

He made an exasperated sound and started lacing her up. "Don't you dare suggest a hotel where anyone can just walk in."

"I'm not. I'll stay with Richard and Anne in Belgravia. My brother has kept a bodyguard on retainer since his father-in-law's trial."

"You think those nobs in Parliament don't want to see Grey taken down a peg after he revealed Sheffield's involvement in concealing child murder? You think they'll forgive his wife for sharing their secrets?"

He finished lacing her up, and Alexandra slipped on her dress. Without her needing to ask, he fastened the buttons for her and stepped back as she adjusted her skirts. "Of course not," she assured him, fixing him with an unwavering gaze. "But I'll be safe there."

"You'll be safe here," Nick said firmly.

"That man was in my bedchamber because I am married to you." Alexandra was not in the mood to mince words. "That body in Whitechapel was to taunt *you*. So perhaps you should consider your very long list of enemies and narrow it down for me." She threw up her hands. "Where are my bloody boots?"

Nick crossed to the bed and reached underneath. Thrusting the boots at her, he said, "So, you're going to put your brother's life in further danger, along with his wife? That one narrowly missed being married to a bloody killer. Are you going to risk her unborn child, too?"

Alexandra reared back in shock. "Who – who told you...? *Anne* is with child?"

"Grey has a loose tongue," Nick said with a hint of sarcasm. "He talks too much."

She pressed her lips together. It was difficult enough to be in the same room with Nick, but staying here, night after night? Separate rooms weren't enough. The span of the ocean might not even be, but it was a start. Then another four years. Ten years. Twenty.

Enough time for her to learn to trust someone again.

"Fine," she muttered through gritted teeth. "I'll stay."

Then, when this was over, she'd pack her things and leave him.

∽ 10 ∽

Richard Grey was at the Earl of Kent's residence when they arrived. The moment Thorne entered with Alex by his side, Richard's eyebrows shot up, and a wide grin stretched across his face.

"Hello, little sister," he said to Alex. "What—"

"I'm not speaking to you," Alex retorted, striding past her brother and thudding up the stairs. The sharp click of her boots reverberated through the foyer. "I can't believe you didn't tell me I'm going to be an aunt," she hollered over her shoulder.

Richard cast a sidelong glance at Thorne. "You *told* her?"

Thorne mused on the novelty of being involved in something as commonplace as a family drama. It was a welcome change of pace. The lads he grew up with in Whelan's dingy basement always had problems of the more challenging variety – ones that typically culminated in death.

"How was I supposed to know you hadn't given her the news?" he responded nonchalantly, shrugging his shoulders.

"It's been four years since you two separated," Richard said, his voice tinged with annoyance. "Letting you in on the secret was like telling any random bloke on the street."

Alexandra's muffled shout emanated from the upper floor. "Send one of them my way. They'd make for a better husband."

Richard's lips twitched, and Thorne couldn't determine if he was stifling a chuckle or a scowl. "You're not currently reconciling with her, I take it," Richard remarked.

"Not even remotely," Thorne retorted.

Richard gestured towards a nearby door. "Care for a drink? Or several?"

"God, yes."

In the study, Richard poured generous amounts of brandy into two snifters and handed one to Thorne. The last time Thorne had set foot in the room was three months prior. He'd barely savoured the brandy then; it was a poor distraction from his contemplations of murder. Richard had uncovered that the Duke of Kendal was clandestinely adopting children from the orphanages in the East End, and they were never seen again.

Richard and Thorne had broken into the duke's home and found a child in a cellar there. Had they been a day later, they might not have saved the lass. Thorne keenly felt some of the blame. He was responsible for the East End children – to look after them if he could – but even he didn't have the power to stop every piece of shite in the city from doing unspeakable acts. He'd do his best, one case at a time. One threat at a time.

One murder at a time, if necessary.

And now his wife had seen the monstrousness that people in this city were capable of.

The sweetness of the brandy suddenly seemed too cloying; a good Irish whiskey would have suited better. Something that burned and satisfied in equal measure. Being in such proximity to Alex after all these years... Thorne's nerves were frayed beyond reckoning. As she stripped down that morning, he felt the sting of loss. He'd kissed her once, skimmed his calloused palms over her smooth skin. Christ, he even missed their swimming lessons together. She used to laugh so freely at Stratfield Lake. He hadn't made her smile for years.

"Are you going to sit there and down that entire bottle, or will you tell me what the hell happened?" Richard demanded.

Thorne battled with his guilt, shoving it down where it belonged: lodged beside the permanent dagger that Alex had plunged into his heart when she left Roseburn. The one he deserved. "What makes you think something happened?"

Richard swirled his glass of brandy thoughtfully in his palm. "Maybe it's to do with a household of panicked servants summoning me when they found out their mistress had vanished into thin air and, oddly enough, taken a blasted carpet with her." He glared at Thorne. "I don't suppose you'd know anything about that, would you?"

"Was it a nice carpet, at least?"

"Who gives a toss about the carpet? It was expensive and conspicuously *gone*."

Thorne leaned back in his chair and crossed his legs. "I'll buy your brother a new one."

"Forget the damned carpet," Richard snapped. "Three days ago, you wouldn't even spare a word to my sister, and now I find out she spent the night with you. Now tell me what happened."

Thorne made a noise and polished off his brandy. "Some

bastard tried to abduct her from her bedchamber last night. Because she's my wife."

Richard stood up, alarm filling his features. "Say that again."

Thorne had no intention of revealing Mary's murder to Grey. The last thing he needed was Richard getting tangled up in this mess when he had a pregnant wife to fuss over.

"A man like me has a lot of enemies, Grey. I've made more than my fair share while helping you blackmail those poncy politicians in Parliament."

The other man grimaced. "I'm sorry."

"No need for that. They wouldn't pass a sodding reform bill if their lives depended on it."

A thump from upstairs caught Grey's attention. "So, Alexandra will be staying with you at the Brimstone?"

"Just as soon as she gets her clothes. And before you think of getting involved, you'd do well to keep an eye on your wife. You've got enough problems. Don't burden yourself with mine."

Richard looked angry at that. "You're my bloody brother-in-law now. She's my *sister*."

"I'm taking care of it, Grey."

"And the man who attacked her?"

"Dead," Thorne said tightly. Then, meaningfully: "Sorry about your brother's fancy bloody carpet."

He wouldn't tell Richard Grey that his sister was the one who had dealt the killing blow. As understanding as he was, murder had a way of changing a man's opinion of someone. It was no skin off Thorne's hide to imply he was responsible; he'd committed enough unsavoury acts in his time. Sometimes he had to remind Grey of what sort of man he'd allied with.

Grey levelled a severe look at Thorne. "If you hurt her again, I'll stand by and watch as she beats the hell out of you, and then I'll help her burn your life to the ground."

"Duly noted," Thorne said with a dry laugh. He finished his brandy and stood up. "She's been up there a while. I hope she's not bringing her entire wardrobe."

Grey directed him to Alexandra's chambers, and Thorne departed from the study. As he made his way up the stairs, he examined the paintings that lined the walls, all portraits of Grey's family. He wondered how his wife felt, surrounded by reminders of her illegitimacy, of her father's role in destroying her life. The old earl was dead now, and the house and title had passed to his heir. But Thorne knew from experience that death didn't make memories less painful. It only eased the hurt for a brief time.

The door to Alex's bedchamber creaked open like the rusty hinges of a long-abandoned cellar door. Thorne stepped into the room and was met with a sight that stopped him dead in his tracks.

His wife was huddled on the floor, her fingertips tracing the bare floorboards with a despairing touch. The look on her face was like a punch to the gut, a reminder of the last time he saw her at Stratfield Saye, when she banished him from her life.

Thorne closed the door with a soft click, but the silence was suffocating. Alex didn't look up at him, didn't acknowledge his presence.

"Alex," he breathed, afraid to shatter the stillness.

"You can see the blood, can't you?" she asked him, barely above a whisper. "It stained the wood."

The floor was clean, scrubbed until it gleamed. The air was thick with the scent of lemons, an attempt to mask the stench of death that lingered like a spectre. O'Sullivan and his men had done an admirable job of cleaning up the evidence, but the memory of what had happened here would never be erased. Thorne knew that better than anyone. He had lost count of the number of times he had covered up a murder, the number of bodies buried on his orders.

This time, it was different.

This time, it was personal.

But Thorne comprehended her; it didn't matter how many men he'd had killed. The first was the hardest, the one that haunted you long after the blood had dried and the body was buried. A weight that you carried with you wherever you went.

"Alex," he said again, softer. He knelt beside her, his hand hovering over her back. "Sweetheart, look at me."

She didn't respond, her fingers tracing patterns on the floorboards. Thorne could see the pain etched into every line of her features, an almost palpable grief. "I killed him right here. He had me on the ground, and I killed him."

Thorne recoiled at the memory those words evoked. He watched as she curled her hand into a fist, a bruise on her wrist that spoke of violence and pain. He was a curse, a poison that infected everything he touched. She could have been so much more, could have had a life beyond the blood and the violence. But he had taken that from her, had dragged her into a world she never wanted to be a part of.

Stolen a better future from her.

Thorne's heart was heavy as he gazed down at her, his hands framing her face like a prayer. "Alex," he said, rough with emotion. "Look at me."

Slowly, her eyes lifted to meet his, and Thorne felt his

world shift. She was his anchor, the only thing that kept him grounded in a world that had long since lost its moorings. Without her, he would be adrift, lost.

With sins heavy enough to sink him.

"I wish I could take those memories away," he whispered, his thumb tracing her cheekbone. "But I can't. All I can do is promise I'll never let harm come to you. Do you understand?"

But Alex shook her head, her eyes clouded. "No," she said. "I told you I don't—"

"You don't believe my promises," he finished for her. "Listen to me, anyway. I'm a bastard for what I did to you. You have every right never to trust me again because God knows I don't deserve it. But I'll protect you with my life. Understand?"

Thorne's thumb traced a gentle path across her cheek, needing to touch her. He had missed her, missed the way she fit into the curve of his body, the way her caress set his skin on fire. He was hungry for her, starved and ravenous with want.

As he shifted closer, drawn in by the pull of her gravity, he couldn't help but whisper, "Remember what I told you back at the Brimstone? I protect what's mine."

Alex pulled away from him, her eyes flashing. "I'm not yours."

Thorne made a frustrated sound in his throat, but he knew better than to push her. "Fine," he said, his voice clipped. "Call yourself whatever you want. But I'll still offer you protection, regardless."

There was a weight to her silence, a sense of impenetrable fortitude that Thorne could almost touch. She was a fortress made of steel and stone; he was just a man who had broken her heart.

"I need to make something clear to you," she said, finally, calm and measured. "This is not a choice for me. I'm doing this for survival. When we find who contracted my attempted abduction and Mary's murder, I'm leaving."

The knife in his chest twisted. "Alex—"

But she wasn't finished, her words cutting through the air like a knife. "This is not a second chance, Nick. Next time I walk out that door, it's for good."

Thorne knew she was right, and there was no going back to the way things had been before. He had shattered her trust, had destroyed any future together.

Thorne had no dreams of a future that would never be. He didn't wish for second chances or pray to the stars above. The East End was where dreams went to die, where the only truth was what you could see with your own eyes.

Thorne dealt in simple honesty: she owed him nothing, and he owed her everything.

Thorne reached out slowly, his movements deliberate and measured. Alex tensed, as if preparing for battle, and Thorne felt a pang of regret. Perhaps she expected him to lay some claim on her. To remind her of their vows in Gretna and the register they signed as proof.

But he wasn't like a child in the Nichol, about to cage a bird to hear it sing. Confining something untamed always killed it quicker.

"I let you go before," he said, "and I won't stop you from leaving again. It's not my way. But you ought to know a few things before you walk out that door one last time."

Her breath came out in a slow exhalation. "Like what?"

"It wasn't all lies," he said softly.

11

STRATFIELD SAYE, HAMPSHIRE

Four years ago

Alexandra's heart raced as she departed Roseburn. She had agreed to rendezvous with Nick at the lake for their maiden swim, and while the idea of seeing him once more thrilled her, meeting him in such secrecy was risky business. If anyone were to find out – if anyone were to witness them...

Alexandra's reputation would be in tatters.

For now, she wanted to keep their friendship a secret and let it blossom without the expectations of courtship. Alexandra dismissed her maid's help and dressed, concealing her bathing costume under a simple walking dress. With determination in her step, she headed towards Stratfield Lake.

It was another scorching day in Hampshire, with the distant hills providing a perfect backdrop of fluffy, white clouds. Alexandra hummed a tune as she strolled down the path, the sun filtering through the trees and dancing on her skin. As the lake came into view, a smile played on her lips.

Her smile faded when she saw Nick.

It's only an infatuation, she told herself, swallowing hard. *Only an* – he turned and spotted her – *infatuation.*

Oh, lord.

How had she never realised that a man's bathing costume could be so revealing? His sailor-style black suit, coupled with a shirt that showed off his chiselled arms, left Alexandra breathless. But the shorts were the true killer. The material clung to his powerful thighs and ended at the knee to reveal shapely calves. It wasn't just the smooth expanse of his golden skin, but the corded strength of it that made Alexandra's heart skip a beat. This man hadn't achieved his physique in a classroom; he had worked for it.

His gaze met hers. And his smile – God, that smile – rendered her speechless.

"Been there long?" he asked, with the satisfied awareness of a man who had caught a woman blatantly admiring him.

"If I was?" She kept her voice light as she approached.

If he was surprised by her confession, he didn't show it. He merely looked pleased. "I'd ask if you've been enjoying the view."

"Aren't you bold?" Alexandra teased, placing her towel on the nearest rock. "Next, you'll have me compose an ode."

His amusement was infectious. "An ode? Go on, then. Impress me."

"*With a strut and a swagger, he preens like a king. His vanity inflated, a comical thing. I share this verse, with a grin and a tease. To rib the grand gent, who struts with such ease.*"

Nick laughed in genuine surprise. "Did you make that up just now?"

"I told you I'm a writer," she said with a wink. "How was my poem?"

He tilted his head. "I was hoping for something more like, *The rose is red, the violet is blue, your face is a poem, and your body, too.*"

"Ugh." Alexandra cringed. "That's horrible. I should push you into the water and see if you swim better than you rhyme."

Nick leaned against the tree on the banks of the lake. "But what will happen to the scandalous things we do together if I die? Who could possibly replace me?"

"You're not my only friend in Stratfield Saye." She had other friends. Older ones. Near their dotage. They enjoyed needlework and spoiling small dogs.

Nick scoffed. "The village ladies? What would you say to them about swimming unchaperoned with a bachelor? Caught red-handed admiring his backside? You're a writer. Use your skills."

"Maybe I'd compose an ode to your backside. Something like this," Alexandra retorted as she set her food basket down. "*On the lake's shore we stroll, a picturesque scene. His alluring backside, so firm and so lean. With a charming ode, his assets I toast. A gentleman's rear, that deserves the most boast.*"

"Oh ho!" Nick laughed. "Quite a rhyme." He crossed his arms, and the movement distracted her. She had never seen bare biceps on a man who wasn't one of her brothers. He caught her look. "I see you enjoy my front, too."

Alexandra snorted and unbuttoned her day dress. He watched as she took it off and set it beside her basket. "I think I loathe you."

"I think you like me," Nick replied confidently, his eyes sparkling with amusement. Then he studied her bathing dress, bemused. "Is it common for women to wear two complete dresses?"

"Two… sorry?" She motioned to her outfit. "This is my bathing dress."

It was a shapeless attire comprising a short blue garment worn over wide trousers. Unlike Nick's, it concealed every inch of her body. Nick frowned as if she had made the absurd choice to bring a horse blanket to their lessons.

"That's an entire dress. What's it made of?"

Alexandra rolled her eyes. "Flannel."

"Huh. How can you even swim in it?"

"Magic." Without waiting for him to answer, she gestured towards the water. "Come here. I'm going to teach you how to float."

"Float?" He said the word in astonishment, as if she'd just declared they were having eel for luncheon.

"Learning to float requires trust." She waded into the lake and threw a glance over her shoulder. "And perhaps I need to learn to trust you before I teach you how to catch me in the middle of the lake."

A strange look crossed his face, one that held secrets she had yet to uncover. "Is that what you'll teach me? How to catch you?"

Alexandra gave him a sly grin. "I'll think about it."

She crooked a finger at Nick like some temptress beckoning him for a kiss. Even in that silly bathing costume, she was more enticing than any woman he had ever met. He watched water drip from her hair down the column of her throat and envied its journey.

"Come in, Nick. You're not scared, are you?"

Control yourself. She's just like any other mark.

So why didn't she seem like it?

Nick waded in. The water was cool, but not overly so. It was a balm in such warm weather. "Not afraid of much."

"Oh? Here, lean back against my arm." She drew closer and slid a hand across his back. A jolt went through him, and – *Christ* – his cock stirred. He curled his fingertips into his palm. *Control. Control.* He did as Alex asked.

"Good," she murmured, her voice as beautiful as birdsong. "Lean into me now. That's it. And relax."

He closed his eyes and allowed her to pull him further into the lake, her breaths and the gentle splashing of water lulling him into a state of relaxation. It was one of the rare moments in his life where comfortable silence enveloped him, a luxury he had seldom encountered. The East End was never still, the streets pulsating with sounds from every direction. The noisy tenements, the rumble of traffic, the lively taverns, and the machinery clanging in the factories.

He had never truly experienced complete stillness until he found himself in Stratfield Saye that first night. He woke up to an eerie quietness, and the only sound he heard was the rhythm of his breath.

Alex's voice was as soothing as the water lapping around them. "So, what are you afraid of?"

Nick tried not to stiffen. The quiet shattered. Replaced with—

The cold and dark. The dripping of the cellar and the harsh winter and numb limbs. A hunger that gnawed in his gut, the pain of it as sharp as teeth through skin. Failing the

*men who survived it with him if he didn't seduce and marry
one last mark.*

One. Last. Mark.

The reminder forced him to relax once more. Thorne
could not afford failure.

"What if it were something silly?" he asked lightly. "Like
rats?"

*Down in the cellar, the scratch of claws against stone.
They could smell the lads closest to death.*

"Rats?" She sounded amused. "I'd say you're in the
perfect place to avoid them here, in the middle of a lake."

She jostled him with a soft laugh, pushing him farther
into the water. Thorne was floating now, but Alex had
yet to release him. Not that he minded. He loved how
her hand lingered on his spine, the smooth press of her
palm against his skin. How he longed for her to touch him
everywhere.

"And what about on land?"

"Why, Nicholas Spencer," she said, and he could hear the
smile in her voice. "I'll just have to save you from the rats
on land, won't I? Mice, too, if your fear extends to them."

Nick opened his eyes, and Alexandra smiled down at
him, her golden hair glinting in the sun. He wondered if she
was a vision he had conjured up during his hungry nights in
Whelan's cellar. But no, she was tangible, and the longing
in his heart was real.

He could feel her hands now, the soft stroke of a thumb
against his shoulder. How easily she could leave him in
the middle of the lake to drown. No wonder she said this
required trust. Thorne was learning to trust her.

And she was learning to trust Nicholas Spencer.

At that moment, he loathed the schoolmaster. He hated the imaginary collection of Southwoldian children, the house that wasn't his, the title that didn't belong to him, this accent that was as fake as his background. He wanted her to see Nicholas Thorne and like *him* – scars and all.

It wasn't to be. The day she learned his true name was the day she'd learn to hate him.

"You're so serious now," Alex murmured with a frown. "Was it something I said?"

"Just thinking I like you," he said softly. "Ratcatcher that you are."

She ducked her head, but not before he saw her blush. Nick felt her grip tighten. "You're trying to distract me with your masculine wiles, I think."

"Masculine wiles?" He leaned back into the water. "Never heard of those."

"Oh, my brothers have them. They give women a certain look, as if they've crooked a finger. But yours is more effective. I suppose it's because your eyes are so black."

Thorne gave a short laugh. "Are you this candid with everyone?"

"Yes." She pressed her lips together. "That's my problem. I do all the wrong things, which is why my father banished me here before the end of the season. He considers me an embarrassment. Said I was ruining my marriage prospects."

She said this last part with a forced smile that gutted him. Thorne longed to tell her the truth: her father sent her to Stratfield Saye to be seduced by the confidence artist he had hired to steal her money.

Thorne had no right to be so angry. She was his mark.

But he'd heard the hurt in her voice, and rage coiled inside him. He liked her. She deserved better than this.

Better than *him*.

"You could never be an embarrassment," Thorne told her gently.

"A woman who speaks her mind is amusing for conversation, but not in a wife. Suddenly, that entertaining conversationalist becomes a political and social liability." Water dripped from Alexandra's lashes onto her cheeks. He wanted to kiss those droplets, hear her laugh again. Make her smile always. "But perhaps the ladies in Southwold are permitted to speak more freely."

Those damn nobs. They understood nothing of value. Tell them a rock was an antiquity, and they'd pay a fortune. Present them a dusty sapphire, and they'd all query, "Pray tell, what is this pebble?" If they had looked beyond appearances, they would have recognised her worth the moment she spoke. They would have seen her anger and passion and wanted her just as desperately as he did.

Thorne thought of all the women he knew in the rookeries, and wrath was how they survived. Sometimes, it was all you had left to burn on a cold night. They would not understand these rules about keeping quiet. He certainly didn't.

"They're formidable," he said to her, thinking only of East End women. "And fierce. They speak their mind and don't find shame in work. I think you'd like them."

Her expression softened. "They sound wonderful."

Nick almost touched her, stroked his thumb across her cheek. He wanted to remove her bathing dress and know the feel of her skin, the look of it in the light. But her garments covered so much of her; fabric was another way to keep a woman hidden.

"That they are."

"Nick," she whispered, leaning in so close that he thought she might kiss him. But she didn't. "I never told you what I was afraid of."

His lips twitched. "Not rats."

Alexandra worried her lip. "Not rats," she confirmed. "I don't suppose you've met my father?"

Nick shook his head, adding a small lie to the growing list.

"He's not known for pleasant company. Neither was my mother, from what I understand. Their marriage was arranged when they were very young, and it was clear from the beginning that he hated her. She died while giving birth to me. James, my eldest sibling, practically raised my brother Richard and me – quite a responsibility for a mere boy. I saw my father four times a year at most. He despised his children because of how much we resembled our mother. None of us favours our father, me least of all."

Nick felt her fingers brush his skin in the water, an idle movement as she considered what to say next. "Nick, have you ever loathed anyone so much that the mere memory of them angers you?"

He held his breath and thought of Whelan. "Yes," he said simply.

"Then you'll comprehend my fear." Her fingertips were at the nape of his neck again, stroking. "I'm terrified my father will force me to marry someone I'll hate until the day I die."

Nick froze. Her soft words stirred something in his chest,

tight and painful. He was to be that man she hated, the one forced upon her.

A wild notion lodged in his mind: if he told her everything, she might understand. Maybe even wed him, still. Give him the means to seize power from Whelan before the old bastard hurt anyone else.

No. You can't risk that.

O'Sullivan was hiding in the East End, waiting for him to return. Callahan was still monitoring Whelan's movements. The others depended on Nick to see this through – he'd told them he had a mark to end it all, and he couldn't fail them.

Play your role. You are Nicholas Spencer.

And so he smiled Nicholas Spencer's charming smile and said, "Perhaps you won't end up with someone so bad. You might even like him."

"I'm glad you think so. Maybe we'll meet in the ballrooms of London one day, long after you've learned to swim."

Christ, she was beautiful. Thorne had never felt like more of a bastard. "May I have the pleasure of a dance with you?" he asked, attempting to regain some of his composure.

"Of course," she whispered back, her voice as sweet as a lark's song. "I'll save you a dance."

When Thorne returned to Fairview House – the manor he had borrowed for his scheme – the earl was waiting for him.

Thorne entered the sitting room and found Kent staring out the window with a glass of sherry. Thorne was not a fool; he understood what these occasional visits meant. The earl would make himself comfortable as a reminder: he owned everything in this residence. Thorne was hired help, paid for like a butler or a valet. His presence at Fairview House was to complete the ruse, nothing more.

Kent was immaculately dressed in dove grey trousers and a coat. His blond hair was brushed back, pristine. His features were stern, made more severe by high cheekbones and silvery eyes. They were the colour of gunmetal and every bit as cold.

That icy gaze swept over Thorne's clothes – still damp from his lesson with Alex. "Good God," Kent said with a short bark of laughter. "Before today, I could almost have been fooled. How uncivilised you look."

Thorne went to the sideboard and poured himself some sherry. "You didn't want a gentleman. So you got me." He toasted with his glass and tossed back the spirit in a single swallow. Then Thorne splashed more liquor into the snifter, sat in the leather chair, and propped his boots up on the table – pointedly uncivil.

Kent grimaced. "The servants tell me you've met Alexandra. Several times now."

Ah, so the old man wanted an update. "She's a fine woman. Has a kind heart."

He said those last words just to see what Kent would do, what he'd say. The earl only sneered. "I don't care about her heart. Have you seduced the chit yet, or not?"

Thorne took a sip of the sherry but hardly tasted it. "No."

Kent drew himself up. "If you're wasting my time—"

"You want to force her to marry me, catch us swimming alone," Thorne said sharply. "But I'll not force my attentions on any woman. Not for one hundred thousand pounds, not for a bag of jewels, and certainly not for you."

"A thief with principles," Kent said. "How shocking."

"Seduction and marriage were our deal. So make a choice: will you force her to wed me or not?"

Kent's lip lifted. "No. Alexandra is too headstrong. She'd run to her brothers before I dragged you to the altar, and neither of my sons would suffer if I cut off their finances in retaliation. She has to come to you willingly."

"Then let me do my job."

Thorne didn't intend to tell Kent that he was sure Alex was growing to trust him. He wanted longer with her before revealing that he was precisely the man she feared most: someone she'd hate for her whole life.

"I'll concede your point, Mr Thorne." Kent sipped his sherry thoughtfully. "However, I can move things along."

A wintry chill settled in the pit of Thorne's belly. "How?"

"Leave it to me. Alexandra won't be able to resist something I've forbidden her from having."

∽ 12 ∽

LONDON

Four years later

Alexandra couldn't concentrate.

For the second night in a row, she barricaded herself in that opulent bedchamber at the Brimstone. Even with the connecting door to Nick's room locked, every noise from that direction jolted her into awareness. After four years, her husband was only a room away.

Separated by one door and a single lock.

She did her best to throw herself into work. Notes were scattered across her bed, the tea table, and the small writing desk that was barely adequate for composing a letter. The chaos had some organisation: these were times of shipments, these were men and women transported to Australia, locations, manifests, interviews. Crimes this intricate were filled with minutiae – and there was her problem. Minutiae required concentration, diligence.

And all she could think was: *It wasn't all lies.*

"Stop this," she whispered to herself. "Stop it." She groped for the wooden box under her pillow, for what seemed like the thousandth time that day. "He is a liar, and *this* is the truth," she continued, telling herself the same thing she had over the years since their separation.

Alexandra opened the box and lined up the columns she'd cut from newspapers. This one, written by Nicholas Spencer in *The Examiner*:

Lady Alexandra writes admirably of the difficulties of East End workers. However, it is easier to notice oppression while standing at the top of the factory gazing down from that lofty height than it is to acknowledge the ways in which every man and woman of her station benefits from the exploitation of their labour.

And this, from the *Saturday Review*:

Lady Alexandra's work in charity, like many women of her station, comes with the problem of picking and choosing recipients based upon moral judgement, rather than an understanding that every man and woman serving in the gaol for thievery began their crimes as a starving lad or lass who stole a loaf of bread to help feed a hungry family.

These eight passages she had cut from the literary reviews and newspapers revealed his real thoughts: marriage didn't change the fact that their backgrounds were insurmountably different. He had written reviews of her work under the name *Nicholas Spencer*, knowing she was the only person in London who would ever connect that name to Nicholas Thorne.

Alexandra would ask him about these one day, when she could shove the box in his face and convey nothing of her hurt. But she was not there yet. His words still held weight.

His lies still hurt.

A rap at the door drew her attention. "M'lady?" The young maid, Morag, entered the room and gave a startled noise. "Jesus, Mary, and Joseph," the girl squeaked, gawping at the mess.

Alexandra put Nick's articles back into the box and shut it with a thump. She ignored Morag's shock at the collection of notes scattered across the room. "Yes?"

Music drifted from the hall as Morag opened the door wider. "I just…" She scanned the room with wide eyes. "I just came to ask if ye were wantin' dinner soon, m'lady."

"Thank you, no." Laughter roared from downstairs. Nick's business, it seemed, was crowded tonight. The noise was breaking her already fragile concentration on her work. "Later, perhaps."

Morag cleared her throat. "Would ye like me to tidy the room for ye?"

"*No.*" At Morag's stunned expression, Alexandra tried again. "That is, please tell the other staff that the room must stay as it is. If a note is missing, I'll know."

"Aye, m'lady," Morag said, no doubt thinking Alexandra was a complete lunatic.

More hoots of laughter came from below stairs. Alexandra frowned in irritation and shifted her notes into better-organised piles. "Is it always this obnoxiously loud?"

Though Alexandra had arrived two nights ago in the middle of business hours, the private suites, kitchens, and staff rooms at the back of the club muffled the noise from below.

"Sometimes louder, if the orchestra is in a mood." Morag didn't seem bothered by it. "If not dinner or tidyin', would ye like help dressin' for bed?"

Alexandra gave a distracted shake of her head. What was it Nick did during these nights? Was he downstairs now laughing with the other gentlemen? Flirting with Maxine's girls? Counting his pounds, shillings and pence? "I might as well take a look at what my money built," she muttered, passing the maid. "Goodnight, Morag," she called over her shoulder. "Take the night off."

All Alexandra had to do was follow the raucous noise, and it led her to a balcony overlooking the gaming hell's ground floor. She stared at the sea of men and women below in amazement. Now she understood why everyone from aristocrats to businessmen patronised Nick's club. The decor at the front was decadent, everything draped in gilt, gold, and crimson. The ceiling fresco completed the opulence; without the gaming tables, the hell could have been mistaken for a palace ballroom in France. The busy tables were full of men laughing and chatting, with women draped across their laps.

Alexandra leaned forward, resting her elbows against the railing. This was what Nick had betrayed her for, what he had used her fortune to build.

A monstrosity to line his pockets.

Some heavy ache settled in her chest. This had been worth everything to him: a building. Just a mere building covered in gold trimmings, where he ruled as lord and master. His East End palace. This place had been worth destroying her.

A gusty, bitter laugh escaped her. She hoped Nick felt cold at night, knowing the Brimstone was what he sold his soul for. She hoped it brought him comfort in the days to come, long after the divorce petition had been settled. While he counted money and card decks, *Alexandra* would be travelling the world. It was time she made up for the years she'd wasted hurting over him.

"My lady," came a voice behind her. "Was there something you needed?"

Alexandra looked over to see Nick's factotum – the one with the spectacles and the pretty face. She could study him properly now, in the bright light of the candelabras. She had been in such a rush when she showed up on the Brimstone's doorstep. Few men were more beautiful than Nick, and this one was his opposite: gold in the way of an angel, with tawny hair and startling eyes the colour of a tiger's. He certainly seemed more predator than angel – or, at least, as fierce as a heavenly warrior. Right now, his full attention was on her, and if Alexandra had not grown used to Nick's scrutiny, she might have been unnerved by him.

"You're Mr O'Sullivan, yes?" At his nod, she extended her hand. He stared at it, as if he wasn't certain what to do with it. "It's not a snake, sir. I prefer the informality of a handshake."

Mr O'Sullivan seemed reluctant, but grasped her hand and gave it a firm squeeze before releasing it. "Is there something I can do for you?"

"No. I wanted to see the Brimstone for myself. Assess its value."

"It's a gaming hell, not a stable of thoroughbreds," he said.

Unlike Morag, Mr O'Sullivan did not defer. He did not regard her as a staff member might, when faced with his boss's wife. Rather – behind his cool demeanour – Alexandra had the unnerving suspicion that he considered her an unwelcome burden. Trouble that had shown up on his doorstep and now seemed content to linger.

Well, that was hardly *her* fault, was it?

"Mr O'Sullivan," Alexandra said calmly, "I have a pair of working eyes. As a married woman, I may not be permitted to own property, but I'm nevertheless relieved Nick didn't waste my money purchasing a stable. If he had, I might have strangled him."

His lips twitched, and Alexandra wondered if Mr O'Sullivan was trying to suppress a smile. "You're blunt for an aristo."

"So I've been told." She scrutinised him. "I hear you're very close to my husband. I assume this means Nick told you the truth before our marriage went public in the newspapers."

"Yes."

"Then perhaps you'll understand why I place a high value on honesty."

Mr O'Sullivan stared down at the bustling club. Alexandra wondered what he thought of this place, of the money that created it. What had Nick told his friends after returning to the East End? Had he laughed about her? Called her a fool, a pigeon, a mark? Worse?

"What about loyalty?" Mr O'Sullivan asked, breaking his silence. At her puzzled expression, he added, "You ought to ask him why he went to Hampshire sometime. God knows every man in his employ owes Nicholas Thorne their lives. One of them even gave it for yours."

Alexandra flinched at the reminder of O'Malley, the man Nick had hired to protect her. He had been murdered in her garden. What had they done with his body? Had he a proper burial? A headstone? God, she'd not thought to ask.

"I'm very sorry for Mr O'Malley's loss, and that you had to take care of my..." Alexandra bit her lip. What did she say? *My murder? My mess?* She left behind two bodies for him to clean up. Two horrors foisted upon this man and his friends. "I'm very sorry," she repeated softly. "May I contribute to his burial? To his family, maybe? I... I owe him this small thing."

"Taken care of," he said, clearing his throat. "But that's a kind offer."

"You sound surprised." At his guarded expression, a realisation struck Alexandra. "You think me unkind."

"I don't know you."

"Indifferent, then."

Mr O'Sullivan leaned against the railing. "Let me tell you something. Even if Thorne hadn't built this place – even if we had nothing in our pockets but some thread and a stray button – we'd bury our own, and we'd do it proper. Wouldn't be the first time, wouldn't be the last. I don't think you unkind or even indifferent. Thorne and I, we take care of our own." His cold, golden eyes met hers. "So when a woman comes along and breaks his heart, I notice. My lady."

Break Nick's heart? Is *that* what he had claimed? Likely, his pride had been damaged. Perhaps Nick had thought of Alexandra after leaving Stratfield Saye, wondering if she was pregnant with their child. Or maybe he thought she'd be fool enough to forgive him.

Nick was not the kind of man one abandoned on a gravel drive. She hoped the memory of her refusal infuriated him. She hoped it plagued his dreams.

A movement on the floor of the Brimstone caught Alexandra's attention.

Nick.

Yes, he stood out, even in the crowded club. Alexandra was struck again by how foolish she had been to believe his lies back in Stratfield Saye, for a suit did not hide his lethal grace. If anything, it enhanced the effect. That suit was a camouflage, she understood, enabling him to playact the gentleman. But he was no gentleman.

"He never gave me his heart," she said, watching her husband shake hands with the men below. "I can't break what I'm not given."

O'Sullivan made some dismissive noise. "I've read your work," he said, to her surprise. "Thorn'd boast about it. Funny, none of those essays and pamphlets ever led me to believe you were a fool."

"Boast about it?" Alexandra's laugh was dry. "Perhaps you're not aware of the criticisms he published about my work in the newspapers. You'll find them written under the name Nicholas Spencer, the alias he assumed in Hampshire. He's called me every word in *Roget's Thesaurus* for *fool*."

The factotum stared at her with an expression Alexandra found unreadable. "You don't know him at all, do you?" he asked.

"No." Alexandra pushed away from the balustrade. "I was Nick Thorne's unwitting dupe. So you see, Mr O'Sullivan, I couldn't have broken his heart. Not when he left my own in pieces."

Before O'Sullivan could respond, a shout came from below. Alexandra looked down to see a commotion on the floor – men shoved at each other, circling something. What was it? One man threw a punch. The other?

Oh, bloody hell. The other was her husband.

∽ 13 ∽

"Mr O'Sullivan?" Alexandra's alarm rose as the factotum made no move to leave, not even when Nick took a second punch. "What in God's name is going on down there?"

His expression remained unperturbed, as if this was a regular occurrence. "Aristos have a habit of becoming angry when they play too hard and lose everything."

The men disentangled from their brawl, gasping for breath. Alexandra's lip curled in disgust when she recognised Nick's adversary as the Earl of Latimer. The bloke was a complete git, and she had once cautioned his betrothed, Lady Elaine Featherstone, about him. Everyone knew that the maids in Latimer's household worked in pairs because he had a reputation for cornering those who tidied up alone. Besides, the earl had a chronic gambling habit.

Lady Elaine jilted Latimer a fortnight later, and it seemed the earl had no luck finding another bride to accept his suit. Last she'd heard, he was looking among the wealthy American debutantes.

Latimer swung a hard right hook at Thorne's jaw. Alexandra gritted her teeth in frustration. Was her husband even trying? "Do something!" she hissed at O'Sullivan.

The factotum was unbothered as he observed the chaos unfolding below. "Thorne has it in hand."

Latimer hit Thorne again.

"He does *not* have it in hand," Alexandra snapped, stepping forward. O'Sullivan's grip tightened on her arm. "Let go of me, Mr O'Sullivan, or I'll punch *you* in the face."

His lips quirked up in amusement. "For someone who claims to despise him, you seem awfully protective of him." He shrugged off Alexandra's scowl. "Just watch and wait."

She turned to the scene below, cringing as she watched Nick take the beating. It was foolish to defend a man she despised, but she couldn't bear to witness him getting pulverised on the floor of his club. The crowd of drunken idiots was no help, cheering and jeering at the fight below. It was a bloody nightmare.

But then, something shifted.

Nick stood up, wiping the blood from his mouth with a low chuckle. And then, in a swift motion, he slammed his fist into Latimer's face.

The earl stumbled back into the throng, who shoved him towards Nick. They were a pack of wolves, hungry for blood, clearly determined to see this fight through until there was a clear winner. Alexandra had feared that Latimer would triumph, but she needn't have worried. Nick was...

Magnificent.

Alexandra leaned forward, captivated by Nick's graceful

strikes and calculated blocks, as fierce and ruthless as a hunter on the prowl. She recognised the movements of his body – they were still profoundly familiar to her. He had been feigning weakness with Latimer, masquerading as the prey when he was truly the predator.

"Why...?" Alexandra shook her head, unable to comprehend.

O'Sullivan lifted a shoulder. "Thorne makes the fight look fair. Better for business if he gets hit a few times."

As memories of Hampshire flooded back, Alexandra went rigid. She had once taught him how to float, how to swim, how to be vulnerable. Thorne's ability to make the fight appear even was just one of the many techniques he had honed in Stratfield Saye, a deception in his arsenal. He made you believe you were his equal, only to reveal it had all been a ploy. To Thorne, this fight was a game.

Another lie.

Alexandra stepped away from the balustrade, unwilling to witness the bloody spectacle any longer. But then, she caught sight of something that stopped her heart.

Latimer had a knife.

"*Nick!*" she cried out without thinking.

Her scream drew Nick's attention for a fleeting moment – too long. Latimer took advantage of his distraction, swiping the blade deep into Nick's shirt. Alexandra gasped as fear stole her breath.

She surged past O'Sullivan and raced down the stairs.

The group of men gawping at the fight blocked Alexandra's progress. She dived into the hollering crowd, elbowing a few imbeciles out of her way. Alexandra came to a halt as she reached the front. Nick's waistcoat was stained with blood, and his coat was torn at the sleeve. Latimer may not have been as skilled in combat, but he compensated for it with raw anger.

Latimer lunged. Nick sidestepped with ease, more annoyed than afraid. "Put the knife away, Latimer, and I won't snap your wrist."

"You stripped my house, you Irish piece of shit." Latimer's words slurred. Alexandra couldn't tell if he was inebriated or if Nick had hit him too hard. "You left me with *nothing*."

Nick's smile was grim. "Left you the house. Unless you want to bet that, too."

Latimer snarled and swiped. Nick dodged and delivered a rough smack to Latimer's cheek. Was he even *trying* to end this? She suspected he was giving everyone a show.

Enough of this.

"Latimer," Alexandra's voice sliced through the chaos. "Put down that knife this instant."

The earl didn't bother to acknowledge her. "Bringing your wife to a brawl, Thorne?"

"Alex goes wherever the hell she pleases." Nick flashed her a grin that left no doubt in her mind. He had known she was there watching, and he *was* showing off.

Only not to the crowd – *her*.

Alexandra scowled at her husband, then returned her attention to the earl. "Latimer, put the knife away, or I'll—"

"Or you'll what?" Latimer sneered. "You're the reason Lady Elaine called off our wedding. You and this bastard have ruined me." He spun around to confront Nick, brandishing the weapon. "How did you manage to bed this one, Thorne? I didn't know a single man who would dare to touch her. We all thought her frigid cunt would freeze our cocks off."

Nick's chin dropped. Rage clouded his dark eyes. Gone was the man having a bit of fun with an idiot aristocrat before throwing him onto the street. This was the King of the East End, whispered to have eliminated his enemies in the shadows.

His gaze shifted to Alexandra's, as if asking permission. No. *He's mine to deal with.*

A flicker of a grin danced across Nick's lips, acknowledging her unspoken command.

Alexandra stepped up behind Latimer. The earl was a fool, distracted by the larger opponent rather than the woman he'd insulted at his back. She grasped his arm to whirl him around. The moment of surprise worked: Alexandra slapped the knife out of Latimer's grasp and punched him in the nose.

Latimer howled. "You *cunt*."

She hit him again. The surrounding men cheered as Latimer crumpled to the floor, blood gushing from his nose. "You never had a chance with me because I deserved better than any of you."

Alexandra glared at the crowd of onlookers, demanding their attention. "Gentlemen, stop standing there like a bunch of slack-jawed idiots and return to your business," she commanded. When they hesitated, she snapped, "*Immediately*."

She signalled for some of the club's staff to attend to the wounded Latimer. "Escort this man off the premises, please. Then have someone deliver clean bandages to Mr Thorne's quarters."

"Alex," Nick's voice was soft.

Alexandra closed her eyes before turning to her husband. He gazed at her with a mixture of surprise and desire. A look that spoke of lust and carnal desires – of tangled sheets and feverish lovemaking. Perhaps she was just as perverse, but the image ignited a fire within her.

She pushed those emotions aside. "*You*." She gestured sharply. "Your suite. *Now*."

Nick followed her obediently up the stairs. "Alex."

"Not yet. Still fuming."

"I know," he said casually, putting his hands in his pockets. They reached the private wing. "Listen. What Latimer said—"

"*Don't* repeat it."

"Wasn't going to." He looked askance at her. "You were magnificent."

"Nicholas."

"And I adore you."

She shook her head and released an amused huff of laughter. "Flattery won't get you anywhere." She opened his bedchamber door more forcefully than necessary. "Inside. Take off the waistcoat and shirt."

He smiled slowly. "I like where this is going."

God, he was beautiful, all fierce power and confident sensuality. But she couldn't forget the things he had done, the lies he had told. "You're still bleeding through your clothes," she said sternly. "Let me see your wound."

"Now I hate where this is going. Let's try something else. I remove my shirt, and you...?"

"I'm about to throw a vase at you, Nicholas."

At her exasperated look, he chuckled. "Fine. Then be my nurse."

He deftly removed his waistcoat, then lifted his shirt over his head and dropped it.

How could Alexandra have forgotten Nick's beauty? He was a man of lean muscles and sharp edges, shaped from years of rough work and experience. She wished she could have touched him more, explored him, learned all the curves of his body. At the inn where they'd first made love, the candlelight had hidden so much from her. Then on the train, they had been covered with blankets, as he had taken her hard and fast on the narrow bed in their private sleeping car.

He'd made it seem as if they had all the time in the world. And he'd smiled at Alexandra precisely like that.

The next day, she'd discovered how many lies that smile hid.

Nick's eyes locked onto hers in a wordless challenge.

Daring her to look away.

Daring her to come closer.

"Nothing you haven't seen before," he repeated her words from the other night, his voice low and husky.

A pang went through her. Did Nick hurt at the reminder of what they shared? Had he imagined their journey to Stratfield Saye in the darkness of his bedroom? Did he touch himself at night and recall the swaying bed on the train where they'd spent so many hours? She did – and she hated herself for wanting him.

But Alexandra would not retreat. Admiring his beauty was not the same as approval. She had to recall he was not like a lion. Lions only acted out of survival; this one *chose* to betray her.

"Turning my words around on me?" she asked. "It's unnecessary. I remember."

A soft knock came from the door. Alexandra took the bowl of warm water, towels, and bandages from the maid and dismissed her.

Nick settled in the wing chair like a feline predator, watching Alexandra as she approached. The pulse at his throat beat fast, as it always did when she was near. She longed to press her lips against it, feel the rush of his blood. Maybe then she would understand why her heart raced whenever she was with him.

"Do you wish you could forget?" he asked.

Forget? She could never forget. The memory of him moving against her, the feeling of being so thoroughly claimed by him, was burned into her mind. But the idea of that intimacy, of loving him and then losing him, was too much to bear.

Yes, she almost said. But then, no.

She couldn't bring herself to lie.

"Do you want the answer to that question?" she asked, turning to inspect the cut on his shoulder. His skin was hot under her fingertips.

"Not really."

Of course he didn't. He was too busy playing games, too busy trying to prove her weaknesses. She had to remind herself that she couldn't fall for his charm again. Not after he shattered her heart into a million pieces.

"What did Latimer mean about Lady Elaine?" he asked.

She took a deep breath, letting her hand linger on him longer than necessary. "He proposed to Lady Elaine Featherstone at the start of the season. But she came to me, asking me to investigate him. And I found out he was a bastard with a gambling problem that nearly bankrupted his family. It's all kept quiet. He had enough to keep up appearances, so Elaine wouldn't know he was after her fortune. She broke things off after I told her."

Nick chuckled, the sound low and rough. "That's my girl."

She tried to ignore the way her breath caught. "Don't call me that."

"You used to love it when I called you that."

"That was *before*," she said, pulling away from him. "Did you *really* take everything he had?"

"Left him the house." Nick shrugged. "And the shirt on his back."

"Generous." Alexandra rolled her eyes. "Maybe we should add Latimer to our list of suspects. He hates both of us, and he's clearly unstable."

"He's an idiot," Nick replied, grimacing as she pressed the bandage to his wound. "And he wouldn't know his arse from his elbow. It's not him."

"Good reason. Back to the drawing board, then."

Nick watched her slowly bind his arm. "Have you investigated potential husbands before? For other women?"

"A few," she said lightly. "I've some experience with husbands hiding things."

Nick fell quiet. Alex held her breath for what he'd say next, regretting that she had brought up their catastrophic marriage. But Nick only asked, "And where did you learn to defend yourself?"

"Perhaps that secret ought to stay mine."

Nick looked up at her through his eyelashes. "What if I promised to keep it?"

When his gaze lingered on her like that, she wanted to spill every truth she had hoarded over the years. She yearned to be with him, drifting on the serene waters of Stratfield Lake, sharing everything. But her secrets were all she had left to protect her.

Alexandra forced a smile. "Maybe I'll tell you another time."

They both knew she wasn't going to. After this was over, she wouldn't be this close to Nick again. Alexandra focused on her future of distant shores and foreign lands, of the adventures she'd embark on without him. She imagined the guidebooks she'd read, the maps she'd memorised, and the unknown territories that awaited her.

Far away from him.

Alexandra's attention shifted to Nick's gash. "The blood made it look worse than it is," she reassured him. "You should recheck it in the morning, but I don't think you'll need stitches."

Nick made a sound of indifference. "Wouldn't matter if I did."

Another scar to add to the many that intersected Nick's body, old wounds that spoke of a past he'd never shared. She had wondered once where a gentleman could get such injuries – perhaps he had fought in foreign wars or been caught in a tragic accident.

But deep down, she knew those were just excuses.

His scars were a map of his brutal history that she had never dared to inquire about. Wheals crisscrossed his back, and star-shaped marks etched into his skin, some ragged and thick. There was one particular cicatrix along his chest...

Her fingers danced over it before she could stop herself.

Nick's palm closed around hers, keeping it there. They stayed like that, lost in each other's touch. Was he waiting for her to say something? Or was he holding her hand for different reasons, ones she couldn't begin to imagine or didn't want to?

"You going to ask?" he said, breaking the silence.

"Ask what?" she replied, though she already knew.

His regard grew intense as he guided her fingers over his scar. "You know what. You never demanded answers from me. Never asked about my past. Never even asked me why."

Alexandra couldn't admit that she had investigated him, too. That she kept her notes in the box with his articles, a reminder of her youthful foolishness. But knowing more about him never seemed to ease the pain.

"Isn't that the problem?" she said. "I shouldn't have had to. I married you because I trusted you."

Nick's grip tightened. "No secrets between us, Alex. Not anymore. Don't make me out to be like the men you've uncovered, known for their lies."

"But you are," she whispered.

Nick's eyes were bright, feverish. "Ask me. You ought to know who the man is whose name you carry."

Say something, she urged herself. It would be easy to tell him she didn't intend to bear his name any longer, that she intended to divorce him. Such words would be the final blow to their tragic tale, a period at the end of their story. If she wanted to twist the knife, she could bring up the ship, the ocean, and the distance she would one day put between them.

But the words wouldn't come. For the first time, Alexandra saw him at his most vulnerable, and something in her wouldn't walk away without knowing who she was leaving behind.

Alexandra's gaze lowered to the scar – just one of many. None of them made him any less beautiful. His secrets marked in the topography of his body. "Tell me this one, then. Only this one."

Nick closed his eyes and loosed a slow breath – heavy with pain or relief. She couldn't tell. "When I was a kid in the Nichol, there was a toff who took a liking to my mam. She worked the streets, did whatever she could to bring coin home and raised me as best she could. He treated her like shite but paid her better than most, so she kept him around."

Alexandra noticed the subtle thickening of his Irish dialect, the lulling cadence of it. When she'd known him as Nicholas Spencer, his English accent had been lovely. But this? Oh, she loathed that he'd had to hide it from her. Nick's voice was the most beautiful thing she had ever heard.

"Anyway," he said, running his fingertips along the back of her hand. "He showed up looking for a quick tumble. He'd been paying our rent, so who was Mam to say no? He roughed her up, of course. When I tried to defend her, he whacked me with his cane. That's when I realised it had a blade hidden inside it. He slashed me here and told me to remember it the next time I dared to interfere."

Alexandra fought the bile rising in her throat. She had always known Nick's past was filled with brutality. A man like him couldn't have become the King of the East End without knowing a thing or two about savage thugs. But she felt sick at the thought of someone hurting him.

"How old were you?"

He lifted a shoulder. "Seven, I think. Mam died not long after, anyway."

"I'm sorry, Nick," she whispered.

"I don't want your pity. That's not what this is for."

"What is it for, then?" she asked tiredly.

He reached up and cupped her cheek. "Just truth, Alex. Nothing else."

No, this was too intense. Too much. Who was he to stir up these feelings in her? He wasn't her infatuation anymore. She wouldn't be dazzled by his handsome face and charming smile. He had lied to her, betrayed her, abandoned her, and insulted her.

Alexandra put distance between them, a chasm that felt as vast as an ocean. She didn't need a ship to cross it. "You gave me the truth too late."

He didn't look angry. Not frustrated, either. Only understanding. "I know it. But you still have the right to demand an explanation from me. Doesn't matter how many years pass, you'll always have that right."

She stared at him, at the scars now bared to her. *Tell me about that one on your wrist*, she wanted to say. Then another, then another. All those missing pieces of his past accumulated like the notes in her box.

Perhaps she needed those answers before she could put her youthful foolishness behind her for good.

Before she could answer, an insistent knock came on the door. "Thorne?" It was O'Sullivan. "We've got a situation."

Thorne didn't look away from Alexandra. "What is it?"

"The lads found a body."

14

"**S**tay here," Thorne said to Alex as he pulled on his coat. The movement made him wince. *Damn Latimer to hell.*

"Absolutely not," Alex said, jerking open the connecting door to her bedchamber. She disappeared inside, and he heard her rustling through her wardrobe. "I'm coming with you," she called out, voice muffled in the depths of her closet.

"It's out of the question."

"Someone paid a man to abduct me from my bedchamber," Alex said as she stomped about her room. "He's now responsible for the murder of three people. What am I supposed to do? Toil away in your club? Worry about you all night?"

She'd worry? Thorne came to the doorway. "You'd—" He paused, scanning the chaos within. "What happened here?"

Alexandra looked offended. "Happened? Nothing

happened." She gestured towards the piles of paper all over the place. "This is what work looks like."

"That's not what my office looks like."

"This is what *my* work looks like." She buttoned up her coat. "Don't change the subject. I'm coming."

Thorne blocked her escape. "You don't have to see this."

"Nicholas Thorne," she said, tapping her foot impatiently, "you seem to be labouring under the delusion that I need your permission. Let me clarify: I do not. Move aside, or I'll shove you out of the way."

With a muttered curse, Thorne flung open the door. Alexandra swept past him, and they rushed down the corridor to the back stairs of the Brimstone.

O'Sullivan eyed Alex as they approached. "I wasn't aware her ladyship was coming."

"Is surveying a corpse some sort of exclusive male bonding ritual? Is there a placard proclaiming 'Dead Body: No Women Allowed'?"

O'Sullivan seemed to ponder this. "Solid point."

"Mr O'Sullivan, you" – she flashed her teeth – "are not an idiot. Well done." She slid out the door.

O'Sullivan looked over at Thorne. "What just happened?"

"You agreed with her, you damn fool. Now she thinks you're on her side."

"Oh," O'Sullivan said. "Shit."

The Nichol stirred up a maelstrom of memories for Nicholas Thorne. He remembered racing through these serpentine alleys, lifting wallets, committing more sinister deeds. The

East End wasn't for the meek; one needed a certain hardness to weather the life it gave you.

It was peculiar how a place could evoke such diametric emotions in him, joy and sorrow woven in equal measure. Like his mother's occasional indulgence of sweets when they could spare the coin, some recollections shone like beacons in his otherwise murky past. Others still haunted him. The fear after his mam died. The gut-wrenching hunger that drove him to thievery for survival. He recognised every twisted alley, alcove, and crevice. He'd sought refuge in them all, at least once, during dire times.

Back then, the East End had been in worse condition: filthier, the buildings unsafe and crowded. It wasn't a pretty place; the Nichol, though, had got a sight better since he'd gained control over the parish. Not by sitting on the board, of course, but in the way he knew best: bribery, intimidation, violence. They weren't kind things, but Nicholas Thorne couldn't afford to be benevolent to some men. So he put fear into them.

Thorne cast a sideways glance at Alex, curious about the thoughts that lay behind her serene expression. Was she repulsed? Did she breathe in the stench and yearn to return to St James's?

But no, Alex remained unperturbed by the decrepit structures and the repulsive drunk who ogled her as she passed by. Thorne couldn't blame the bloke; she was stunning, determined, her strides purposeful. She stood out like a vibrant rose amid the gloom.

"Oi, there!" O'Sullivan called out as they neared a pack of lads gathered around a body concealed in the darkness.

The flickering gaslights close by projected lengthy shadows onto the damp, glistening street.

"Mr O'Sullivan!" The smallest boy raced over and clung to O'Sullivan's legs.

O'Sullivan gave the boy's shoulder a hearty pat. "Thomas? What are you doing out here, lad? You should be home with your mother."

"Tommy insisted," said another voice. George, one of the elder boys, strode over and tipped his cap to acknowledge Thorne. "Nasty bit o' work ower there, Mr Thorne."

Thorne put a restraining hand on Alex's arm to keep her from investigating. "You see anyone around this way, George?"

"Nah. Empty by th' time I got 'ere. That bloke were cold a while." George's gaze lingered on Alexandra, as he was still learning the ways of women, and Alex was not one to miss. "Pretty piece. Heard you had a woman up at the Brimstone, but I thought Dot and Lottie were tellin' tales again."

"Never say you saw her," Thorne said. He pulled some coins from his pocket. "Take these. Get Thomas and the lads some supper. And the rest to your ma. Don't even be thinking of spending it on a woman, or I'll have your hide if I hear of it."

George laughed, taking the money. "Aye, sir."

"Good lad."

The boy caught Alex's eye and winked. "Bye, lady."

As George, Thomas, and the other boys raced off, Alexandra observed their departure pensively. "They didn't seem affected by such a gruesome sight."

"It's a common sight for them," he murmured to her.

Murder, disease, starvation, accidents; there were plenty of ways for someone to meet their demise in the East End. Misfortune was unavoidable.

Thorne yearned to understand her expression, but Alex turned away, her face shrouded by the dull glow of the alley.

Let her feel what she wants to feel. Pity or disgust. It'll make it simpler for her to leave when the time comes.

Thorne exhaled slowly before approaching the body. He had seen his fair share of brutality and death. Whelan had contributed a good number of corpses to these streets, with some bullet chips in the bricks and bloodstains on the pavement. Nick had assisted him when protection money was short.

But this was something else. The man was shirtless, his torso a gory mass of knife wounds. If Thorne were to estimate, he would place the figure around seventy. Someone had taken their time, making their victim suffer, and likely continued to stab him even after he had expired.

The man's face, however, remained unscathed.

"Joseph Ayles," O'Sullivan said. "We're going to have to tell his daughter."

Another family broken apart. Another death to report. O'Sullivan and Thorne had become experts at comforting those who had lost someone to tragedy in their territory.

"She's got an aunt over in Spitalfields," Thorne said, reaching out to shut Joseph's eyes. From the neck up, he looked as if he were sleeping. "Lives with her ma. Make sure they have enough for the funeral and whatever else they need to take in the lass."

"Sure, boss."

"Someone you know?" Alex's voice echoed as she

approached. He heard her sharp inhale as she stared down at the dead man. "My God. Ayles."

Thorne glanced at her sharply. "*You* know him?"

"He was another of my informants, like Mary Watkins, for information on Sir Reginald Seymour's smuggling scheme. Joseph was a crew member on one of the ships." Her face twisted with guilt. "I always took precautions when meeting them, but apparently, they weren't enough. Do you think Sir Reginald took out a contract on my life?"

"And the lives of your sources," Thorne said, his voice gentle. "Two of them turning up murdered is no coincidence."

O'Sullivan's eyes narrowed behind his spectacles. "Seymour? The MP of Cambridgeshire?"

Alex nodded. "Yes."

O'Sullivan let out a gusty laugh. "Damn me. When you go after an aristo, you sure know how to pick them." O'Sullivan glanced at Thorne. "Thinking we should pay him a visit? Make him pull the contract?"

"No," Nick replied, although he hated to say it. Seymour didn't deserve to live, but charging in without a plan wouldn't help Alex. "Not until I find out who took the contract first." He turned to his wife. "How much information do you have on Seymour?"

"Enough," she said, still staring down at the body. "But I have to be cautious with the details. Sir Reginald has powerful supporters in Parliament, and public opinion will be in his favour, not mine—" She leaned in closer to the corpse, her eyes narrowed. "*Mr O'Sullivan*. You carry a handkerchief in your right pocket. Give it to me, please."

What was she up to? "Alex—"

"Quiet, Nick. Mr O'Sullivan, the handkerchief."

O'Sullivan dug into his coat and handed her the cloth. To Thorne's astonishment, Alex used it meticulously to pry open Joseph's mouth.

O'Sullivan scrutinised her. "What are you doing?"

"I'm not certain, but I believe…" she trailed off, holding her breath as she shoved her fingers inside the dead man's maw.

Good Lord, this woman had nerves of steel.

"There." She pulled out a scrap of paper. It was rolled around something, but she focused on the print. "Oh," she said softly, lowering her eyes.

"What is it?" When she didn't answer, he prompted, "Alex?"

She slid her finger across the paper and murmured, "I agonised over these words when I wrote them. And now it's being used like a mockery." The pain etched on her face was a knife in Thorne's gut. He knew how much her writing meant to her. "I have two more informants. I need to warn them."

Thorne's hand rested on her arm, gentle and firm. "Not tonight." She was trembling, and he was reminded of when she'd shown up at his office days ago. Some things, once seen, could never be forgotten. "It's safer during the day. Give me those."

She passed him the paper and something else that had come out of Joseph's mouth – a cigar. Thorne held it up, perplexed. Why would the killer leave this? He lifted it to his nose, trying to catch a scent.

The reek of the speciality tobacco hit Thorne like a punch to the gut. He doubled over, gasping for air.

"*Nick!*" Alexandra sounded alarmed.

O'Sullivan snatched the cigar from Thorne's hand, took a whiff, and then retched. He immediately recoiled, retching again. "God." He dropped the offending item and ran his fingers through his hair. "My God." His voice was raw, like sandpaper on skin.

Memories crashed into Thorne – of being ten years old and trapped in the darkness, surrounded by that same noxious smell, as they treated each other's wounds. Some died from infections. Others perished in unspeakable ways – freezing to death, dying in turf wars in the Nichol, or falling victim to murder. So many murdered. There were thirty-one boys at first, then twenty-eight, twenty-three, twenty, fifteen, ten.

All of them sent to an early grave by the man Thorne had dethroned as the King of the East End.

The man he had betrayed Alex to defeat. Her wealth had given him the leverage he required to rescue those who had shared his shadowy existence – the boys who had defied the odds and grown into men.

The bastard who had starved them, beaten them, and turned them into killers and thieves was still breathing.

He was still bloody breathing.

And now he was coming for Thorne's wife.

"When we get back to the Brimstone, alert everyone," Thorne barked at O'Sullivan, his grip on Alexandra's arm tight as he dragged her towards the club. "Two of my men on her door at all times, and someone at every entrance. If he took the contract from Seymour, he won't act alone. You know the score."

"Who?" Alex stiffened under his grasp but allowed him to lead her. "What does the cigar mean?"

O'Sullivan shook his head frantically, racing to keep pace with Thorne. "It can't be him."

"His body was never found," Thorne reminded him.

"You shoved a blade in his gut and tossed him over the bridge. If he didn't drown in the Thames, infection would have got him. We made damn sure no one fished him out. Whelan is dead."

Thorne's skin crawled to think the bastard had survived and pulled himself out of the Thames four years ago. That he had recovered and planned for the day he could return and get revenge on Thorne. On *everyone* who betrayed him. O'Sullivan, too.

Alex tensed in his grip as Thorne led her down another alleyway. "*Who* is Whelan?"

"Patrick Whelan controlled the East End." He placed a hand on her back to urge her forward. O'Sullivan's pace was brisk beside them. "He used to snatch kids off the streets to pilfer or kill for him. Always told you how much coin you owed him for food and shelter, so debt and terror kept you loyal. Anyone who tried to leave him ended up with a knife in their back."

"You think Seymour hired him?"

"Aye. I've a lot of enemies who would ally themselves with Whelan." He lowered his voice. Now that he knew Whelan was alive, every street corner seemed to be filled with eyes, observing them from the darkness. "The bloke you offed was just one of many."

"Makes sense," O'Sullivan said. He sounded breathless. "Whelan did business with toffs. If Seymour suspected your wife was gathering dirt on him, hiring someone who despised you both would be the perfect incentive to get the job done."

"*Me?*" Alex looked surprised as she came to an abrupt stop. "Why should he hate *me?*"

O'Sullivan raised an eyebrow at Thorne. "You gonna tell her?"

Thorne made an impatient noise. His old nemesis wouldn't strike now, but he wanted his wife safely ensconced inside the Brimstone, guarded by his trusted men. "I took the East End from him," Thorne told her, urging her forward again. "And he hates you because you gave me the means to steal it."

15

STRATFIELD SAYE, HAMPSHIRE

Four years ago

Alexandra smoothed her palms over the front of her dress, studying her reflection in the mirror. Her cheeks were pink. Despite seeing Nick every day for weeks, she still felt nervous before their swimming lessons. It was an odd sensation, this fluttering in her belly each time.

She had never experienced so many emotions in her vast vocabulary until she met him: craving, yearning, longing.

Desire.

More than that.

Alexandra could be honest; no one was about to witness her folly.

She was falling in love with Lord Locke.

Stupidity was another word reserved for a woman who fell in love with someone who did little more than engage in harmless flirtation. His smile was devilish; it made her blush. But he had made no move to kiss her. If his touch ever seemed to linger, it could easily have been in her imagination.

Foolish. That word, too. In the sanctity of Alexandra's bedchamber, she spent far too many hours reliving the way Nick's swimwear hugged his form. The contours of his muscles were discernible through the fabric, taut and sleek like those of a magnificent feline. She frequently pictured herself stripping him down to lick the water off his skin. She longed to envision the noises he would emit, how he would touch her everywhere, his fingers trailing down her hips to discover the mound between her thighs.

Quim, a word from one of her naughty books, stored away in her mind, so little used.

Alexandra's fingers would wander towards the waistband of his swimwear, yearning for the skin beneath. *Cock*. Another expression she retrieved from the depths of her vocabulary. It was forbidden, unsuitable for a lady's vernacular, but its frankness appealed to her. It belonged in the bedroom. *Cock*. What would Nick's look like? How would he react if—

A faint tap at her chamber door jolted her out of her reverie. Alexandra pressed a cool palm against her cheek. "Yes?"

A maid entered with a quick curtsy. If she noticed Alexandra's flush, she didn't breathe a word of it. "Apologies for the intrusion, milady, but Lord Kent is askin' for ye in 'is study."

Alexandra scowled. George Grey may have been her father, but he was practically a stranger to her – a stranger who found her company repugnant. He did not mask his disdain for Alexandra's opinions on political matters, her unladylike demeanour, and her uncultured conduct in polite circles.

Granted, Alexandra was not known for her modesty, a fact that her siblings enjoyed ribbing her about. But George Grey despised his daughter for a straightforward and indisputable reason: Alexandra bore a striking resemblance to her mother.

It was peculiar to be an utterly redundant and unwelcome offspring in a union characterised by such animosity. Kent's heir and spare were conceived in rapid succession – the marital obligation fulfilled – yet the earl and countess bore another child to torment each other. *Her.* Alexandra did not pretend to comprehend that disastrous marriage. After all, she had not known her mother beyond the few minutes following her birth.

Now Alexandra existed merely as a reminder of the woman her father loathed. Death had done little to change that.

Alexandra dismissed the maid and strode across the hall to her father's study. She discovered him hunched over his desk, etching tidy figures into rows and columns, and felt a surge of annoyance. The Earl of Kent was a virtuoso in money management, and estate matters were responsible for much of his absence. Alexandra might have seen him no more than three in the last eight months.

"Good morning." She tried to mask her impatience. "Was there something you needed?"

Alexandra's notice slid to the longcase clock. Nick would be at the lake now; she would be late.

George set down his pen. "Do you have somewhere you need to be?"

"No." Her answer came in a rush. "Only my afternoon walk. My maid said you asked to see me." A wordless way of saying, *for heaven's sake, hurry up.*

His eyes snapped to meet hers. *Cold eyes*, Alexandra thought. The colour of gunmetal. Her brothers had inherited them, but James and Richard's were warm and full of laughter.

"It's been brought to my attention that you've been seen in the company of our new neighbour, Lord Locke." George leaned back in his chair. "More than once."

Had he been *spying* on her? Alexandra tried to keep her expression even. Who could have seen her? A servant? The gamekeeper? If they had – *oh goodness*, someone would have witnessed them swimming together.

Without an escort. It wasn't proper. It wasn't *done*. A woman's standing was gossamer thin, as fragile as tissue paper. A hint of impropriety – the slightest bit of force – and it collapsed to ash. Ruination.

No, Alexandra thought. Nothing had happened. She had nothing to be ashamed of. "What of it?" Her voice didn't tremble.

The earl's stare hardened. "You're not to see him again, Alexandra."

Her mouth fell open. She had expected strong words about having a care for her reputation. If Kent had a mind to do so, he could visit Nick and issue some idiotic demand that they marry to keep village tongues from wagging.

But this? He was forbidding her? "I *beg* your pardon?"

"Did you lose the ability to understand English? Shall I speak in another language you know?" At the absurd suggestion, he continued his cruel lecture in French. "You are to end your acquaintance with Lord Locke. No daughter of mine will be compromised by a penniless peer, let alone one previously employed as a common schoolmaster."

Alexandra's lips flattened. She would not play his game. "You've barely acknowledged me as a daughter," she said in English. "Why do you care to whom I show affection?"

"If it reflects on my name—"

"*You* were the one who insisted I rusticate here after deciding I was ruining my marriage prospects in London. I've finally met a man whose presence I can tolerate, and you're telling me to reject him because he was a *schoolmaster*?" She gave a dry laugh. "I don't even have words for how patently idiotic that sounds."

Kent rose and planted his hands on the desk. "Listen to me," he hissed. "If you want to fall into bed with a glorified commoner after you've wedded a suitable gentleman, that's your business. God knows you take after your whore of a mother as it is."

Alexandra slapped him. The sound seemed to echo in the small room, and the red mark of her palm was stark against his shaved cheek.

George seized her wrist and yanked her forward. Alexandra's face was so close to his that she could smell the brandy on his breath. "I've never struck a woman, but you try my patience. If I hear about you seeing Lord Locke again, I'll marry you off to someone without the same restraint. Do you comprehend me, or shall I repeat it in French?" When she didn't answer, he squeezed her so hard that she almost cried out. "*Do you?*"

Alexandra glared at him. "*Yes.*"

His eyes narrowed, but he released her. "Good. *Stevens!*" The butler appeared at the door and bowed. "Escort Lady Alexandra to her bedchamber. Make sure she stays there."

Stevens seemed apologetic as he escorted her. Alexandra

knew her father's voice carried; the butler likely heard their conversation. But she was in no mood for pity. She did not want condolences. Such emotions would not save her if her father wanted to marry her to a cruel and abusive husband.

Alexandra paced her bedchamber. Nick would wonder where she was.

Would he be disappointed if she didn't show up today? If she never showed up again? Compromised or not, Alexandra would force nothing on Nick; her tattered reputation was not his concern. He'd made no promises to her. Their lessons were not vows.

But he deserved some goodbye – an explanation for her future absence.

"*Damn* this," she muttered. No, she couldn't let Nick wait. She'd end it today.

Alexandra pulled open her bedchamber window. She had climbed this tree many times in her youth, the scrapes and bruises angering her brother James. He'd called her reckless. She wished he were here so she could tell him climbing up and down trees was the simple part.

What came next would be the hardest.

Thorne paced along the banks of the lake.

Alex was late, but Thorne had already sifted through sand and stone with her name on his lips for over an hour. Meeting her had become the best part of his day – her laughter a brief respite from the hell of his own making. Joy had been so fleeting before – a warm meal here, a bed there, scarce moments of comfort and security.

An intoxicant. Difficult to gain, easy to lose.

The irony was too delicious. The master manipulator had been played by the only person who ever truly saw him. Punished by the sweetest torture possible: happiness. He had no right to it, not after everything he'd done, and yet here she was – proof that even monsters can stumble into second chances. Until they don't last.

He laughed bitterly. "What cursed luck," he murmured.

A movement in the trees had him look up, and his breath caught. Had this woman been fashioned at birth just for him, she couldn't have awed him more. She moved through the world with her gaze as sharp as an executioner's axe; but softer metal can be bent or chipped away. No, Thorne could only describe Alex in terms of a summer storm: powerful and electric.

And storms always made Thorne feel alive.

"You're late," he said, a smile ghosting across his lips.

As ever, she wore her usual attire: a shapeless gown atop her bathing dress, her hair woven in a tight plait. She looked wilder than the sea sirens of old tales. "Yes," she said shortly, "I must—"

Their gazes locked, and a moment passed between them then. Secret and unspoken.

"What's wrong?" he asked softly.

The space between their breaths seemed to stretch into infinity. Then Alex looked away, breaking the tension like a bursting dam. "Nothing." Alex began unfastening her over-dress, dismissing Thorne's question altogether. "It's nothing at all."

"Alex."

She took the gown off and tossed it into the grass. Even the thick, nun-like material of her bathing costume didn't hide the agitated rise and fall of her chest. Soon her boots joined the discarded dress.

"Swim with me," she said, wading into the water. "I don't want to talk."

"No. Not until—" Nick's answer was cut off as she dove in. "Damn it! *Alex*."

But she was already swimming away from him, her strokes sure and fast. Nick muttered an oath. Clothing was shed with reckless abandon until all that remained was his swimming costume before he plummeted into the watery depths. Alex was swift – she moved like a siren of legend, swift and merciless.

His chest heaved with the effort of catching up to her. Sheer desperation drove him – what choice had she made? What had happened? Why was she late? – and perhaps some emotion slowed her.

Or, perhaps, she wished to be caught.

With a strong lunge, Thorne grasped Alex around the waist and hauled her against him. Her chest was heaving, hair plastered to her cheeks. A siren captured in a fisherman's net. He had a wild urge to kiss her and tamped down the impulse. He was no fisherman, and she was no fey creature at his mercy. This was Alex – and he cared for her.

And she was upset.

Thorne released her and drew back in the water, placing distance between their bodies. *Tell me*, he longed to say. *Give me your burden, if that's the issue. Let me share it.*

Before he could question her, she spoke. "You won," she said.

Thorne's gaze devoured her. He wanted her like an open book, words and thoughts written in stark black ink. He was a hypocrite. "Yes, I won. But that's not why you're upset."

She ignored his remark. "What now?" Alexandra whispered. She lifted her chin, almost challenging him. "Am I to be your prize?"

Was this a test? Her tone had taken on some strange emotion he couldn't place: anger, yes, but at what? Was she angry with him? What had he done to draw her ire?

Thorne reached for her. He couldn't help it anymore; touching Alex was like an instinct. It was necessary. Her breath caught as his thumb slid across her cheek and stroked the water from her skin. No, she was not unmoved by him. Not angry at him. He wondered at the cause.

"I've never given the impression you were something to win, have I?" he murmured. "That's not how we got here."

"Then how did we?"

He brushed her lip with the pad of his thumb now. "You taught me how to catch you."

"I did, didn't I?" Her words were a low whisper, and Thorne bit back a groan when her tongue darted out to lick his finger. "Are you to take no reward?"

Thorne lowered his hand. "Tell me why you're upset."

Alex's laugh was dry as she looked away. "I was asking you to kiss me, Nick." She turned and swam to shallower water, where she began her walk to shore.

"Alex. *Wait.*"

She paused. Her eyes, the colour of the sky above them, met his. He wanted to lose himself in them, forget the world and all its troubles. But he couldn't. Not yet.

"Are we friends, or more?" she asked, low and urgent. "Say something before I make a fool of myself."

Thorne should've felt a wave of relief wash over him. Finally, the question he'd been dreading had been

asked. Weeks of lying and keeping secrets had led to this
moment. Weeks of restless nights where he couldn't help
but wonder about the fate of Whelan's lads. Wondering
if the money he'd left behind was enough or if they were
being squeezed for more. He thought of O'Sullivan, holed
up in that godforsaken flat in the slums, fighting for scraps.

These worries consumed him during those rare moments
of solitude when his desire for this woman threatened to
override his common sense. When he wished he truly was the
accidental baron and not a slum rat. When he wished
the land beside Roseburn was his instead of just another lie.

But the lives of his friends depended upon his response.

Bastard. The word echoed in Thorne's mind as he stepped
closer and claimed her lips. *Fool.*

A desire rose in him, born from long hours of imagining
her mouth on his, the taste of her, the gasp that escaped her
lips when he touched her tongue with his own. But all those
fantasies had not prepared him for this exquisite agony. Her
fingernails scraped through his hair, pulling him deeper into
the embrace until he forgot everything but the feel of her
against him. She was as wild as the seas of Ireland, a storm
in a kiss – pushing herself against him as if it would be the
last time they ever shared breath.

She broke away with an unsteady exhale and whispered,
"More?"

A demand for an answer: *Friends or more?*

And seven words echoed in his mind: *I will love you until
I die.*

But he said none of them. He knew that one day she'd
hate him for this response: "More."

And then he was kissing her again, lost in a maelstrom of

emotion that threatened to drown them both. She pressed herself closer, her clever hands sliding up his arms, coming to rest at his back.

God, aye. Just like that. Her nails clawed at his shirt, dragging the scratch of wool against his skin. Christ, how he wanted her. Roughly – there in the water. On the banks of the lake. Under blue skies that were so unfamiliar after a life cloaked in coal smoke. He wanted to bury himself between her legs and lap at her cunny until she shuddered with pleasure. He wanted to be inside her, buried as deep as he could go.

Maybe then Thorne could forget how he got there: not because he won, but because he cheated.

Thorne froze. *Bastard*, his mind repeated. *Cheat. Liar. Villain.*

"Nick?" Her beautiful eyes opened, and he felt himself sinking further into the depths. "What's wrong?"

It took every ounce of willpower not to take her back in his arms and kiss her again. Instead, he stepped away, cold water closing around him like a reminder of cruel reality.

Laughing hollowly as if she amused him, Thorne forced out a feeble response. "You're distracting me. Will you tell me why you were angry before?"

"I prefer kissing. It improved my day immensely."

"Alex." Her silence set him on edge. "Something's happened, hasn't it?"

She exhaled sharply. "My father found out about our meetings here. He forbade me from seeing you."

Alexandra won't be able to resist something I've forbidden her from having.

But how far had Kent gone with that plan? He had

proven himself ruthless; hiring Thorne was proof of that. It was clear he extended no kindness to his daughter, not in any circumstances.

A thought struck Thorne that he hadn't entertained before. "Did he hurt you?" His voice was steady, hiding the anger that nearly boiled over. Let her think he was in control. It was easier than admitting the truth – if that bastard had laid a finger on Alex, Thorne would break him.

Alex shook her head firmly. "No, my father has never harmed me. He prefers to alternate between ignoring me and making my life miserable."

So Thorne wouldn't have to resort to murdering an aristocrat – but there were other ways he could make Lord Kent pay. "But he threatened you."

"Yes, he threatened to force me into a marriage with a man who wouldn't hesitate to strike me."

So Lord Kent's plan to push Alexandra towards Thorne involved coercion and intimidation. Thorne seethed with anger at how Kent must have spoken to her to reduce her to this state. He would atone for the rest of his existence; if she desired it, he would destroy her father.

Thorne glanced down at their intertwined fingers, savouring the intimate touch. Once she discovered the truth, she would never permit him near her again.

"Is this goodbye?" Thorne spoke low, hesitant.

Alex's eyes met his. "Do you want it to be?"

"No," he breathed, meaning that answer with his entire heart. He meant it knowing Alex would come to hate him for it. "Do you?"

"No." Then she drew his wrist up to her mouth and kissed it. "After all, you've only just caught me."

16

LONDON

Four years later

Alexandra couldn't sleep.

Rather than make a third attempt at shutting her eyes, she sat at the small desk in her room and attempted to write. Each sentence was worse than the last, and her efforts were rewarded with little more than cramped fingers and an aching back.

"Useless," she muttered, rising from her chair to pace.

Crumpled paper littered the floor – wasted sentences, wasted ink, wasted time. Suddenly the written word felt like a foul bargain. It took lives, didn't it? Three now, by her count. With the stroke of a pen, she'd sealed their fate.

With a surge of anger, Alexandra began to compose a letter to her publisher.

Dear Mr Allendale,
After much consideration, I have decided this manuscript cannot be published. Please accept my—

"Still working?"

Alexandra looked over to see Nick leaning against the frame of their connecting door. After delivering her to the Brimstone, he had left to patrol the nearby streets for any sign of trouble. He had been gone for hours – another reason for Alexandra's poor sleep.

She had worried about his safety.

Nick's countenance was weary, his clothes stained with the mud of the streets. His hair was windblown and damp. Small details that amounted to the same thing: her heart still ached at the sight of him.

Alexandra turned back to the unfinished letter. "The opposite," she muttered, picking up her pen once more. "I plan on writing to my publisher and telling him I refuse to complete this work. Or maybe I'll set it ablaze. I haven't decided yet. I need to think of another way to deal with Sir Reginald."

Clothing rustled. "Why?"

She felt his presence there like a stroke of fingertips across her nape. For a moment, it was like they were breathing in unison, sharing a single set of lungs.

And years of shared memories that hurt.

Alexandra's grip on the pen tightened. Ink stained her fingers. "I don't have the political clout to accuse him publicly, even with evidence. And I'm responsible for the deaths of three people—"

"No." Nick's voice was steady and firm. "You didn't order their deaths or hold the weapon that killed them."

Alexandra's shoulders slumped. "But I might as well have."

Nick's hand covered hers, warm and steadfast. His lips

ghosted over her skin. "You can write your letter if you want," he said softly, "but Seymour won't stop until he silences you. Will you let him?"

"Would you think less of me if I did?"

How strange – how *stupid* – to value his opinion, even now. His newspaper articles had painted her as shallow and superficial, yet here she was, asking him to yield a verdict on her character. She had forgotten what his nearness could do, the power it could wield.

And that meant he could still hurt her.

She braced for his response, wishing she had never asked the question. Wishing she was already aboard that ship, sailing away from England and all its troubles. To a destination unknown, far enough to forget him.

"What do you want me to judge you for?" he asked softly. "Tell me what fault I'm supposed to find in this letter."

"Cowardice."

He made some small noise – a half-smothered laugh. "Alex," he said, low and intimate, "there's no cowardice in knowing that bravery always comes at a cost."

She squeezed her eyes shut, fighting the urge to turn in his arms and let him take her, let him pleasure her. She wanted distractions – from the worries, the memories, *everything*. The words of intimacy were easy, after all. They were simple syllables that rolled off the tongue effortlessly. *Yes* and *no*, or if their lovemaking was as good as last time, *yes* and *yes* and *yes*. If he kissed her now, she'd let him. She'd whisper her assent without hesitation.

But that wouldn't solve anything.

"Then what would you have me do?" she asked him.

Nick's lips brushed against her skin as he whispered,

"Burn his life to the ground. And let this," he tapped her pen, "be your match. I'll be here for you whenever you need me."

With those words, he withdrew his hand and left her holding the pen. The door between them clicked shut.

Alexandra tossed the letter into the wastebasket.

Alexandra was roused from her slumber by the sound of girlish giggles. The bed shook slightly as two small bodies climbed on it, and then a tiny voice said, "Mornin', lady."

She slowly opened her eyes and found herself face-to-face with a child. What time was it? It must have been early since neither of the children was in school yet. She must have slept only a few hours.

No wonder she felt like the devil.

"Lottie?" she asked with a yawn. "Or are you Dot?"

The little girl stared back. "Lottie. Dot's just behind ye."

At her name, the other girl bounced on the bed and rested her chin on Alexandra's shoulder. "Why's yer room covered in paper, lady?"

Alexandra's bleary-eyed scan of the environment around her bed made her acknowledge the justice of this observation. The maids respected her request not to touch her work, and now notes and discarded pages had accumulated across the floor.

"My work involves paper," she said, muffled against the pillow. "Excessive amounts of it." The clock on the mantel read some ungodly hour. Were children *always* there this early? "Don't you both have school?"

"In a bit," Dot chirped. "Tried to get Mr Thorne up, but

he told us to go bovver Mr O'Sullivan, but Mr O'Sullivan is busy, and I'm *hungry*, lady."

Nick got to sleep in? Damn him.

Alexandra sighed. "Does your proprietress not feed you well?"

"Nah, she's a kind 'un," Lottie said, cuddling against her. "Dot wants one of them pastries. Never had food like that afore we came to Mrs Ainsley's. Covered in crawlies, ours was. Ain't it, Dot? Them swells sometimes dropped a treat or two on the main road if they were in a rush. Ma used to brush the bugs off."

Alexandra fought to keep her expression neutral. She knew all too well that children in the East End lacked basic needs. These girls were fortunate in some respects, having food at all – so many went hungry.

Nick had told her that was why he and the other children had turned to Whelan. Food, safety, and shelter came at a steep cost in the East End. Alexandra refused to let these children pay that price.

"Very well, then," she said, throwing off the covers. It appeared sleep would have to wait. She smiled at the girls. "We'll ask a maid to have Mr Burke bake a batch of pastries while I get dressed. Then we'll take them with us to the orphanage."

Dot squealed, and Lottie tentatively smiled back. "You're a good 'un, too, lady," Lottie said, and her small dimple flashed.

After dressing, Alexandra led the girls down to the kitchens, where she found Mr O'Sullivan instructing the cook on the evening's menu.

"Good morning, Mr O'Sullivan. Mr Burke."

Burke's warm grin revealed one missing tooth. Mr O'Sullivan returned her greeting with a brisk nod that improved his earlier frosty demeanour. Then he spotted the girls behind her. "You two." Mr O'Sullivan gestured between them. "Isn't school starting soon?"

"Don't scold the children, Mr O'Sullivan. It's my fault they're still here," Alexandra interrupted before the girls could reply. She looked at Burke. "Pastries?"

The cook reached for the basket on the table and passed it to her. "Fresh out of the oven, my lady."

"Thank you, sir." Alexandra beamed at him, then turned to Mr O'Sullivan. "I have a favour to ask of you."

"I'm busy. You'll have to ask Thorne." The cook clicked his tongue, causing O'Sullivan to scowl. "Didn't ask for your tutting, did I, Burke? Don't you have a shipment to check?"

With a shake of his head, Burke vanished through the side door, leaving Alexandra and O'Sullivan alone in the kitchen with the children. She hated to pull the factotum away from his work, but... "Nick was out all night and only returned a few hours ago."

"He wouldn't wake up, Mr O'Sullivan," Lottie chirped. "Said not to bovver him."

"That's because you escape from Mrs Ainsley's and pick the locks on his door," O'Sullivan said to Lottie, then turned to Alexandra. "I recall seeing the light in your room when he came in. Didn't get much sleep either, did you?"

Nick must have assigned him to guard her bedchamber. "No. But I wasn't patrolling dark alleyways for hours." When he still seemed hesitant, Alexandra said, "Please, accompany us to the orphanage so I can give the other children some pastries before school. Mr Burke went to great lengths to make them."

Lottie added, "And Mrs Ainsley's more forgivin' if we show up with pastries. She likes 'em, even if she pretends she don't. Caught her eatin' one in a closet once, didn't we, Dot? She was cryin' like someone died."

O'Sullivan frowned. "Telling tales again, Lottie?"

"No, sir! On my ma's soul, I saw it." She bit her lip. "You won't tell her I picked the locks, will you, Mr O'Sullivan?"

He sighed. "Just don't do it again, sweetheart." Before Lottie could answer, he took the basket from Alexandra. "Fine. I'll go."

"Wonderful," Alexandra said with a bright smile. "Come along, girls. Lead the way."

They followed the two delighted children out of the kitchens. She pulled up the collar of her coat, attempting to ward off the chill. The weather was brisk with the promise of autumn, the East End redolent with the coal smoke that stained its buildings black. The stench had been difficult to grow used to once, but it hardly affected her anymore.

Lottie and Dot scampered down the muddy lane, darting around passers-by with ease. Alexandra had to admit she was impressed by their agility.

"Stay in sight, girls!" she called after them, barely audible over the din of the bustling street.

It was a vibrant community, brimming with life in these early hours. Drunkards stumbled home from the taverns while factory girls chatted on their way to work. The bakers peddled their wares from the storefront, and a pair of lovers passionately embraced before parting ways. It was a world less formal than what Alexandra was used to, but these small moments of joy made her heart sing.

"The girls like you," O'Sullivan said quietly.

Alexandra slipped a coin into the palm of a boy gazing hungrily at the bread displayed in the baker's window. The child gave a crow of delight. "I fascinate them. Most of their experience with the gentry is limited to stern-faced ladies fussing over their charity or sneering at them from their carriages."

O'Sullivan released a weary sigh. "What's the difference?" he said, eyeing Alexandra with a hint of disdain. Seeing the confusion on her face, he continued, "Ladies like to support orphanages because the kids are too little to realise that their patrons don't give a shit about them. They're just grateful for the crumbs they get, so they'll take whatever scraps of snobbery they're offered." He gestured towards the two girls, walking a safe distance away. "But Lottie's not a baby anymore. She's starting to see the world for what it is."

"See what?"

"The distinction between truth and lies. It's easy to trust the ones with the pretty smiles, but their betrayals cut deeper. The ladies in the carriages might be a bunch of hags, but at least they're honest."

Alexandra fell silent, watching as the two girls strolled through the twisting alleys. Their heads were bent together, whispering secrets. It dawned on her that Lottie's candid remarks about her life before the orphanage were a way of testing her. Was Alexandra just another lady from the carriage, full of fake smiles and empty promises?

O'Sullivan's harsh words rang true; charity was another

currency in Alexandra's world. Everyone, from the daughters of dukes to the wives of baronets, boasted about their good deeds not because they cared about the poor, but because it earned them the approval of their peers. After all, many had husbands and fathers who sat in Parliament, passing bills that only benefitted the wealthy, leaving the rest to fend for themselves.

"You think I am like another patroness," Alexandra said. "Picking and choosing the worthy poor. Don't you?"

How could she blame him if he did? He had grown up here, worlds apart from her upbringing. He had been forced to survive the same streets of Nick's childhood when Whelan demanded loyalty at a high price. Aristocrats cared nothing for this place or the people in it.

O'Sullivan let out a soft exhale. "I don't know what you are. Patroness or a carriage lady, it makes no difference to me. I don't trust aristos. You all demand a high price for your attentions."

Alexandra measured her words carefully. "You have a lilt in your accent that comes and goes. Sometimes it's Irish. Other times it's Her Majesty's English. I assume you might understand something about this 'price'?"

His grip on the basket tightened until his knuckles turned white. "I do," he said simply, cutting her off. Before she could press the matter any further, he gestured to the nearest building. A grand structure with lovely carved letters spelling out the words: *Mrs Ainsley's Home for Orphaned Children*. "We're here."

"Lady! Lady!" Dot ran over and grasped Alexandra's hand. "You gotta meet the others!"

Alexandra laughed as the girls dragged her inside the

orphanage. The building was immaculate, with a welcoming atmosphere that exuded warmth and comfort. Chintz furniture, freshly bought floral draperies, and polished hardwood floors all spoke of a caring environment. The air was thick with the scent of freshly baked bread and lemon-scented cleaning solution, while the sounds of children's laughter and chattering drifted through the halls.

"Come on, lady," Dot said, tugging Alexandra. "I'm ever so hungry!"

"Mr O'Sullivan's the one wiv the pastries, daftie," Lottie said, rolling her eyes.

"Charlotte," came a new voice. "Don't call your sister a daftie. Please apologise."

A young woman with jingling keys at her waist descended the stairs. She carried herself with an air of authority that suggested she was the manager of the place, Mrs Ainsley. She was a striking figure, tall and beautiful, with hair as black as coal and eyes that gleamed like emeralds. Her expression was welcoming as she regarded the two girls.

"Sorry, Dot," Lottie muttered. To Mrs Ainsley: "Can lady join us for breakfast?"

"I'll consider it," Mrs Ainsley said, her gaze appraising them both. "But first, do you have anything you need to confess?" When Lottie shot O'Sullivan a desperate look, Mrs Ainsley shook her head. "Mr O'Sullivan won't help you this time. Dot? You first."

Dot hung her head. "We sneaked out again."

"Ah, now we're getting somewhere. Charlotte?"

Lottie wrinkled her nose. "And I picked the locks again," the girl mumbled.

"I appreciate your honesty." Mrs Ainsley glanced between

them. "I'll think of your punishment, but until then, go join the others. Tell everyone I want them to have their boots on for school."

The two girls ran out of the room, and Alexandra stared after them in amusement. "They're a handful, aren't they?"

Mrs Ainsley sighed. "If that girl keeps picking the locks, I'll have to Charlotte-proof the orphanage." She offered her hand to Alexandra. "My apologies. You must be Mr Thorne's wife. I'm Mrs Ainsley, but you must call me Sofia."

Alexandra gave her hand a firm shake. "Pleasure. Thank you for allowing me to borrow your clothes the other day. I hope you'll let me replace them."

"How kind of you, but I have everything I need."

"Things for the children, then. You only need to ask." Alexandra scanned the room, noting the meticulous cleanliness once more. It must have been hard work keeping an orphanage so clean. "Do you run this entire home yourself?"

"I've some staff Mr Thorne hired after he asked me to become the manager. The previous mistress was not" – her lips thinned – "a kind woman. I shall leave there." Sofia looked at O'Sullivan. "Mr O'Sullivan. I'm happy to see you again."

The factotum was staring at Sofia with an odd expression on his face. "Can't stay," he muttered abruptly.

Sofia's smile faltered slightly. "I never said I would hold you here against your will. You may come and go as you please. You, of all people, should know that."

In the short time Alexandra had known him, she had never seen the Irishman so rattled. It was as if he was fighting some inner demons. "Leaving," he said through gritted teeth. "I need to go." With that, he thrust the basket into Sofia's hands. "These are for the kids," and was gone. The door slammed shut behind him.

Alexandra couldn't help but wonder aloud, "What was that all about?"

Sofia's expression was pensive as she stared at the door. "Unfinished business, I'm afraid," she said softly. Then, with a forced smile, she turned to Alexandra. "Shall we check on the children?"

∽ 17 ∽

Alex was not in her room, and no guards were at her door.

Thorne tried to calm his surge of panic. Whelan's return had him frayed at the edges. The memories of that old, musty cellar haunted him, so vivid he could practically taste the cigar smoke clogging his lungs. Thorne had jolted awake in a cold sweat, barely reaching the water closet before he vomited up his guts. He'd lurched back to his bed, curled up in a ball, and sucked in deep, heaving breaths.

When Dot and Lottie had stumbled upon him like that, he'd been too sharp with them. Lottie, bless her, had given his shoulder a pat, taken her sister's hand, and left him be.

Hours later, Thorne had cleaned himself up, dressed, and gone to check on his wife.

Empty chamber. Scattered papers. Alex's mess, or someone else's?

Thorne pounded down the hall, finally spotting one of his men. "Clements," he said sharply, aware that he must have appeared half-mad. At that moment, he didn't bloody well give a damn. "Lady Alexandra isn't in her room." The other man spluttered some response that was more like a panicked gurgle. "Spit it out. Where is she?"

"She's at the orphanage," another voice said wryly.

Thorne whirled to see O'Sullivan coming out of his offices. The factotum looked at Clements and dismissed him with a nod.

"Someone is supposed to be guarding her," Thorne said. "At all times."

Thorne had searched throughout the night for any sign of Whelan's whereabouts, but to no avail. He'd scoured Whelan's favoured pubs, gin palaces, and gaming dens – everywhere except for the only place Thorne feared to tread: the cellar where he had endured his tormented childhood. He'd bought the decrepit building from the landlord, paying whatever it took, and left it to rot. He wished he had burned it to the ground. Salted the earth. Let the pigeons shit on its ashes.

But over the years, all he'd wanted to do was forget.

O'Sullivan removed his spectacles and rubbed them on his shirt. "If you intended to keep her locked in there, you should have informed me. I wasn't aware we were keeping her captive."

Thorne felt a stirring of irritation. "Don't be an idiot."

"Stop threatening Clements as if he were a gaoler and not an employee," O'Sullivan snapped, adjusting his glasses on his nose. "Your piece is safe. She's with Sofia and a merry band of ecstatic children."

Sofia was the sole reason O'Sullivan was breathing and not rotting in a ditch. Thorne recalled the day Whelan lined up all his lads for some fancy gent to pick out his favourite from the pack. Thorne was a young fourteen, and O'Sullivan was two years his junior, with a pretty face that caught the attention of the wrong crowd.

On that day, Whelan had sold O'Sullivan.

Thorne spent three years searching for the toff who had bought his friend. Fortune smiled on him when a girl approached him in the Nichol and revealed the earl's identity. O'Sullivan had been locked up and kept like a caged animal in the earl's London residence for the entire time.

When Thorne finally found O'Sullivan, his body was covered in scars, but he was alive.

Years later, when Sofia came to the Brimstone and said she needed to go into hiding, Thorne and O'Sullivan didn't ask questions. They hid her. Now she was known as Mrs Ainsley, the manager of the children's home.

Thorne turned to O'Sullivan. "Did you say anything coherent to Sofia, or did you just stand there, looking like a bloody eejit?"

"Don't start," O'Sullivan said warningly.

"I haven't even begun. She's a stunner. Got a heart of gold. She saved your arse from the Earl of Sunderland. What's the problem?"

"About twenty, give or take," O'Sullivan muttered, shoving his glasses up his nose. He let out a deep sigh. "Go to your wife, Thorne. I'll handle matters here."

Thorne clapped O'Sullivan on the shoulder and made his way to the orphanage.

As the maid ushered him inside, he couldn't help but smile at the cadence of children giggling. Since Sofia took over the orphanage, it was filled with joy and mirth. Before

Thorne owned the building, it was managed by Mrs Foley, who stank of gin and spent half of her day sloshed. Thorne's first order of business was getting rid of her.

Sofia had performed wonders here. The children were thriving under her care.

Moments before reaching the sitting room, Thorne caught a familiar sound: Alex's laughter. Thorne peeked through the door and discovered his wife assisting Sofia in organising the children. He leaned against the frame, savouring the view of Alex. Her blonde tresses were tumbling out of her chignon, and her eyes glimmered with merriment. He hadn't seen her look so happy since Gretna when the blacksmith had bound their hands with ribbon. After their train journey, she had been weary and rumpled, but her smile had been the most beautiful thing he'd ever seen. Still was.

But this one wasn't for him.

"Mrs Ainsley always tells us a story before school," a little girl informed Alex. "Right, Mrs Ainsley?"

"Children," Sofia was saying. "We really must get you ready. Oh my goodness, Mary, those pastries have made your fingers all sticky. Come here, darling."

"One story," Lottie said, flopping into the armchair. Her bootlaces remained untied. "Please, Mrs Thorne?"

Alex released a throaty laugh that made Thorne's chest tighten. "Very well," she agreed, kneeling to tie Lottie's laces. "Are there any requests?"

Dot bounced next to Lottie. "Tell us one about Mr Thorne!"

"Ohhhh," Lottie said. She twirled her hair around her finger and said, "Tell us about *you* and Mr Thorne. Is it ever so romantic? I wanna know."

Alex's grin faltered.

Sofia picked up on her discomfort instantly. "Perhaps another tale," she suggested softly. "How about the diamond and the loadstone? Or—"

"*Pleaaaaaaase*, Mrs Thorne?" Lottie cried.

"Lottie, my love." Sofia spoke sternly now. "It's Lady Alexandra, and don't harangue her. She's our guest."

"No, it's all right." Alex straightened. Though uncertainty flickered across her features, she found her resolve. "Mr Thorne and I—"

"No, you got to start right-like," Dot said, picking at her just-tied bootlaces. "Like in them fairytales."

"Of course," Alex murmured, her face etched with pain. After all, their marriage was no idyllic tale to inspire children. If this were a fairytale, Thorne would be the villain. "Once upon a time, there was a young woman. She had two caring brothers, but a cruel father who relished any opportunity to remind her that he viewed her as a burden, a mistake. You could call her a princess since she attended grand balls. However, she never danced."

Dot gasped. "Ohh, but why not? Didn't she wanna?"

"Of course, she wanted to very much. But she didn't fit in with her peers and was expected to make herself smaller." Seeing their puzzled expressions, Alex clarified gently, "Pretend to be someone she wasn't. And when she refused, her father banished her to the countryside as punishment. One day – when she was very lonely – she met a man."

"Oh my goodness," Lottie sighed. "Did she kiss him?"

"Not immediately," Alex replied. "But she was very fond of him. He was the first person who truly understood her.

They spent nearly every day together, swimming in the lake or sitting beneath the trees, chatting for hours. He was…"

Alex paused, and the knife twisted in Thorne's chest. He knew what was coming next, all too aware of how the story ended.

He still remembered her entering the carriage and leaving him on Roseburn's gravel drive.

Four years was a long time.

Alex shook her head as if to clear it. "The man was kind to her. That was what she fell in love with: his kindness. But her father considered this man beneath her, so she was forbidden to see him."

"No!" Dot cried.

"How awful," Lottie added. "Did she run away with him?"

"Yes, sweetheart." Thorne heard the sadness in Alex's voice. "They eloped, and she married him." Alexandra looked towards the door, as if sensing him. Their eyes met across the room. Thorne held his breath, waiting for what she'd say. How she'd tell the children that he wasn't a kind man at all, but a liar hired by her father to deceive her to that altar. But she only smiled at the rapt children. "And that is the story of Mr Thorne and me."

Happy sighs from the children. The room filled with the applause of a dozen small hands clapping.

Sofia, who had been listening with a tender expression, stood and addressed her charges. "Time to leave our guest and head to school. Lottie, please help Miss Margaret with the little ones."

The children's exit left the chamber oddly hushed. Thorne felt as if he'd been submerged in a warm bath, and the water suddenly drained away. He turned to Alex, taking her in. She was like a bird poised to take flight – quick, light, and watchful.

"Good morning," she said.

Sofia noticed Thorne in the doorway. "Oh, hello, Mr Thorne," she said pleasantly. "I didn't see you there. Have you come to inspect the inventory?"

"I suspect he's here to accompany me." Alex's countenance remained wary. "As Mr O'Sullivan seems to have vanished."

Nick couldn't help but think of last night, that moment in her room after he returned to the Brimstone. He would have given anything to kiss her, but in the end, he retreated to his chamber and had a sleep plagued by nightmares.

"O'Sullivan's at the club." Thorne addressed Sofia: "I'll leave one of my men to watch the premises. The children may have to stay inside after school for a few days. Make sure Lottie can't pick the locks."

Sofia's hands twisted at her skirts as if she was hiding a secret. "I've heard whispers about some murders nearby—"

"Nothing for you to worry about." Thorne's tone softened. "O'Sullivan and I promised to keep you safe, and we don't break our vows."

Still looking worried, Sofia nodded. "Very well. My thanks."

After exchanging pleasantries, Thorne and Alexandra departed the orphanage. The East End was buzzing with life in the few minutes Thorne had been there, with hawkers calling out their wares and machinery humming. He glanced at Alex, wondering what she thought of the noise. For him, these sounds were home. But she was raised in peaceful Hampshire. Thorne remembered the quiet of the countryside, how it made him restless, and how Alex had filled the space in his heart that yearned for comfort.

And how he'd squandered it.

Silently, Alex strode down the street, away from the Brimstone. Thorne caught up with her. "The Brimstone's the other way."

She didn't look at him. "It's a shorter distance to hire a hack this direction, and I need to make two stops."

He nodded in understanding. "Your sources?"

"Yes. First St Giles, then Mayfair." Alex hailed a hack, gave the driver the first address, and settled across from Thorne. With a sigh, she looked out the window. "I'm worried they're already dead."

Thorne didn't know how to console her with words. So he took her gloved hand in his, surprised and relieved when she interlaced their fingers. It had been four years since he'd held her hand like this. Four long years.

His thumb grazed her wrist, feeling the warmth of her skin even through the leather. He longed to brush his fingertips along her cheek or kiss the curve of her neck, but he didn't dare. This was the only touch she allowed, and he would be content with that. He wouldn't ask for anything more than she was willing to give.

"You didn't tell the children the rest of our story."

Alex fixed her gaze on their joined hands, watching him trace circles on her palm. "How should I have ended it?"

"You could have told them I held you in my arms for four days. How we travelled up north and back, and how I woke up each morning with your kiss on my lips," he said, his voice low and husky. "But when you smiled and called yourself Lady Alexandra Locke, I didn't correct you. I let the name stand."

Pain flashed across her face, and Thorne felt it too. "The name might have been a lie, but my feelings for Lord Locke were real." The carriage stopped, and she withdrew her hand, taking all the warmth with her. "Let the children have their happy ending, Nick. It's better than the one we got."

18

STRATFIELD SAYE, HAMPSHIRE

Four years ago

Alexandra bit her lip and gazed absently out the window of the private rail compartment. The scenery flew by, but she scarcely noticed the changing landscape as the train sped north.

That morning, Alexandra had barely had a moment to think. The sun had just risen, painting the sky a beautiful shade of pink, when she hastily packed a single valise and escaped through the window. She met Nick's carriage at the end of the drive, and they embarked on the journey to London. Their sole option was to take the train from London to Carlisle and catch a second train to Dumfriesshire. And once they reached Gretna Green, the local blacksmiths were the only ones who could officiate their wedding at such short notice.

Alexandra's nerves were frayed as they sat on the train with nothing but time ahead. Nick was uncharacteristically quiet during their daring escape from Stratfield Saye to London. It had been five torturous days since they kissed

– ample time for him to make arrangements he hadn't bothered to explain to her. Was it long enough for him to have second thoughts? To realise he had made a mistake?

Alexandra studied him. Nick was dressed elegantly in his dark grey suit, which hugged his broad shoulders and trim waist. Although he initially appeared to be at ease, Alexandra could sense the tension in his fingers as he clutched his hat and drummed it against his thigh.

Say something, she mentally urged him. *Look at me. Kiss me. Anything.*

The train rocked. Alexandra heard the soft laughter of passengers elsewhere in the carriage. If they were to pass the door of Alexandra and Nick's car, they might assume it was unoccupied.

Fidgeting with her dusty travel dress, Alexandra cleared her throat. "Should we be worried about the Scottish law? Twenty-one days' residence prior to nuptials?"

Nick didn't so much as glance her way. He continued to gaze at the outside world with an inscrutable expression. "If I pay the blacksmith enough, he'll say we were born and raised in Scotland."

A hush fell over their compartment once more, leaving nothing but the sound of Nick's tapping hat. *Tap. Tap. Tap.* Elsewhere in the carriage, glasses clinked. More laughter.

Tap. Tap. Tap.

"Will we live at your house in Stratfield Saye?" Alexandra asked, trying a different tack now. "Maybe discussing their future might draw him out. "Or somewhere else? Perhaps we could buy another…"

Nick turned to face her, his eyes ablaze with an intensity that Alexandra couldn't quite read. Was it anger? She felt a flush creep up her neck. They had not discussed his finances, but her father had remarked on Baron Locke's near-empty coffers.

"I have money, Nick," Alexandra hastened to reassure him. "My mother put it in a trust to ensure my father could never withhold my dowry. I'll be able to access it once we're married."

His jaw tightened. "Let's not discuss this now."

"Very well." Alexandra's voice was soft.

She watched him cross his legs, creating even more distance between them in the confined space. The sound of his tapping hat grew more incessant. *Tap. Tap. Tap.* Alexandra couldn't bear it any longer – the silence, his clipped responses, the notion that he might be second-guessing their impulsive elopement.

Tap. Tap. Tap.

Alexandra reached out and placed her hand over Nick's, stopping the ceaseless rhythm. "Nick. You've made no vows to me. If you've changed your mind – if you regret—"

"No." Nick's eyes bore into hers as he interlaced their fingers. "I don't regret."

A lump formed in Alexandra's throat. "If it's money—"

Before she could finish her sentence, Nick leaned in and captured her lips with his own. The kiss was gentle, but it left Alexandra lightheaded and dizzy. "It's not money," he murmured, shifting to sit beside her. With a possessive grip, he wrapped his arms around her waist and trailed hot kisses along her jaw. "It's not about regret, or you. Never about you."

Her neck arched in response. "Then what's the matter?"

Nick breathed against her, his heartbeat strong beneath

her fingertips. He closed his eyes and kissed her again and again – until Alexandra forgot he'd never given her an answer.

Their arrival in Gretna Green was delayed, and they reached the blacksmith's in the dead of night.

Thorne paid the blacksmith and his family a generous sum to overlook the Scottish law that mandated a twenty-one-day residency before a wedding, designed to prevent elopements like theirs.

But every man had a price, and the smithy had ten mouths to feed.

His wife and eldest daughter stood as witnesses, watching with kind smiles as Thorne and Alexandra exchanged vows over the anvil and had the ribbon wrapped around their hands.

Alexandra's lips curved in a smile as the ceremony ended. She looked every inch the glowing bride, unaware that she'd just completed one of the ultimate steps in Thorne's swindle. She embraced the smithy's wife and daughter and didn't even notice when her new husband signed *Nicholas Thorne* instead of *Nicholas Locke* in the register beside hers. If she had, she would have known him for a liar and refused the final step in his deceit.

The marriage bed.

Don't bother returning unless you've consummated the marriage, the Earl of Kent had said. *The last thing I need is my sons helping her obtain an annulment.*

"You have that look again," Alexandra said, sipping her ale.

They were in their private room at the inn in Gretna. It wasn't as luxurious as his suite at Fairview House, but it was a damn sight better than anything he would have found in the Nichol. They had already enjoyed a hearty meal of meat pie and dark ale, and Alex's initial distaste for the beverage had quickly dissipated with each passing gulp.

Mid-meal, Thorne had noticed Alex fidgeting with the neckline of her dress, and that innocent motion had released a torrent of carnal thoughts. The slow removal of her garments, the taste of her skin on his tongue, the texture between her thighs as he pleasured her, the twisted sheets as they fucked until dawn.

But he couldn't forget that this was borrowed time, and soon enough, she would despise him for what he was about to do.

"What look?" Thorne returned his gaze to the last swig of ale in his tankard. He needed to keep up the pretence of being the happy new husband and flash a smile for Alex. It was only a few more lies.

No one had ever told him that lying could hurt so damn much.

"As if you're somewhere else." She made a soft noise. "Somewhere I can't reach."

It was the cellar in the Nichol that had occupied his thoughts on the train. Memories had flooded his mind, driving him towards his purpose, a reminder that this deception was not only about her. It was about everyone back in the East End living under the weight of Whelan's boot. Otherwise, he might have been tempted to get down on his knees.

Tell her the truth.

I'll be the poorest bet you've ever made, but I swear I'll make it worth the gamble.

Thorne knew a thing or two about playing the odds. If it were just him, he would take the risk and put himself at her mercy. He would confess his deceit.

But not for the others. Not for O'Sullivan or Callahan. This wasn't roulette, not a game of luck. His was a game of power, and it took skill and cunning.

And cheating.

He'd bear the weight of his artifice in the morning.

Thorne stood up, the wooden chair scraping against the floor. Alexandra watched as he approached her side of the table and set aside her tankard.

He brushed his lips over her wrist, feeling the erratic pulse beneath. "I'm sorry," he said, pulling her closer. "I've been neglecting you, haven't I?"

Ah, her laugh. God, her laugh. He'd miss it when the truth came out. "It's been a long day," she said, her voice low and husky. Thorne suppressed a groan when she flicked her tongue against his earlobe. "But you can apologise to me."

"Where should I start?" His mind was already running wild with possibilities.

She nuzzled his cheek, then turned in his arms. "Undress me."

In the morning, he'd regret not telling her. He'd regret that she didn't have a choice – not really. When he put his hands on her and unbuttoned her clothes, he did it with guilt and something far worse: love.

Thorne loved Alex.

And he hated himself for what he was about to do.

★ ★ ★

In a whisper of fabric, Alexandra's dress cascaded to the floor. Nick had nimble hands. His movements were deft and practised as he unlaced her corset and pushed down her petticoats.

An indrawn breath. Alexandra knew what he saw: her combinations were as gossamer-thin as cobwebs, her skin visible through the material. She lifted her arms, a silent plea to remove them. Nick complied – but when she thought he might touch her, press his hands to her back, her shoulders, kiss her – he only stepped away.

Why was he so hesitant now? If she faced him, would she find Nick in that same distant reverie that seemed beyond her? The place in his mind she couldn't reach?

But she refused to have a husband who kept himself at arm's length. She wanted the man who had kissed her at the lake, who couldn't get enough of her.

Alexandra pulled down her drawers and heard his soft hiss. *There*. She could still reach him.

She turned and almost faltered at the hunger in his gaze. His eyes touched her all over – legs, hips, breasts, up, up. They were fevered when they met hers.

"You will stay here with me," she said, reaching for his coat and removing it. Her eager fingers worked on his waistcoat, undoing the buttons one by one. "Not in that place in your mind, Nick. Here, with me."

Braces off his shoulders. His shirt was in the way. Alex lifted the material over his head so roughly that she heard the fabric tear. He was a work of art, his muscles like carved marble, each line and curve a testament to his strength and power. It seemed almost criminal to cover him up. She traced the scars that crisscrossed his torso.

Nick's expression was so grave. So grim. The candlelight highlighted the harsh set of his mouth, the intensity of his dark stare as he regarded Alexandra. As if he challenged her to ask.

Alexandra teetered on the brink of something vast, unknown, and terrifying. It did not suit her mood.

"With me," she snapped, her hands going to his trousers, ripping open the smallclothes with ease. When she had him naked, she reached up and touched his cheek. "In this room."

Nick's hand came up to clasp hers, and he uttered her name through clenched teeth. "Alex."

It sounded like a confession. Guilt spoken aloud. She wouldn't listen. Not tonight. She did not want to know what was at the bottom of the precipice – what came after the fall.

Alexandra tangled her fingers into the softness of his hair and grasped him roughly. "You and me, Nick. Nothing else. Nothing between us."

Nick seemed to come to a stark and sombre decision – a promise in the air, a secret knowledge shared between them.

Then he dipped his head, and their lips collided like lightning striking tinder. Yes, this was what she needed. The warm strength of his body against hers, pushing her back until the mattress cushioned her fall. His hands, hot and tender on her skin as he mapped out her every detail.

Not enough.

Alexandra was famished, an insatiable hunger clawing through her veins. She dragged her nails across his flesh, ravenous, the void within her never-ending. His answer came in a low growl as she parted her thighs to accept his offering.

"Patience," Nick whispered against her lips, teeth lightly grazing.

"No," she answered back, hips rising to meet him.

Nick groaned and pressed her wrists into the mattress. Then he lowered his head to whisper in her ear, "If you're patient, I'll slide my tongue inside your pussy and make you come so hard, you'll see stars."

Alexandra's exhale was unsteady. "I'm open to being convinced."

His smile was fierce and confident as he let go of her wrists. His kisses trailed from the base of her throat, down, down. When he hesitated, it was with his mouth hovering a breath from where she desired him most. "Still need convincing?"

"*Nick*." She would accept nothing less than complete satisfaction. She wanted his mouth on her, his hands on her skin, to never stop touching her.

He set his lips to her. Alexandra arched up, gasping as he licked and sucked the sensitive mound between her thighs. He knew just how much pressure, where to press his tongue and use his fingers.

Trembling, Alexandra said his name in a ragged prayer, barely coherent. "Please," she begged, not knowing for what she asked. "Please."

Nick rose over her, the muscles in his arms straining. When he stared down at her, those black eyes glittered like the ocean at midnight. "I don't want to hurt you," he whispered in a voice as rough as shale.

Alexandra slid her legs against his, cradling his hips

between her knees. "It's only once, Nick." She smiled at his grave expression. Was this his earlier worry? Hurting her? "Make it up to me next time," she said, and kissed him.

He drew back abruptly. "I'm so sorry," he breathed.

Then Nick bridged the gap between them, pressing himself deep within her with one swift thrust. He must have seen the flinch on her face because he pressed kisses to her throat, murmuring apologies into her skin. But Alexandra wanted no apology – she had dreamed of this moment for weeks, longed for its blissful agony.

Alexandra lifted her hips off the bed, gratified by his sharp intake of breath. Fine, he would not move? She'd move. She'd break his control.

Alexandra shifted beneath him, teasing him with shallow thrusts until he grabbed her wrists and held them tight against the bedsheets.

His eyes were bright and fevered again. "Tell me how you want it," he panted, his voice hoarse. "If you prefer it slow, tell me now." Nick's tone had a soft lilt that she had never heard before, which made her flex her hips again. He responded with a rough sound and pressed her wrists harder into the bed. "*Alex*."

The wildfire in his gaze blazed brighter. Her name had sounded like a plea.

"I don't want slow," she said.

Desperation honed his stare to sharp steel, his words frank and vulgar. "Speak plainly. How do you want me to fuck you?"

Alexandra shivered at his directness, the raw need that ignited every nerve in her body. She lifted her head to lick the shell of his ear. "Hard and fast. Now."

Nick went still for a moment before a hoarse laugh escaped him. "Thank God."

Then he reared back and slammed into her.

Alexandra went slack against him as a conflagration spread through every part of her. This was what she desired: Nick driving into her with savage force, muscles straining with each thrust. The scrape of his teeth as he marked her, pain mixed with pleasure.

He adjusted his position and pushed even deeper, yet it wasn't enough – it would never be enough. She wanted him beneath her skin. Deep within her bones. She wanted to discover every inch of him, to hear the thunderous roar of his breath in her ear as he whispered filthy words that should have made her blush.

"Finish," his husky plea stroked against her like smoke, hips moving faster now. "Alex. *Finish*."

Alexandra didn't understand, but she loved hearing him beg. A wicked grin curved her lips. "No."

"No?" Nick slid an intimate hand between their bodies, pressing his fingers to that sensitive place between her legs where pleasure built like a storm-tossed wave waiting to crash down upon her senses. "Still no?"

Her spine went rigid, toes curling tight into the mattress beneath them. "Nick."

"That's it," he murmured, circling with his fingertips. "Finish for me, sweetheart."

He swirled circles with gentle touches until everything blurred around her. The warmth became too much for Alex, and she braced herself against him for support. His skin bore rosy marks from her nails as she grasped him close – her anchor amid the chaos, the only thing tying her to the earth.

A jagged gasp tore from her lungs – a harsh entreaty of his name.

Almost immediately, he gripped the headboard and shuddered above her as he found his release. Her power over him was intoxicating; she had brought him pleasure. Made him come apart.

But it wasn't enough.

Alexandra wanted to put him back together and unravel him again. Every day. Every night. For the rest of her life.

Hours later, Alexandra lay sprawled in bed as Nick softly kissed the arch of her neck. With a smile, she asked, "Is it always like this?" as he trailed his lips along the wings of her collarbones.

They had dozed for a while, and Alexandra had never slept so well as in the cradle of Nick's arms. The warmth of his body pressed to hers had brought safety as much as comfort. Then, when she woke later, all she wanted was to have him inside her again.

Alexandra had made her intentions known by taking Nick's hand and pressing it to her wet quim. *Fuck*, he'd breathed, and that filthy word had burned her ears. In the space between heartbeats, he was on top of her once more, his cock filling her, and her release crashing over her with such force that sparks burst behind her eyelids.

Nick stiffened at her question, his mouth ghosting over her pulse. When he spoke, his words were hoarse and heavy. "No. Only with you."

Alexandra smiled and slid her hands into his hair. "Good. Then it will always be like this between us." Nick's muscles tensed above her, his body growing rigid as stone. "Nick?"

Nick lifted his head. Those eyes were deep pools of black in the candlelight, as unfathomable as the space between stars. He was beautiful, high cheekbones stark and shadowed, lips swollen from kissing her. But a distance was creeping over him again, a gulf of isolation threatening to swallow them whole.

"Don't," she whispered. "Don't go."

He frowned. "I'm not going anywhere."

"You are. You're leaving me for that place in your mind I can't reach."

He opened his mouth to say something, then seemed to think better of it. "I love you," he told her. "I love you. Remember that when we return to Stratfield Saye."

And he pulled her close and held her so tightly that she felt his heartbeat against hers.

"Let me speak to your father," Thorne said, his eyes scanning the lavish foyer of Roseburn. The butler had greeted them with a glare that could curdle milk, but Thorne was used to the look of judgement from those who believed themselves to be his betters.

"Why not go to your house?" Alexandra's voice trembled as she bit her lip. "We'll send for my brother, James. He'll make Father see reason."

The train ride to London had been torturous for Thorne. With every passing moment, he longed for more time with her. More hours. More minutes. More days. Thorne had lost count of the number of times he'd taken her in their private cabin, made her scream his name until she was hoarse. He'd stolen her pleasure like a common thief, fully aware he didn't deserve her.

Thorne was no hero. He'd never been one, not for a single day of his wretched life. Every coin he'd ever earned had been drenched in blood, every secret he'd ever kept a betrayal.

But he was more terrified of losing her than anything else in the world.

Thorne gritted his teeth, knowing what he had to do. He had to confess to her. He couldn't let her father reveal the truth and twist it to hurt her. It would break her heart, but he would be the one to tell her that he meant his words from last night.

He loved her.

Thorne gently cupped her face, and she leaned into his touch, trusting him completely. It was painful to realise that this would be the last time she'd do this. Today, he held her trust.

And today, he was going to lose it.

"Your father needs to hear it from me," Thorne said, his voice firm. "Will you wait for me here?"

Alexandra hesitated, her eyes filled with worry. "You shouldn't go in alone."

The butler returned, announcing that the earl was ready to receive Thorne. Thorne dropped his hand from Alexandra's cheek, his heart heavy. "Don't worry about me, Alex," he murmured. "I don't deserve it."

He left her, following the butler down the hallway to the Earl of Kent's study. Kent was standing by the window, holding a glass of brandy. As Thorne entered, the earl dismissed the servant without a second glance.

"Please tell me you wed the little baggage," Kent sneered.

Thorne's hands clenched into fists, his temper rising. So this was what it felt like to make a deal with the devil: to gain everything you desired, only to lose everything you held dear. "We're married."

"Thank God for that." Kent strode over to his desk, placing the snifter down with a clink. "When you hadn't seduced her yet, I was beginning to think I'd made a mistake investing in you." He glanced over at Thorne. "You bedded her, yes? Her brothers won't care if she's my wife's bastard. My heir isn't without resources for an annulment."

Thorne was a heartbeat away from punching the earl square in the jaw, but he held himself back. He couldn't afford to be thrown into gaol for assaulting a lord. He didn't have enough power to avoid punishment.

But one day, he would.

He would make sure of it.

"We had a deal," Thorne said icily. "And I've held up my end of the bargain, as agreed." *You filthy bastard.* "Now pay me what you owe me."

The earl's smile was as frigid as a winter's night. There was no mistaking the look on his face: they were both mercenaries conducting a business transaction. And Thorne had come to collect what he was owed.

Even if it meant selling his soul to do it.

"Of course." Kent opened a drawer and retrieved a pouch and a stack of papers. "Her trust is yours. Her money is yours. Take these jewels" – he flung the bag towards Thorne, who easily caught it – "and our business is concluded. Congratulations, guttersnipe. You're a rich man now."

A soft gasp behind him made Thorne's heart clench.

Slowly, he turned to the door. Alexandra stood there, her chest heaving with emotion. She stared at the velvet bag in his hand – which suddenly felt as if it weighed a bloody ton – before her gaze shifted to the papers on the earl's desk. Though she couldn't read them, she must have known what they were: the contents of her trust fund.

All one hundred thousand pounds.

And everything, down to the last penny, now belonged to Thorne.

She flinched, realisation dawning on her, and the pain etched on her face nearly destroyed him. "Alex."

"No," she breathed, putting up a hand. "Don't. Just don't."

"You didn't tell her," Kent said with a chuckle of disbelief. "My word, she still thinks you're a peer, doesn't she?"

Alexandra's eyes locked onto his, and a pang of guilt tore through Thorne's chest. He thought of her earlier in the foyer, her expression full of trust. Now that trust was shattered, and Thorne knew he was to blame. He was a monster.

"Who are you?" Her voice quavered, pleading for reassurance that what she overheard was untrue. That there was a reasonable explanation. Something that wouldn't hurt her. "Tell me."

He would not lie to her, not anymore. Never again.

But it was her Kent who answered. "He's a nobody," he said. "Some criminal from the East End I hired to take you off my hands."

Thorne glanced at him sharply. "*Enough*, damn you."

Alex took a step back, inching closer to the door. "Why?" Thorne heard the pain in her question, the understanding that the man she believed was her father hadn't just neglected her; he had worked to destroy her. "What have I ever done to—"

"Don't you understand, you stupid girl? You're. Not. Mine," the earl said through his teeth. "Your mother never thought I'd find out that she humiliated me by siring a bastard under my roof. I'll be damned if I let another man's by-blow marry a peer using my reputation. You're lucky she secured you a trust; otherwise, you and your new husband would be scrounging for scraps in the gutter."

"I said that's *enough*," Thorne snapped.

His words drew Alexandra's attention. The betrayal in her expression was like a knife through his heart. He wanted nothing more than to fall to his knees and beg for her forgiveness. He'd give her anything, if only... if only...

Tears rolled down Alex's cheeks.

Her father smirked, taking pleasure in her distress. "You must have been quite the lover, Thorne. I've never even seen her cry."

Thorne spun, about to punch Kent in his arrogant goddamn face – to hell with prison, he'd risk it – but Alexandra let out a sob and took off.

Thorne cursed as he watched Alex storm out of the house. He couldn't let her go, not like this. He ran after her, his heart pounding in his chest. "Alex! Wait!"

She didn't slow down, fuelled by anger and hurt. Thorne finally caught up to her and reached out for her, but she yanked away. "Don't touch me, Nick," she snapped, her hand pressed against her stomach. "My God, is that even your real name? He called you Thorne."

"My name is Nicholas Thorne," he said quietly. "My Christian name was the truth."

Alex panted, her voice shaking with emotion. "And everything else?" At his hesitation, she balled her hands into fists. "Tell me, Nick. *Everything else.* How we met? My father forbidding me to see you? Was it all a pack of lies to get my money?"

Thorne fought to keep his feet on the ground, his pulse thundering in his ears. These were only hints of the emotions that boiled inside him. It would have been easier for him to kneel and offer to cut out his heart for her. Surrender it on a silver platter. Let her decide what to do with it.

But it was worth nothing. Thorne had nothing of value to give her.

"Yes," he whispered. The word tasted like ash on his tongue. "I lied to you for your money."

"Oh, God." She covered her mouth with her palm, looking as if she would be sick.

Thorne's hand shot out reflexively, but she flinched. He had grown too accustomed to touching her, and now he wished he hadn't taken those moments for granted. "Please, let me explain—"

"*I said don't touch me.*"

Alex recoiled, her fingers clutching her gown so tightly that they turned bone white. She gasped for air, her form quivering with the strain. Gradually, her breaths became more measured. Her body loosened. But as she stared at him, a cold, implacable glint took hold in her eyes. He knew it to be a barrier, one she was constructing piece by piece. He was marooned in the frigid wasteland beyond those ramparts, pacing in circles until he had no choice but to concede. Her heart was a keep, and he was denied entrance.

"I'm taking the carriage to my brother's," Alex said flatly. "You won't come with me. And tell my..." She clenched her jaw. "Tell *the earl* that if he notifies a single person about this marriage, I'll inform everyone who will listen that his wife made him a cuckold."

Thorne would do more than that. He'd make threats, do what she asked – anything she wanted. He owed her that much.

"All right," he said gently. "There's a tavern in Whitechapel called the Hare and Hounds. Will you send word—"

Alex returned his stare, her face set with grim determination. "I'll only send word if I am with child," she said. Her expression was hard. "Legally, I can do nothing about the fact that my money now belongs to you. Take it. Do whatever the hell you want with it. Spend it all, if that's your wish. But don't contact me. I don't want to see you. I don't want to know you."

He felt a tightening in his chest, as if his lungs had been bound with iron chains. *You deserve this. You deserve this for what you did to her.*

But he had to tell her there was one truth – the one thing he knew was real amid a sea of his lies. "I love you."

She stiffened, and Thorne's heart shattered as she uttered her last damning words: "I don't believe you."

Alex spoke to the coachman and got into the carriage. He watched as the conveyance disappeared down the drive.

∽ 19 ∽

LONDON

Four years later

The hack wouldn't go into the St Giles rookeries.

Thorne kept a watchful eye for pickpockets as they strolled past the tenements. Just from Alex's appearance, it was apparent that she didn't belong. Her plain grey walking dress was too immaculate and well-crafted for these parts.

"Up here," Alex said with a gesture. She disregarded the old drunkard who gawked at them, his trembling fingers fiddling with the buttons on his frayed trousers as he relieved himself against the wall.

"Who precisely is this woman?" Thorne asked as he trailed her across the street.

"Millicent Kirkpatrick was transported to Australia to work in Sir Reginald's opal mines." She led them down a narrow alleyway. "A guard there took a liking to Millie and helped her escape. Miraculously, she ended up back on English soil. She provided me with all the details on the opal trade conditions." Approaching a tenement door, she knocked.

As a group of youths passed by, Thorne instinctively placed himself in front of Alex. "How frequently do you come here?" he inquired.

She rapped again. "Often enough."

Thorne's muscles were taut. She wasn't safe in the streets while Whelan was still alive. He fought the temptation to take Alex back to the Brimstone with him. "Alone?"

Alex bit her lip and hesitated. "Yes," she said finally, gesturing to her clothing and knocking again. "Usually, I wear more functional attire."

Thorne made a noise under his breath. "Whether it's functional or not, it's not—"

"Safe? Few places in London are for women." Thorne would have protested further, but Alex muttered something impolite and glanced at him. "You're a thief. A competent one, from what I've heard."

"Retired thief. I'm practically respectable now."

Alex snorted. "*Practically*." She took two pins out of her coiffure and handed them to him. "I presume you can pick a lock. Do me the honour, if you please."

Thorne plucked the pins from her grip. "Stop deflecting."

"I'm not interested in receiving a lecture on safety," she replied, her gaze intent on his nimble fingers as they worked the lock. "But I have to ask: where did you learn to do this?"

A wistful smile graced his face. "From my mam," he answered, feeling for the subtle give and resistance of the lock's inner mechanisms, listening for the telltale clicks. "She ran with a crew in Dublin. Only took what they needed, looked out for each other. But then the famine hit hard, and they had to choose: stay and starve or leave and try their luck elsewhere. The others went to New York.

Ma came to London." He shrugged. "She wanted to return home someday."

"Did she ever…" she trailed off, biting her lip.

"No." The lock yielded, and Thorne pulled it open with a soft click. Whelan insisted on efficiency, so Thorne could pick a lock in mere seconds with his eyes closed. But he toyed with the mechanism a moment, wanting to bask in her company just a little longer. "She never went back. Sold herself to the wrong man one night. He wasn't quick with her."

Her features softened as she considered something, lost in thought, as she often was. "Did you ever find that man?"

Thorne couldn't dawdle with the lock any longer, or she'd notice he'd opened and closed it multiple times. He swung the door open and gestured for her to enter. "I found him some years later," he answered. "And I wasn't quick with him."

She brushed past him, then hesitated, her expression inscrutable. Alex was a lock he could never quite pick, her mechanisms complex and steel strong. The only way inside was if she let him.

Her gentle touch on his arm made Thorne's pulse quicken. It was as if a tiny mechanism had yielded a weakness in the lock on her heart. "Good," she whispered before disappearing into the tenement.

As they ascended, the narrow stairway creaked and groaned beneath their feet. The building was quiet, residents already toiling in London's factories or seeking solace in gin palaces and taverns. The doors were all shut tight, save for one that stood ajar.

Alex's hand trembled as she pushed open the door, and

they stepped into the small flat. It was barren, devoid of any sign of life. The bed was stripped, the table and stool the only furnishings. Millie, whoever she was, had clearly vacated the premises.

Alex sat heavily on the bed, its springs screeching in protest. She gazed despondently out the window.

Thorne wanted to comfort her, but his words sounded trite even to his own ears. "Maybe she moved on. Rent was high around here."

A harsh laugh escaped Alex's lips. "I paid her rent."

Think of something else to say, fool. "Perhaps she—"

"Please," she interrupted, her eyes snapping open. "You promised no more lies. Remember?"

Damn. She had him there, didn't she? "I'm sorry, Alex."

They lapsed into silence, Thorne grappling for the right words – only to realise that all he had were lies. And he'd vowed the truth.

Finally, after what felt like an eternity, she released a heavy breath. "Do you know anything about opal mining?" she asked him.

It was an odd change of subject, but as Alex gazed at the roofs of the other tenements in St Giles, her mind seemed to be working again. Perhaps it was a question meant to distract from her worries, to renew her focus.

Thorne shook his head. "Just seen the gems. Very pretty."

"Very pretty," she repeated with a hollow laugh. "Indeed. Australia is vast and hot, and the sands surrounding the opal mines are more effective than iron bars. The gems are extracted from deep within the earth through narrow passages that go for meters. Millie used to say that it was hard to breathe in that darkness. You yearn for the sight of opals because finding them meant something to eat. Think what she went through to survive, only to—" She made a soft noise and clenched her dress in a white-knuckled grip. "Can you even imagine?"

The dark felt almost tangible. Closing in and suffocating. He learned to tell time by the space of his breaths and would do almost anything to leave it: kill, maim, or steal. What did it matter? They took place in fresh air.

"Yes," Thorne said, his voice barely audible. "I can."

Alexandra's muscles tensed. "Is that so?" she queried.

His reply came out in a rush of breath. "Ask me."

Thorne scrutinised her as she nervously bit her lip. Her hesitation didn't last long. "You've got scars on the side of your torso, just under your arm. Eleven of them," she said, her gloved digit running along the fabric of her dress as if to follow the lines there. "They look deliberate, like notches."

Thorne's body went rigid. "Yes."

"Tell me about them." She continued to trail her finger. "In Gretna, they seemed fresh, less faded."

"They're reminders," he said in a low tone. "I marked them myself before I left for Hampshire. When I was there, surrounded by riches I'd never experienced before, I needed to remember why I went. What I was risking if I failed."

"Reminders," she repeated, struggling with the word.

"They represent every friend I lost to Whelan."

Alex's hand stilled, her gloved fingers curling into her palm. "And he... put you all in a dark place? Like an opal mine?"

Rats scratched the walls. The stones pressed in, the stench of cigar smoke lingering in the air. Thorne's grip tightened on O'Sullivan's shoulder in the blackness, urging him to hold on. *They had to make it through.*

"A cellar in the Old Nichol," Thorne replied in a calm voice, one that he had practised for years. "We were let out for tasks. Whatever Whelan needed."

"Tasks?" Alex prodded.

He held a knife, slick in his grasp. Killing meant sustenance. A means of survival in the dark. Each successful kill made him stronger, one step closer to escaping.

"Killing," Thorne said bluntly. "Stealing. Kids can fit into tight spaces, hide more easily. They're more eager to please, and we had no family. There was nobody to look for us or miss us if we died. Nobody who cared. You learn what you're willing to do for a full belly, a hint of kindness, and the promise of fresh air." Thorne looked out the window, gazing at the rooftops of the East End. He had climbed many of them, even when his body was weak and trembling. "We were set free from that cellar when we grew into men and were replaced by other children Whelan wanted to train. But we never forgot. I didn't, when I took your father's offer."

It was the same gaze she had given him in Stratfield Saye, the kind that had lured him into the water. The type of look that ensnared sailors, promising both passion and destruction. As she rose from the bed and closed in on him, Thorne found himself rooted to the spot. Held captive in a spell.

He watched as she slipped off her glove and reached for him with her bare hand. She nudged his jacket aside, pushed under his waistcoat to find the lawn cloth of his shirt. With brisk movements, she untucked the fabric from his trousers.

There. The heat of her fingertips on his skin, sliding up his torso. Thorne didn't dare breathe. Didn't dare move. He was afraid that she would stop touching him at any moment. She was the untamed fey creature in the lake, holding his fate in her grasp and deciding whether to love him or drown him.

Her fingers found his scars, the eleven ridges he had etched there the night before he left London all those years ago. Names he had thought of on the train ride to Gretna. Names he had meticulously catalogued in his mind before every lie he told her.

"If you had told me everything back in Stratfield Saye before we married, I would have been furious," she said to him.

"That's why I—"

Her fingertips dug into his scars harder. "I would have been bloody *furious*," she repeated, as if he hadn't spoken. "I don't know how long it would have taken for me to forgive you, but you need to get something into your thick skull." Her eyes were fierce now. "I still would have gone with you to the anvil."

Those words hit him like a rock, nudging the blade even deeper. For four years, he went to bed every night, wishing he'd told her everything on the train. He cursed his stupidity for saying nothing.

"I couldn't take that risk," he said, the excuse sounding hollower with every passing second. *Idiot. Imbecile. Fool.*

Ever so slowly, Alex withdrew her hand from his shirt, and when she looked at him, it was with a sense of sadness. "The problem wasn't the risk, Nick. It wasn't the lives etched into your skin, or your lies, or Whelan. It was that you didn't trust me."

CC> **20** CC>

The journey to Mayfair was quiet.

    Their conversation in Millie's flat had been a double-edged sword for Alexandra, offering relief and unease. Nick had carried the weight of the East End on his shoulders for years, yet he had kept her at arm's length, never fully confiding in her.

The realisation had torn open Alexandra's old wounds, wounds she had believed were long healed. Memories of his articles deriding her work came flooding back. Words that suggested, in no uncertain terms, *Stay away. I have no use for you.* But they were also cautionary: *We live in different worlds. We can't be fixed.*

And how could she blame him? He had been raised with lies; trust was a luxury he couldn't afford.

But despite that, it still hurt.

Perhaps she ought to heed his words and take them to heart. Opportunities awaited her over the vast ocean; it promised a fresh start with new people who would know nothing of Nick – a necessary journey if she wanted any chance at mending.

But first, she had someone to warn.

Before the hackney driver could even open the door for them, Alexandra spotted their destination – the back entrance of the Masquerade. She paid the man quickly before jumping out and striding across the cobblestone street towards the wooden door.

"Should we be entering a nunnery in broad daylight?" Nick asked.

Nunnery was an old canting word for a brothel, where the ladies of the night were called *nuns*.

"It's a club," Alexandra corrected him, her voice clipped. "And this is the entrance for the staff. I have my own knock." She then stepped forward and tapped three times in quick succession on the door's thick wood.

Nick chuckled and arched an eyebrow. "Isn't 'club' just a fancy name for a brothel?"

"No. Membership can be bought, but companionship is not for sale. Do you plan to use every term in your vocabulary for a brothel?"

Her husband grinned slowly. "Cavaulting school."

"Sweet Lord," she muttered, rolling her eyes. It was tough to hold on to her earlier anger when he smiled at her like that – the kind of smile that made her melt, leaving her bones like butter and making her as docile as a kitten. Curse him.

"Smuggling ken," he continued, apparently uncaring of the danger they were in should someone hear him. "Nugging house? Buttocking shop?"

The last remark made Alexandra lose her composure. She laughed out loud as the door swung open, revealing

Charlie, the doorman. The man in front of them was built like a fortress – his crisp suit was unable to conceal his rough features and brawny physique, let alone his gravelly accent that gave away his upbringing in the non-genteel parts of town. Charlie's job was to oversee the entrance and ensure that no one in the club felt unwelcome or unsafe, and rumour had it he was excellent at his job.

Blushing furiously and feeling more than slightly mortified, Alexandra nudged Nick out of the way before smiling sweetly at Charlie. "Good morning," she said, praying he hadn't heard Nick's garish comment about buttocking shops. "Is Madame in?"

Charlie lifted an intrigued eyebrow at Nick, recognising the King of the East End. "Afternoon, Mr Thorne." Then he returned his attention to Alexandra. "Is th' mistress expecting ye today, miss?"

His question confirmed that Madame was still breathing, and Alexandra sighed in relief. "I'm afraid not, but I must speak with her. It's urgent."

"Of course. If ye'll but wait a moment." Charlie gave a curt bow and left them to go down the main hallway.

Nick surveyed the foyer, his eyes sweeping over the dimly lit wallpaper, flickering wall sconces, and the soft melody of a harp drifting from one of the chambers. The Masquerade was all about decorum, even when there was no grand ball – lovers could discreetly reserve rooms for secret rendezvous during the week and experience flawless service from an army of staff generously compensated for their discretion.

"What sort of patrons frequent this club?" Nick inquired, his hands tucked into his pockets as he approached a painting on the far wall that depicted Apollo basking in the sunlight. "Is there anyone I'd recognise?"

Alexandra narrowed her eyes. "Don't play coy with me, Nicholas. You're seeking information that you can use for political blackmail, aren't you?"

"Potentially," he replied with a sly grin. "You never know when those politicians in Parliament need a little push to pass a progressive bill."

Alexandra couldn't help but concede the point. Nick and her brother Richard often worked together to whip bills. It took enormous effort to enact reforms in chambers dominated by a wealthy, self-interested aristocracy.

"I can't say," Alexandra replied. "Masks are a requirement for membership. The members' identities here are only known to Madame, and she's very protective of her secrets."

Charlie returned, the metal toecaps of his polished black shoes clicking on the marble. "My lady, if you go through the east wing, Madame will receive you in her chambers now."

Alexandra thanked Charlie and walked up to the painting of Apollo. She knew these hidden pathways well, having been granted unrestricted access after countless visits to the club. Madame never mingled with guests; even to her closest associates, she was a mystery. No one spoke with her, no one questioned her, and no one ever glimpsed her face.

The only people she showed herself to were Charlie and Alexandra.

Nick whistled softly and followed Alexandra down the secret passageway. "So, how did you meet this Madame?"

Alexandra shrugged, ascending the steep stairwell. "She invited me after reading my work. I don't know what life she leads beyond these walls, but I suspect she could put your knowledge of political secrets to shame."

"Aristocrat?"

"It's possible," she replied, flashing him a smile. "But I won't divulge my suspicions."

He tsked. "You afraid I'll blackmail her?"

"I think it's more likely she'll blackmail you."

Nick gave a surprised laugh. A strand of hair fell across his forehead, and Alexandra had to clench her fists against the urge to reach out and brush it back. Touching him in Millie's flat was a mistake. It had been too brief, had made her want to peel the clothes from his body. As they strolled down the dimly lit passageway, warm thoughts stirred within her – wicked ideas of skin brushing against skin, soft lips pressed together.

Shaking off the thoughts, she cleared her throat and continued down the dark hallways, nodding towards another section. "This way."

Nick walked beside her, studying the paintings illuminated by the wall sconces. They depicted tender moments of intimacy – some couples in a nude embrace, while others held hands and wandered through fields of flowers. In every painting, they donned elaborate masks commissioned by Madame for her club.

Nick shook his head in amusement. "Toffs have such peculiar habits," he murmured, moving on to the next artwork. "I'd want to know who I'm taking to bed."

"It's a matter of preference," Alexandra told him. "Women of my station rarely have their desires catered to. Here, every decision belongs to the individual. All members must agree to become lovers, and to fulfil each other's fantasies."

Nick fell silent as they climbed another flight of stairs. Madame's private suite was on the top floor. "And what of your desires?" he asked her softly. "Have they been satisfied here?"

She lifted her chin. "If they were?"

Their gazes locked. Nick had a way of looking at her that felt almost tangible. It brought back memories of his fingertips tracing the curve of her hip and sliding between her thighs. It reminded her of all the things he whispered in bed, things she could never forget.

"I might inquire how they've changed since I last pleasured you," he murmured. "And if he made you climax, or if that only happened with me."

Alexandra's skin was hot. A primitive impulse surged within her, begging to be unleashed. She wanted to slam Nick against the corridor wall, rip off his jacket, and sink her teeth into his flesh. She'd confide that the last time she reached climax without the aid of her hand had been on the train from Gretna. That when she satisfied herself at night, she only ever came when she thought of Nick inside her, touching her, tasting her, licking her.

Alexandra straightened, fighting against her desires. "Madame's suite is at the landing." Her words sounded hoarse. "Please stay here until I'm through."

Nick smiled, as if sensing her unease, and leaned back against the wall to wait.

Madame had crafted her suite for comfort rather than seduction. Her sofas and chairs were well-loved, patched up in places, and one wingback was particularly piled with cushions, a clear indication of the time spent there. Next to it, a stack of books with dog-eared pages and tea stains lay, speaking of Madame's avid interest in literature, philosophy, and mathematics. At the far end of the room was a writing desk carved out of mahogany and gleaming with a polished finish, cluttered with pamphlets.

Alexandra had lusted after that desk for months, ever since she first laid eyes on it.

Even to Alexandra, Madame's identity was a mystery, but her keen intellect and inquisitive nature were evident in every nook and cranny. It was clear that Madame was worldly, someone who had seen and experienced much more than she let on.

A creaking floorboard caught Alexandra's attention, and she turned to see Madame enter from her bedroom.

"Alexandra," Madame said with a smile. "How delightful to see you."

Madame wore a veil that obscured her features, but what Alexandra could see was a woman of average height, dressed in clothes that showed off a lean figure. Her voice was melodic, the words German, but the accent English, undoubtedly to conceal her identity. Alexandra suspected that Madame was of aristocratic stock, someone she might have met before, but she could not determine Madame's age.

Alexandra lifted the books off the wing chair – astronomy, calculus, botany – and settled into her usual seat. She had interviewed Madame for months, arriving after most members had selected their rooms. Sneaking out was difficult to explain – her friend Emma once asked if Alexandra was meeting a lover at night. The truth was far less pleasurable: Madame fed Alexandra information about Sir Reginald's smuggling operation.

"I apologise for the unexpected visit," she said. "But the matter is urgent."

Madame was quiet as she sat opposite Alexandra. "Shall I ring for tea?"

"No," Alexandra said firmly, leaning forward and clasping her hands. She didn't waste any time. "My work has been compromised."

Madame's stillness became even more pronounced, and Alexandra longed to see her face, to know who she truly was. "Has it?"

"My husband – you've read the broadsheets, I assume?"

"I have." Now Alexandra could hear the smile in her voice. "Nicholas Thorne. Not a choice I expected."

Alexandra ignored Madame's comment, pressing on with urgency. "A man from my husband's past has returned to the East End. We suspect Sir Reginald paid him to murder my informants and me, and he has taken the contract as a personal vendetta. He's already killed two of my contacts – possibly even a third. You're the only one left."

Madame studied Alexandra intently, nothing in her countenance betraying her emotions. "I see," she said.

"I'm not here to ask for your identity," Alexandra continued. "But I suggest that leaving London might be your safest option."

Madame's veil fluttered with her agitated breath at the suggestion. "I'm afraid that's not possible," she replied. "I have obligations here that I must attend to."

Alexandra considered the response, knowing that Madame was more than just a source to her. "My husband's men could provide you with protection. They would keep your name secret, even from me."

Madame stood and approached the bay window, her gloved hand gripping the frame tightly. "As you may have guessed during our time together, I'm skilled in the art of disappearing," she said, the sunlight piercing through the lace of her veil to reveal the slope of her nose. "I don't need to leave this city to vanish. I can do it standing in the most crowded ballroom in London."

Alexandra couldn't help but wonder if she had been guilty of not truly seeing Madame. If her eyes had slid past her beyond the walls of the Masquerade, and if she owed her an apology for it. As she glanced at Madame's stacks of tea-stained books, they took on a different significance. It was strange to think that a woman who engaged in the business of intimacy might be lonely. Perhaps those volumes had become a refuge for a brilliant mind amid people who couldn't even remember her name or face.

"Do you ever wish things had turned out differently?" Alexandra asked softly.

She thought of all the women on the periphery of ballrooms, waiting for a shred of acknowledgement. Alexandra's reputation was scandalous and in ruins now, but she had never been ignored or forgotten. Her face had been the subject of countless illustrations, and her name had been featured in innumerable articles and gossip. It was a curse of opposites.

Madame straightened, a hint of wistfulness in her voice. "If things were different, I would have no secrets to share with you."

"But your club is—"

"You misunderstand," Madame interrupted gently. "I don't gather information in this club. I don't infringe on the privacy of my guests, and I certainly don't take part in the activities. The Masquerade is not for me."

The revelation that Madame didn't participate in any of the Masquerade's activities surprised Alexandra. After all, the club's allure lay in its anonymity, allowing members to explore their desires and take new lovers without fear of judgement or expectations. Alexandra had always assumed Madame indulged her own fantasies.

"If you don't partake, then why…" She trailed off, unsure of how to continue.

"Why start a den of iniquity?" Madame finished, a hint of amusement in her voice. "The truth is, I'm a hopeless romantic. I hope some of my members will fall in love and have no further use for this place." Alexandra sensed Madame was smiling now. "I've heard that your brother and sister-in-law are very happy."

James and Emma had met at the Masquerade a few months back, and Alexandra even lent Emma her mask for the occasion. Although her friend's affair with James had come as a surprise, Alexandra was glad to see them together.

"They're still on their honeymoon, and the post has been slow," Alexandra replied. "I expect they'll return once James hears that I've been secretly married for four years. I never told him."

After confirming that she wasn't pregnant with Nick's child, Alexandra wanted nothing more than to forget the whole ordeal. To pretend that her moment of weakness had never happened. Over the years, her marriage to Nick had taken on a life of its own, becoming a sort of myth. It was easier to remember those days as a dream, something she had imagined while floating on Stratfield Lake on a warm day.

Madame's gaze was assessing again, and Alexandra glimpsed the soft curve of her lips beyond the lace veil. "Were you ashamed, then? Of your husband's background?"

Alexandra shook her head firmly. "No, never that. He hurt me a long time ago. I've spent all this time hardening my heart, and now…"

"And now?" Madame prompted gently.

It should have surprised Alexandra how easily she could speak in front of this woman, but Madame kept so many secrets. Alexandra didn't need to see her face or know her name to understand that Madame was worth trusting.

"It doesn't matter," Alexandra said. "I've already spoken to my solicitor about petitioning for divorce."

She had to prepare herself for the scrutiny of her peers, for the inevitable increase in cruel gossip. Divorce meant revealing to everyone what they had long thought: no man would want her except for her money. She had nothing else to offer.

Madame adjusted the trimming of her veil. "On what grounds will you seek it?"

"My solicitor says adultery is the easiest way." Alexandra fidgeted with her gloves. "Nick won't keep me in this marriage against my will."

"Mm." A small smile played at the edges of the Madam's lips through the veil's lace. "And if he still loves you?"

Alexandra didn't know how to respond. He'd told her he loved her, but she couldn't believe it was true. She harboured too much resentment in her heart to let him near it again.

"It's been four years," she said softly.

For once, Alexandra was grateful for Madame's veil. It hid a gaze that she knew was as penetrating as sharpened steel. "Is that enough time for forgiveness?" Madame asked. Alexandra didn't answer, and Madame turned to the window with a short laugh. "As I said, hopeless romantic."

Nick straightened up as Alexandra descended from Madame's room. "Everything all right?"

Alexandra inclined her head, turning from his piercing stare. She wouldn't allow herself to dwell on the painful memories Madame had stirred up, those emotions she had buried deep within herself. With every moment spent in Nick's company, her longing for him swelled like a foolish dream: to gaze upon him, to touch him, to feel his lips on hers.

The very notion of the ship that was meant to carry her away across the ocean became increasingly elusive.

Focus on freedom. Imagine the undulating waves gently lapping against the vessel, carrying you to distant shores. Think of the thrill of the ship's engine propelling you forward at a speed of fourteen and a half knots. Or perhaps the Continent calls to you, with all its uncharted marvels? You could journey to Germany and witness the Striezelmarkt's festive glory.

Alexandra straightened her shoulders – holding onto the image of an endless sea, unfamiliar sights in other countries – and pressed the latch beneath a painting of Ares and Venus. "Follow me," she said, swivelling the door open. "Madame has instructed us to use this route so we're not caught unmasked when her guests arrive."

"I've seen fewer hidden entrances in buildings populated by spies," Nick said, following her.

"And what do you know about government spy passages?"

"More than enough."

Alexandra gaped at him. "Never say you have Home Office operatives in your pocket?"

His smile sent a jolt of longing through her. "A few of them might be decent operatives, sweetheart, but they're shite at hazard, and some information is as valuable to me as currency."

When he called her *sweetheart*, a dangerous thrill coursed through her veins. Utterly reckless. "How much is a secret worth to you?"

"Depends on how well kept it is."

"For instance?"

"For instance?" he repeated in a velvet whisper, like the promise of something dark and forbidden.

His gaze flicked down to her lips for a moment. The corridor was dim, with only candlelight to illuminate his features. The shadows favoured him, made his eyes glitter like the sky on a moonless night, and caressed him like a lover. As he shifted closer, Alexandra felt the hardness of the wall behind her shoulder blades.

He dipped his head and breathed in her ear, "I would

forfeit every pound, shilling, pence, and property I have to know your secrets. I would sell the clothes off my back."

Alexandra's breath caught in her throat at his words.

"Would you?" she whispered, her voice barely audible.

Nick made some soft noise and turned his face from her. "Yes," he said. "But you shouldn't sell them so cheaply."

If she wanted, she could have leaned into him, rested her cheek against his. She could have slipped her hands under his shirt to feel his skin, just like she did back in St Giles; he would have let her. But Alexandra curled her fingers into her palm. Such a simple action that took so much effort.

"Do you consider everything you have to be of such little value?" she asked, trying to keep her voice steady.

"No." His exhalation slid across her shoulder, sending shivers down her spine. She thought she felt fingertips at her nape. "I consider you to be worth everything."

If she had not been standing against the wall, Alexandra might have stumbled. His words sank into her bones, past the thorns she had erected around her traitorous heart. For beneath its protection, she was still so vulnerable.

I can't. I can't do this again. I won't recover.

As if he heard those thoughts, Nick stepped away. "How about an easy secret, no payment required?" he asked lightly, avoiding her gaze. "What do the coloured knobs on some of these doors mean?"

Of all the questions to smooth over the moment, he inquired about the red and blue doorknobs. Alexandra had to fight to keep her expression neutral. Not one second to compose herself. She was at his mercy, and she knew it.

Alexandra straightened, her heart pounding in her chest. She had to overcome the urge to flee the corridor.

"They're... er... speciality rooms. Red, for those who like to be watched," she said, flushing, "and blue for those who like to watch."

Oh, she was sure her face was entirely red. It wasn't enough that she'd answered – now she wanted to know which room Nick would choose: to watch or be watched?

Nick's smile was slow, sending a lick of heat between her thighs. "Do you have a preference?"

The blush spread across her entire body. "Of course not."

"Very well." Then he winked. "I'll decide." He grasped a blue doorknob and went inside.

"*Nick.*"

Alexandra muttered a curse and followed him. The chamber was a lavish indulgence beyond what she had seen at the Masquerade, with furnishings crafted from rich, dark wood, reflecting the Masquerade's attention to detail. The air was thick with the scent of roses, filling the room with an unmistakable sensuality. A four-poster bed invited them to surrender to the moment, but Nick chose the chaise longue against the far wall. A sliding panel in the middle of the wallpaper was closed. Were there people on the other side? Did Nick intend to—

Stop it. Stop it.

Alexandra slammed the door closed, one hand clinging to the knob. "We shouldn't be in here."

Nick smiled, a wolfish thing that made her heart crash against her ribs. "If some toffs in the next room expect us to watch, I'll give them what they want." He crooked a finger at her. "Come here."

A thrumming heat bloomed inside her chest – desire, untamed and wild. She shook her head, trying to deny the feeling blossoming in her veins. *It's lust*, she told herself sternly. *It means nothing*.

Nick seemed to read the thought on her face. He draped his arm across the back of the chaise longue and asked softly, "You afraid?"

"Of what?"

"That you'll like it," he purred and oh, his smile was wicked enough to make her imagine him disrobed and beneath her.

Stop it. He's baiting you.

Furious now, Alexandra marched over to the panel beside the marble fireplace and slid it open with a clatter – revealing an empty chamber beyond.

"There," she said, trying to mask her disappointment with relief. "Now, can we—"

Nick's grip on her arm stopped her. "Wait."

A masked couple stumbled into the observation room, their laughter fading to soft sounds as the man pressed the woman against the door. They shared a fierce kiss, overcome with a desperate desire. Buttons skittered across the carpet, fabric torn in their haste.

Their whispers barely reached Alexandra's ears through the glass, but she imagined the vocabulary. They were demands she'd made in Gretna, and again on the train to London. Words he'd taught her, that she learned to wield with lethal precision.

Fuck me.

Alexandra willed herself to turn from the panel, to break the spell that held her captive. But her body refused to comply. She remained perched on the chaise beside Nick, mesmerised by the scene unfolding before her. It conjured memories buried deep within her of when Nick had kissed her like that at the inn outside of Gretna. He had stripped her dress and slowly traced her curves with his lips. In her dreams, the details of that night blurred, morphing into different scenarios with each passing year. Sometimes it was intense, other times, it was languorous, but the one constant was how she burned.

And sometimes, when her fury at herself for still wanting him boiled over, she would use his desire as a weapon, taking him beneath her and tormenting him until he begged for mercy.

But when she forgot her anger and surrendered to the pull between them, she would remember the look in his eyes that night.

Is it always like this?

No. Only with you.

"What are you thinking about?" Nick's voice was husky, exhale warm on the shell of her ear. When she only shook her head, he whispered one word, a question: "Us?"

She wanted to confess everything, to reveal the truth about the pieces of her heart that she had carefully stitched back together. But the thought of betraying her vows stopped her. She had taken years to heal.

The man in the next room carried the woman to the bed.

Nick edged closer, his hard thigh pressing against hers. The heat of his breath on her neck was tantalisingly close. "I dream of Gretna every night," he murmured, his words tracking a path down the curve of her shoulder. "The man in there? He has the right of it. Watch him slide his lips down – ah, *there*. Remember?"

The sight made her heart race, the man's actions inflaming

something feral within her. She watched as he knelt between the woman's thighs, his tongue expertly tracing every inch of her skin.

"Yes," she replied, barely able to speak.

Nick's words were a match striking against dry kindling, igniting a blaze of want. "In my dreams, sometimes we don't even make love," he murmured. "Some nights, I lick your cunny until you come so often that you can't leave my bed for hours. Then—"

The man caught the woman around the waist, lowering her onto the bed. He plunged his cock inside her, his movements rough and urgent.

"—I fuck you just like that. You liked it hard and fast."

Alexandra's body burned with heat, her fingers digging into the upholstery of the chaise as she fought for control. She needed something to anchor her, to keep her from surrendering to the pull between them.

But Nick leaned in closer, his whisper like a caress. "Answer me one question, Alex." His lips brushed against the skin of her throat. "Are you wet right now?"

The query scorched her ears, and she couldn't stop herself from answering, from admitting the truth that threatened to consume her. "Yes," she breathed.

Nick's forehead dropped against Alexandra's shoulder, his voice a groan of longing. "God. I misspoke before. I would sell every damn thing I own if you let me kiss you just once."

The words hung between them, and Alexandra's heart pounded with the weight of his desire. She wanted to say yes, to yield to the pull between them, but the reality of their situation crashed down on her like a wave.

They were in a club in Mayfair, surrounded by people who could discover them at any moment.

She pulled away from Nick, rising to her feet in a rush of panicked adrenaline. "We have to go," she said, her voice trembling. "I need..." Her thoughts were a jumbled mess, but the truth was clear.

She needed him.

Without waiting for him to follow, Alexandra fled the room.

⌒ 22 ⌒

When they arrived at the Brimstone, Alex strode past the kitchens and up the stairs to the private wing. Thorne ignored the curious stares of his staff and hurried after her. The entire hackney ride home had been tense, Alex huddled to one side, her face a silent warning: *Not now.*

But Thorne had to say something. Apologise? Confess his love? Hell, he didn't know.

"Alex."

She paused at her bedchamber door but didn't turn when he approached. Thorne reached for her, settling a hand gently on her arm. Some ragged sound escaped her – a confession.

Alex wanted him.

Look at me, he willed her. *Look at me.*

But she only pulled away and disappeared inside. The door closed behind her, and then he heard the click of the lock.

Thorne went into his room, wondering at her wordless

admission. Did she spend the journey home imagining, as he had, what might have happened back in Mayfair? Thorne had lost himself in her, every little detail of her composure under his notice. He couldn't help but remember how her teeth dug into her lower lip, the grip of her fingers on the chaise, and the soft sounds that escaped her lips.

Had she even been aware of those? Had she—

Thorne's breaths came in quick gasps as he leaned over his desk. He closed his eyes and reimagined that room in Mayfair. In his fantasy, Alex let him kiss her. Then she took his hand and slipped it beneath her petticoat, guiding him unerringly to the juncture of her thighs, and left him there to explore as he wished.

With a groan, Thorne tore open the buttons on his trousers and grasped his cock. He imagined her slippery quim squeezing his finger as he penetrated her. First one finger, then two, mimicking what he yearned to do to her with his cock. He would have eased her back on the sofa. His tongue would have trailed down her neck as he withdrew his fingers and finally penetrated her.

"*Yes,*" he hissed softly, working his hand fast.

She would be hot, wet, and tight. She would whisper in Thorne's ear a request, a litany, just like in Gretna and then again in their private sleeping car as the train rocked back and forth: *Harder. Faster. Fuck me, Nick.*

He took a handkerchief from his pocket. His orgasm left him dizzy. "Alex," he whispered with a rough groan. "*Alex.*"

After a few heartbeats, Thorne's breathing slowed down. He pivoted to throw the handkerchief into the laundry—

And spotted Alex standing in the doorway, joining their chambers.

Nick shut his eyes and buttoned up his trousers. He wasn't ashamed to be caught – it was evident from her expression that she had heard him pant her name. Heard the illicit fantasies that he'd had while alone in his room. He could not apologize for wanting her – for needing her like air. Even now, his heart quickened at the sight of her.

She opened her mouth to speak.

Nick braced himself.

But she only whispered, "Why haven't you been with other women?"

Nick leaned over the desk again. "You know the answer to that question," he said. "I told you then."

"You told me so many things." Her whisper was so low, it barely reached him.

"One truth. Do you want me to repeat it?"

A sharp shake of her head was the only reply. "No. I don't want to hear those words from you."

And why should she? That truth came too late, offered the night after his greatest deception was revealed. Those whispered professions had been spoken between so many lies – it was pointless now.

He scrutinised her face, so familiar that he could recall every line, every freckle, every detail. It was a terrain he had explored in his dreams for four years. Yet her thoughts were as uncharted to him as the depths of the ocean.

"Then what do you want from me?"

She advanced, and Thorne braced himself. She was like a siren from the lake, with all her grace and loveliness above and secrets unknown lurking beneath the surface. Loving her meant diving into the water without knowing how to swim.

"As far as I'm concerned, this was our only truth in

Hampshire." She reached out and pressed her palm to his arm, but it was as if she had marked him. The heat of her touch seared his skin. "You desired me; I desired you. That was real."

"Alex..."

She turned her nails into the fabric of his shirt. "We will not mince words. You wanted to fuck me in that room in Mayfair. Yes or no?"

His breath came short at her choice of vocabulary. He'd taught her that word in Gretna. "Yes."

"And you want me now," she murmured, her voice low and shuddering with need. "Yes or no?"

"You know I do," he said quietly.

"Then you must understand one thing," she told him. "I don't want pounds, shillings, pence, or properties. I want nothing from you. This means nothing. Do you agree?"

Thorne froze as he grasped her intent; an irreconcilable dishonesty – pretending that making love to Alex had no real significance whatsoever.

"Do you agree, Nick?" she repeated, that faint crack appearing in her shell of steel once more, letting slip a glimpse of vulnerability beneath the glacial exterior.

No, he wouldn't say it; not with a lie between them – Nick had promised Alex that much, at least.

So he showed her the truth.

Thorne inched closer to her, the space between them seemingly infinite yet so close. He took her lips with his own, a soft, tentative kiss, exploring the texture and taste of each other. Her mouth tasted like honey, with the heat of fine Irish whiskey – made for him. Just for him. She deepened the kiss, gripping his shirt to pull him closer.

Slow. Slower. Thorne wanted to linger a moment, to assure himself that she wasn't a dream. That this was real.

She would not have it. Alex's teeth grazed her lower lip, and she gave his erection a firm squeeze.

Four years of yearning, of wanting, of unfulfilled desire – all of it coiled tight. And with one touch, it snapped like a taut bowstring. Nick's restraint crumbled, and he slammed her against the desk. Their lips crashed together. No gentleness now, only frayed control and desperate need. He felt her body tense beneath him, her approval in the rough sound that escaped her lips.

She bit him once more, harder this time – a wordless demand. *Now. Take me.*

Thorne swept everything off his desk and lifted her. She pulled aside her petticoats and parted her thighs to draw him closer.

There. God, yes, there. The slit in Alex's drawers was a godsend. The way she moved against him, the heat of her, her harsh breath against his skin – it was all a revelation. Alex was not the composed woman she appeared to be. Her layers of petticoats, corsetry, and fabric were just another layer of her fortress, her armour. But beneath that armour, she craved him with the same feral intensity he hungered for her.

A ferocity gripped Nick, animal in its strength, and he knew from her response that he was not alone in this. Her fingernails raked across his shirt hard; he could feel them down to his skin. Her lips tracked the line of his jaw, her breath hot.

"This means nothing." Alex panted, her hands straying to his waist as her teeth nipped at the side of his neck. "Nothing."

"Then take it," he growled, feeling her undoing his buttons. "Take whatever you want. Take all of me."

"Now." Her voice was desperate. She guided him in. "Now, now, now."

He pushed into her. *Ah, God.* A rough approximation of her name left his lips as he tilted his head back in ecstasy. She bit down hard on the muscle of his shoulder, and his answer was just as savage, just as bestial – he wanted to bury himself inside her as far as he could go. He wanted to abolish the memory of any other lover she might have had, lay some mark upon her bones. Something that said, *remember me.*

Remember me.

Remember me.

Their union was feral, hungry, and insistent. The yearning in their touch exposed like an open wound, the grasping of hands and hips pushing the craving to reach a crescendo. Alex's response gratified him, the harsh clasp of her hand on Thorne's arse to spur his pace. Her tongue on his neck, the kisses she pressed into his jaw as he satisfied her, the rough words she breathed in his ear.

She tipped her head, eyes shut tight. He wondered what drove her forward, what consumed her thoughts as her body moved against his – another wall, hiding her pleasure from his view.

Another savage urge drove him. "Open your eyes," he demanded, thrusting hard. Alex's lids fluttered open, her expression dazed. *Yes.* "I want you to watch me."

He could feel the thrill of power coursing through his veins. *Keep saying it. Keep commanding her. Look at me. Look at me.*

Heat filled her gaze. It was honest, that look. The barricade around her heart had some vulnerabilities in its armour, fatal cracks in the bricks and mortar she had piled up to keep Thorne out. He wanted to see it demolished.

Thorne reached between them and rubbed his fingers against her clitoris.

Alexandra's nails scrabbled across his back as she came. He didn't last much longer. He climaxed with some quiet moan that brought him back to himself: soft thighs cradling his hips, mouth at his throat, her whispered words there.

"You never answered me."

This means nothing.

Do you agree?

Thorne dragged a hand through his hair. "I promised never to lie to you again."

The reminder seemed to rouse her in some way. She gently pushed at his chest. Wordlessly, he stepped back as she slid off the desk and straightened her skirts. Thorne did the same with his clothing.

Alex started for the connecting door but paused with her hand on the knob. "Nick," she said softly.

"Yes?"

She let out a long breath. "I thought you should know... there was never anyone else for me either."

When she left the room, Thorne shut his eyes. She had let him see the light beyond the high walls of her tower.

23

The account books were a useless waste of Thorne's time. He scowled at the ledgers, filled with columns and figures, attempting to distract himself from the chaos of his life. The scratched-out numbers and corrected sums were an eyesore on otherwise pristine rows of ordered digits. Thorne was a master of accounting. He meticulously kept track of every wager, playing card, debt owed, and every penny earned by the Brimstone, right down to the last farthing. The crisp tallies had no room for error; mathematics had a single answer.

Unfortunately, his wife was not as straightforward. Alex had shut herself in their chamber for three straight days.

Thorne knew better than to interfere with her brooding. On the first day, he had listened to her pacing the room from one end to the other, back and forth, back and forth. Her brilliant mind was thinking too much, grappling with what had passed between them, formulating theories, negating those theories, and developing fresh ones. She had paused at their shared door, and Thorne had held his breath. Hoping she would turn the knob.

But she only resumed her pacing.

On the second day, Thorne mustered the courage to knock and inquire after Alex's well-being. "I'm busy," came her curt response from the other side of the door. Their maid, Morag, reported witnessing fresh clusters of paper littering the floor, Alex's hands covered in ink. Her pen tapping the desk in an agitated rhythm – he'd heard that one, all right, just before dawn.

Then, that morning, a letter arrived for her. This time, Alex opened the door. Her golden hair was dishevelled, and an ink smudge marred her cheek. When Thorne looked into her blue eyes, he felt a primal urge to push her against the wall. Rip off her clothes. Take her until she was replete, then so hungry for him she didn't leave his bed for days.

As if she read his mind, Alex bit her lip and reached out – so close to touching him – but aborted the gesture. Her fingers curled into her palm. "Who is the letter from?"

Thorne held back a sigh and glanced down at it. "A Miss Annabel Dawes. Sound familiar?"

She snatched the missive from his hand and froze, as if she'd been caught in the act of a heinous crime. "It's my solicitor – well, officially, her brother is my solicitor. But she's my…" She cleared her throat. "Anyway. If you'll please excuse me."

Then she'd shut the door in his face.

Thorne cursed under his breath. He'd been staring at his accounts for hours, trying to make sense of the numbers, but the figures just swam before his vision. A knock on his door interrupted his futile efforts, and he looked up hopefully.

But it was only O'Sullivan. The factotum came in with

a look that said, *You, Nicholas Thorne, are a pathetic sod.* O'Sullivan scanned the ledger on Thorne's desk, his sharp eyes darting over each mistake, but he simply asked, "Busy?"

"Please tell me I have the pleasure of breaking a cheating toff's face," Thorne said.

O'Sullivan raised an eyebrow. "Afraid not. But I do have some interesting information. Guess who the lads spotted at his favourite pub tonight? Sean Gibbons. Seems like Whelan's been reaching out to his old allies."

Gibbons was one of Whelan's few surviving loyalists. Once word got around that Thorne had murdered Whelan and marked every last one of his men for death, they scattered like vermin and went into hiding outside London. Those men were cowards without direction or power. It was easy to manipulate boys and force them into unspeakable acts.

None of them thought about what would happen when those abused boys, now trained in the art of killing, grew into men.

Thorne rose from his chair. "Tell Clements I'm heading out. There's some unfinished business I need to attend to."

O'Sullivan stepped in front of the door. "No."

"No?" Thorne arched an eyebrow, giving the man a chance to reconsider.

But O'Sullivan stood his ground. "You heard me. I warned you about Gibbons, but I'll handle it alone."

Thorne's voice turned icy. It was a tone he reserved for those who dared to defy him. It promised violence. "Say that again?"

O'Sullivan shoved past Thorne and stalked over to the desk, flipping open the ledger with a frustrated flourish. "You're so unfocused that you missed two more mistakes!"

"It's just a sodding ledger, O'Sullivan," Thorne growled.

The factotum glared at him, pointing out the window. "And out there, it's your bloody life! You've been distracted for days, and if Whelan is still alive, you're walking into a death trap. You almost got yourself killed four years ago!"

"But we won the war, didn't we?" Thorne retorted, his mind drifting the murky months after Stratfield Saye.

He remembered his guilt for betraying Alex, taking her money to destroy his enemies. His fury at Whelan and his men for all they had done. Thorne had come back to the East End and fought tooth and nail to regain control.

The knife he had carried back then showed no mercy. Thorne didn't care if he lived or died as long as he finished what he had started with Whelan and his crew. He wanted freedom, and he paid the price for it – her.

"Yeah, you won the war. Barely. That lady toff left you a mess after Hampshire. I helped you pick up the pieces last time, remember? Don't make me do it again."

Thorne ignored that. "That *lady toff* is my wife."

O'Sullivan stepped closer, his gaze harsh. "That *lady toff* was your mark."

Thorne made a dismissive sound. "She hasn't been a mark for a long time now. You know that."

"I don't give a rat's arse. If you lose focus and Whelan takes you down, a lot of innocent people will suffer," O'Sullivan warned, his voice stern. "I'm going to take care of Gibbons on my own."

This time, Thorne stood in O'Sullivan's way. "Things have changed. I have more to lose now than I did four years ago," he spoke firmly, adding in a low voice, "And so do you."

"I don't know what you're talking about."

Thorne raised an eyebrow and crossed his arms. "So, you care nothing for the woman managing my orphanage?"

O'Sullivan's lips tightened. "Leave Sofia out of this."

"I may not know what happened after Whelan sold you, but Sofia came to me when you were at death's door. And she went to you when she needed help. I make my living on bets. I'd wager that means something," Thorne pointed out.

O'Sullivan's breathing grew shallow, his eyes cold and hard behind his glasses. "Fuck off."

"Sure. Answer me first: if trouble came for Sofia, would you let me block this door, or would you fight like hell to get past me?" O'Sullivan looked away, his jaw working. Thorne let out a dry laugh. "That's what I thought."

"Fine," O'Sullivan finally relented. "But I'm coming with you. Someone needs to watch your back, or you'll end up with a blade in it."

The Golden Lion was a public house in the Nichol, where Gibbons used to get soused on a near-nightly basis. Where some taverns in the East End acted as unofficial meeting places for anyone from labourers to businessmen, the Golden Lion did not attempt to advertise itself as a respectable establishment. Set within the ground floor of a crumbling tenement, the Lion appealed to men who wanted to drown themselves in pint after pint. Aged prostitutes lingered outside the door, offering a quick one between tankards of the cheapest, foulest ale in London. Near nightly brawls spilled out onto the vomit-spotted pavement, and it was a damned unusual day if you didn't see a man passed out there from either a blow to the face or too much drink.

The Golden Lion was near the tenement cellar where Whelan had kept Thorne, O'Sullivan, and the other lads. If Thorne had listened closely in the darkness all those years ago, he could hear the noise from the public house. He knew how idiotic it was to envy the brawlers and drunkards at the Lion, but when he was a lad, the raucousness had sounded like freedom.

Thorne leaned against the blackened brick wall of a building, hands in his pockets. O'Sullivan stood beside him, quiet, his gaze fixed on the pub's door. As they drew closer to the Nichol, O'Sullivan's expression became more guarded, his mouth pressed into a firm line.

He jerked upright at the faint, indistinguishable sound in the distance. Thorne cocked his head inquiringly.

"All right?" Thorne asked him.

The factotum didn't take his eyes off the Lion. "Just wish we'd gone after Gibbons and the other three that escaped years ago. They all lured young lads into that godforsaken cellar for a fistful of coins."

"Never too late for retribution. But somehow, I don't believe you're only thinking of Whelan's men."

"Sunderland," O'Sullivan said quietly.

Thorne's lips twisted in a cruel smirk. "It's been eight years since I dragged your sorry arse out of that locked chamber. I reckon the earl is feeling comfortable about now."

O'Sullivan's expression went hard. "I want him to sleep soundly," he said. "Think he's safe. Because after I come for him, he'll never bloody sleep again. He and his son, both."

"Good." Thorne pushed himself away from the wall as a familiar figure stumbled out of the Golden Lion. Gibbons, reeling and disoriented, lurched down the murky alley, deeper into the Nichol. "I want to be there the day you ruin them."

Thorne lunged out at the right time, grabbing him by the collar and slamming him against the brick wall. He slapped a hand over Gibbons' mouth to cut off the man's startled yelp. "Hush now. We're going to have a chat."

O'Sullivan stepped out of the shadows with a smile that promised retribution. Gibbons stared back, wide-eyed and terrified, struggling against Thorne's grip. The dim lamplight revealed a man who had changed little despite the years spent away from London. His hair was still greasy and sparse, and the moonlight etched his fox-like features in sharp relief. The stench of sweat and liquor clung to Gibbons like a second skin – always had.

Gibbons bucked, and Thorne pressed him harder into the wall. He wasn't a lad anymore, weakened and trembling from hunger. He had muscles from sparring with O'Sullivan and hadn't gone without a meal in years.

He could break this man so easily.

"Before I take my hand off your disgusting mouth," Thorne hissed, "let me remind you: in the East End, you live by our permission."

"Oh, I gave up my permission years ago," O'Sullivan told Gibbons casually.

Thorne flashed his teeth. "Guess it's by mine, then." Gibbons made some muffled noise, but Thorne dug his fingers into the man's jaw and spoke as if he weren't interrupted. "And I want to know why you would make the idiotic choice to return to *my* city after I was generous enough to let you keep breathing. Speak."

He took his hand away from Gibbons' mouth and waited.

"I got family," Gibbons said in a breathless voice. "Don't fuckin' kill me, I got—"

"I've never heard of any family," Thorne said coldly. "O'Sullivan?"

Behind the glint of his spectacles, O'Sullivan's expression was stony. "He's lying."

"*No.*" Gibbons made some movement, but Thorne had him back against the wall. "I got a cousin" – Thorne's gaze narrowed – "and I need just a bit o' scratch, that's all."

"Now *that* I believe," Thorne murmured. "You need money. And perhaps it's a coincidence that you happened to be here days after some murders in my territory. But you wouldn't know anything about that, would you?"

Gibbons' gaze darted between Thorne and O'Sullivan. "' Course not."

Thorne slid his knife out of his coat and pressed the tip to the other man's face. "Let's try that answer again, eh, O'Sullivan? What do you say about a second chance?"

O'Sullivan's eyes glittered in the darkness. "Not for him."

Thorne felt Gibbons tremble. "Hear that? O'Sullivan wants me to stick this blade in your gut. Why do you think that is?" Gibbons' mouth opened and closed like a landed fish. "Tch. Reckon this one needs reminding, O'Sullivan."

His friend's hands curled into fists. "Oh, he knows. Don't you, Gibbons?"

Gibbons' breathing was rapid. "Now. Now, O'Sullivan, I did a lot of things—"

Thorne gave him a small nick with the edge of the blade. "So many things," Thorne said with a dark laugh. "One in particular. You were there when Whelan sold O'Sullivan to that toff who tortured him."

"I didn't—"

"Quiet," Thorne said, sliding the blade down the man's cheek in a caress that drew blood. Gibbons flinched, releasing a whimper. "Here's what I remember: you and the others taking us out of that cellar for the Earl of Sunderland to inspect as if he was about to buy a damned horse. Fourteen years old, I was. O'Sullivan?"

O'Sullivan's lips flattened. "Twelve."

"Twelve," Thorne repeated softly. "How much was O'Sullivan worth, Gibbons?" When the other man didn't respond, Thorne whispered, "Five pounds. Five. Fucking. Pounds. Did you see any of that coin for forcing us all into that room? Or did Whelan not bother sharing any?"

Gibbons jerked, as if he were thinking of running, but Thorne held him fast. "Don't remember."

Thorne laughed again, the sound echoing through the empty street. Anyone nearby would turn the other way if they heard it in the darkness. "Doesn't remember. See, here's the thing. *We* do." Thorne stuck the knife into Gibbons' chest – not far, but enough for the tip to break the skin. Gibbons hollered, and this time Thorne didn't bother to quiet him. He wanted to hear him scream. He wanted O'Sullivan to hear it after all he went through. "But I requested a conversation. So how about you tell me where you were last Friday eve. We'll start there." The night they'd found Joseph Ayles' body.

"Oh, Christ. You've – Oh, Christ!"

"The Lord ain't gonna help you, Gibbons. Only the devil sullies himself with the Nichol, and tonight the devil answers to me." He leaned forward and hissed, "Talk. Before I sink my blade into your heart."

"I was here! At the Golden Lion. *Here!*"

"You believe him, O'Sullivan?"

O'Sullivan's lip curled. "No."

"Coincidence. Neither do I." His knife sank in further. Gibbons screamed. "I'll ask it again: where were you?"

"*Here!* I swear it. I swear—"

"Fine. Fine, I believe you. I believe him, O'Sullivan." Thorne toyed with the blade handle, revelling in the small sounds Gibbons made when he twisted it a tiny bit deeper. Gibbons had been a master at this particular game when Thorne was a lad. All of Whelan's men were experts in torture. "How about this: did you know that Patrick Whelan lives, and did he tell you to return and help him take back my city?"

There it was – a slight shifting in his gaze. "I don't... I don't know what you..."

"Wrong answer," Thorne said softly, sinking the knife in further, finding satisfaction in how the other man howled for mercy. "Quiet now. You feel that, Gibbons? One more push, and you stop breathing. Do you really want to lie to me?"

"I... may have—"

"Now we're getting somewhere. How about you tell me where I can find Whelan, and I'll *consider* paying someone to stitch you up." But Gibbons was shaking his head, his mouth set in a firm line. "No? That's a shame. My blade hand isn't as steady as it used to be. I might slip—"

"*I don't know.* He always comes and finds me!"

Thorne leaned in. "If you don't know, then give me a good reason why I should let you live."

"I—" Gibbons' breath was ragged. "I..."

Thorne gripped the blade's hilt; he could press it in so

easily now. But not yet. He wanted some last words. "When your very long list of sins decides whether you enter paradise or go straight to the devil, how will you plead?"

Gibbons looked helplessly at O'Sullivan, but found even less sympathy from that quarter. O'Sullivan smiled grimly. "Please," Gibbons whispered.

Thorne paused, rage simmering like a storm inside him. "Please?" he repeated, very softly. Beside him, O'Sullivan tensed. "What did Gibbons do with the lads who said that word, O'Sullivan?"

"He laughed." O'Sullivan curled his lip. "And then he punished them for it."

"That he did," Thorne murmured. "And I've the scars to show for it, don't I, Gibbons? You used to have such a way with a blade. I learned it from you."

Gibbons' chest rose and fell. He knew his time was up. The devil had come to call, and Gibbons was about to suffer the same fate he had meted out to so many others. "You're never gonna find Whelan, you bastard," Gibbons suddenly hissed, baring his teeth. "He's gonna kill you first. You and that cunt wife—"

Thorne shoved his knife in to the hilt. Gibbons sagged against him, muttering some last valediction, lost to the sound of blood garbling up his throat. Thorne lowered the body to the ground and retrieved his weapon with a swift tug. He barely noticed the stickiness of the blood as he wiped the blade against his jacket.

"He died faster than he deserved," Thorne told O'Sullivan.

O'Sullivan looked down at the dead man. "Better fast than not at all."

∽ 24 ∽

Dear Lady Alexandra,

Please find enclosed the documents required for your divorce petition. Should Mr Thorne cooperate with your request, he need only sign where indicated and inquire about further arrangements through our office.
Should he mount an objection, I invite you to make an appointment with my secretary at your earliest convenience.
Cordially,

Miss Annabel Dawes

Alexandra paced the length of her room, tapping Miss Dawes' letter against her dress.

Why had she slept with Nick? Why had she done it? *Why, why, why?* Retreating to the safety of her bedchamber had done nothing to ease her agitation. Her manuscript offered no reprieve from the tumult of her thoughts – being another cause of her troubles.

But now, her foremost concern was a husband. One she thought she'd no longer wanted and now... now...

This means nothing.

God, how she'd wished that were true. When had she taken to lying? She, who demanded such honesty from him?

The marks from his teeth had faded a day ago, but the memory of his touch lingered. She had brought herself to completion the last two nights, imagining *his* hands touching and tormenting her. When she woke in the darkness to find herself alone, she ached to open their connecting door and curl herself against him. She wished to feel his solidity, his scars beneath her fingertips. He had so much more to tell her about each one.

Alexandra sighed and set Miss Dawes' letter down on her tiny desk. Beside it, a scrap of paper documented her pathetic attempts to refocus on the future she had built in her mind:

New York Island has an area of twenty-two square miles and twenty-nine miles of waterfront, about three-fourths of which stretches along the Hudson and East Rivers and the remaining one-fourth upon the Harlem River and Spuyten Duyvil Creek. The streets, roads, and avenues measure 460 miles. 291 miles of these are paved; 169 miles are unpaved. 19,000 gas lights are burned every night—

Boots pounded down the hall outside her room. A door opened and shut. There was movement beyond the connecting door.

Nick was home.

Alexandra stared down at Miss Dawes' letter, then at the

passage she had memorised from a guidebook to New York. In the weeks after her marriage became public, the guides were comforts, and the schedules of sailing ships were, each of them, possibilities – escape routes. But now, much like a ship tossed in a tempest, she was adrift in the ocean without any direction to guide her.

Should Mr Thorne cooperate with your request...

Should he mount an objection...

"It's time," she told herself. Then she set her shoulders.

Alexandra grabbed Miss Dawes' letter and threw open the connecting door. "Nick. We need to t—" She froze at the threshold with a gasp.

Bloodstains marred Nick's shirt and coat. His appearance was dishevelled, hair tousled, jaw clenched. Although he didn't pose an immediate threat, he appeared...

Alexandra struggled to resist the urge to recoil, finally comprehending the source of her unease. The man standing before her was the very figure the East End's criminals dreaded: the ruler of their streets. The man they told tales of and warned others to be wary of. This was the individual who intimidated the most influential figures in the nation.

And yet... Alexandra found this suited him. His eyes were as black and cold as the void between stars. Darkness that begged to be explored.

"What's happened?" she whispered.

"I'm about to have a bath," he said, in some strange voice she couldn't understand. "Perhaps you'd like to speak when I'm finished."

"Don't dismiss me." She came further into the room, close enough to look him over. "Are you hurt? Did Whelan send men to attack you?"

Nick's laugh was dry as he reached for the decanter sitting atop his mantelpiece, pouring himself two fingers of Irish whiskey. Alexandra gasped as she caught sight of his hands, covered in blood and trembling. Did he feel the same fear when she came to him in a similar state days ago? When *she* was the one with blood on her hands?

He threw back his head and polished off the drink. "Concerned about me?"

She frowned. What mood was this? She didn't understand it. "Of course I am. Why wouldn't I be?"

"Three days ago, you declared I meant nothing to you," he said flatly. "I did not imagine that."

Something contracted in her chest. This dull ache had been her constant companion for the last few nights. She was beginning to understand that her heart had never healed, not entirely. Fractured hearts were always so brittle.

She dug her fingernails into her palm. *It wasn't true*, she wanted to say. *It meant too much, and I fear being hurt again*. But in the end, she only said, "You are avoiding my question, Nick."

He poured himself another glass of whiskey. "One of Whelan's old allies was spotted at a public house in the Nichol. O'Sullivan and I went to have a conversation."

"And did you..." She swallowed hard. "Did you have a conversation?"

Nick downed the whiskey and set the snifter on his desk with a sharp rap. "Ask what you really mean." At her silence, he made some noise. "Fine, I'll do it for you: Is he dead? Yes. I shoved a blade into his gut. Ask me once more about the scars on my body, and I'll tell you that this man had a way with a knife. Now ask me why I let him bleed out on the pavement instead of giving the coppers a new prisoner."

"Why?" she breathed.

He stepped closer to her, his gaze as black and endless as an abyss. "Because. I. Wanted. To."

She finally understood his reputation, why some whispered that he had the eyes of the devil, like a man possessed. But she had seen his scars, knew the truth of the matter. The King of the East End was a necessary evil born of cruelty.

She, too, had blood on her hands. Survival always came at a cost.

"Do you want my condemnation or my absolution?" she asked him. "I'll give you neither."

"I need you to understand the kind of man you married. I'm not some schoolteacher, I'm not a gentleman, and I'm sure as hell not Lord Locke," he growled, his voice low and dangerous.

"I've known the kind of man I married for quite some time now." She pressed her lips together and held up the letter from Miss Dawes. "I think you should see this. It's the letter I received from my solicitor this morning."

Nick snatched the page from her hands and read. Alexandra watched him intently, looking for any hint of his thoughts. But his face was as stoic as ever, closed off from her like a locked door.

"I see," he said, very softly, and handed it back.

He turned away, discarding his coat on the floor. His shirt and trousers followed, then his smallclothes, as he crossed the room to the mosaic-tiled water closet. Alexandra couldn't help but stare. She never stopped being surprised by how beautifully made Nick was. Muscular thighs, tapered waist, broad shoulders, strong arms. Golden skin stretched over muscle, with smatterings of scars across his back – reminders of his brutal past.

Alexandra followed him. A bath had already been prepared in the gleaming copper tub, the steam rising. "Do you have nothing else to say?"

He lowered himself into the water. With a soft sigh, he tilted his head back and shut his eyes. "You could make a case for cruelty," he said in that detached tone. "If you want to do it, you might as well do it now before Gladstone reforms the courts."

In an instant, anger coursed through her veins. It was too easy for him to suggest the same thing as Miss Dawes. Women who divorced their abusive husbands found no sanctuary in their own homes. Their husbands didn't provide comfort or affection, much less respect. They didn't even offer to watch over their wives while they slept. Women who divorced on the grounds of cruelty did so out of sheer terror.

"Cruelty," she repeated, her lips flattening. Did Nick believe she thought so little of him that she'd fabricate such a claim?

"Yes, and why not?" His laugh was harsh. "Everyone in that courtroom, from the judge to the gawping audience, would believe any story you told them about me. Make me into a big enough villain, and you might even gain their fickle sympathy."

"Is that what you want me to do?" Alexandra said, her voice sharp with fury. How dared he? "Lie and say you beat me? Threatened my life?"

"Are you worried about my reputation?" What a strange

smile he had, so bitter. "You needn't be. I have none to defend."

"Yes, you do," she snapped. "Here in the East End, you do."

"Here in the East End," he repeated, his voice a dangerous purr. "Where I killed a man mere hours ago."

"A man who tortured you."

"Since when did your opinion of me become so generous?" His mouth twisted. "It's more generous than I deserve."

"Listen to me, Nicholas. I will not stand in that courtroom and call you a monster. You may not have a care, but I do."

He lifted a shoulder. "Say I committed adultery, then, if that lie will better ease your conscience. Isn't that what toffs call a *soft divorce*?"

Once again, he had echoed Miss Dawes' argument with ease. Just eight days ago, in her office, divorce on the grounds of adultery had seemed like the simplest solution. After four years of separation, many husbands and wives would have found solace in the arms of another lover.

But like Alexandra, Nick had remained faithful to their vows.

I consider you to be worth everything, he'd told her. Then why let her go so easily? Did he not want to present his case? Make some argument for gathering the tattered remains of their marriage and attempting to stitch it back together?

"And you would mount no objection?" Alexandra tried to keep her voice calm, fearing he would hear it shake. "Not to any case I bring before the courts, no matter how much I embellish or how abhorrent it made you look? You would do nothing to fight it?" Nothing to fight for *her*?

Open your eyes, she wanted to say. *Look at me*.

But he only let out a breath and said, "No."

Alexandra went over and kneeled beside the bath. *There*, she thought, when she noticed him tense. His hands betrayed him. He gripped the side of the bath hard, his knuckles white beneath the dried blood there.

"Look at me," she said, reaching out to cup his cheek. As if he couldn't help himself, he leaned into her touch, gently nuzzling her. "Nick. Look at me." When his eyes opened, Alexandra found herself almost off balance. No, he was not indifferent to Miss Dawes' letter. He was not indifferent at all. "Do you want a divorce?"

His expression became gentler. Instead of answering, he asked, "If you weren't married to me, what would you do? Would you consider marrying someone else? Make plans?"

"Would that make your decision easier?"

Nick kissed her palm. "Just tell me."

Alexandra's thumb glided across his jawline as she spoke, her words laced with melancholy. She revealed her innermost thoughts to Nick, "When news of our marriage went public, it left me feeling desolate. My brothers were away enjoying their honeymoon, and James seemed content in his letters. Even Richard had found happiness with Anne. While they were blissfully happy in their marriages, I was trapped in a disaster of one. So, I started making plans to travel. I read about far-off places and dreamed of escaping there after our divorce was final. I memorised my favourite travel guides."

Nick brushed his lips against her wrist. "What was your favourite? Recite it for me."

Alexandra exhaled, leaning forward to press her cheek

against his. She whispered into his ear, "'We were standing on the verge of a lofty cliff that stretched precipitously forward like a crescent and formed a bay on whose waters the moon, which had just risen, poured a flood of trembling silvery light; while, on one side, dark, ominous, and frowning, rose the mount, projecting far into the sea, and towering in its sullen grandeur above the rippling waves which bore their snowy wreaths of foam in tribute to its feet.'" She nipped his earlobe, gratified by the involuntary noise he had made. His hands gripped the side of the bath as if for balance. "'Clear and defined against the moonlit sky,'" she continued, trailing her fingertips along the wet, muscular line of his shoulder, "'with no trees or verdure to clothe its rocky steeps, there was something inexpressibly sublime in the aspect of this mountain, and the lonely character of the surrounding scenery.'" Nick tipped his head back with a groan as Alexandra licked the water from his throat. "'No sound invaded the perfect quietude of the hour except the reverential murmur of the sea, and faintly in the distance, the voices of some fishermen, whose barks were gliding forth, their sails filling with the evening breeze, and glistening in the moonbeams.'"

"Where?" It was a breath of a word, as if he could barely find his voice.

"Italy," she replied softly. "Ancona."

Nick's gaze locked with hers, and he spoke almost gently, "I can arrange for witnesses to testify to my adultery if that's what you want. You deserve to go to Ancona, watch the moonrise over the sea, and go wherever your heart desires."

They had been apart for four years, defying the laws of physics that pulled them together. But their collision had brought them together, and Alexandra found that the ship she had envisioned for her future was a lonely one indeed.

"It was never about Italy," she whispered, taking his hand. She picked up the soap from the bathtub's edge and lathered it around his fingers, gently massaging the scars of his childhood. She should have asked him about them years ago. "It wasn't about New York, Greece, France, or any other place on my list. I imagined being on a ship at sea, putting miles of ocean between us. I convinced myself that each new place was an opportunity to write about new experiences. But the truth is, I wanted to be someone else for a while. Someone who didn't know you and couldn't be hurt by you. I wanted to rebuild my heart."

"Then you should write to your solicitor and tell her I'll assist with your case," Nick replied.

Alexandra pressed a kiss to his fingertips. "You didn't answer my question before. Do you want a divorce?"

"If you want—"

"Nick. That's not what I'm asking." She held his gaze. "Do *you* want to divorce *me*?"

His expression softened. "No."

"Good. Because I understand now that my imaginary journey felt so lonely because I wanted you with me. As my husband."

25

Thorne was certain he was in the midst of a fevered dream. His wife had revealed everything he had ever longed for, but never dared to hope for. He couldn't shake off the feeling that this was just a waking reverie or some sort of hallucination.

He had seen her reaction when he returned after taking care of Sean Gibbons. Thorne was not like her; he did not have the luxury of getting covered in someone else's blood just to save himself. It was not an accident.

It was retribution. A message to Whelan: Thorne was no powerless, desperate lad scraping by to survive. He would not be threatened.

But when he had returned to the Brimstone, his old memories took hold. Once nudged loose, those recollections were vicious, unrelenting, and in danger of dragging him under. He'd made it to his room, but only just. He needed a drink, something strong enough to ease the relentless grip of the past – an Irish whiskey, a whole bottle.

Until Alex had burst through the door, this fey woman with a gaze that could ensnare a man's soul. Not for the first time, he had stared down at the blood on his hands and worried about sullying her, because what use did sirens have for mere men when the ocean promised freedom?

The letter she held confirmed his worst fears. She wanted to leave him. To take to the seas and seek her fortunes elsewhere. To object would be to cage her, to hold her back from soaring. It meant confining her when she had chosen to fly.

But no. Alex still held Thorne's hand.

She did not want to leave him.

She wanted him to go across that ocean with her.

Wonder prickled through him like electricity, a sudden awareness that everything between them had shifted. It was as if, on the outer edges of his mind, he had already accepted that he had lost her. The time they spent in Stratfield Saye was long past, and he had caused too much damage to make things right again. But then she had given him something precious: the gift of time. Time to spend with her without fear of discovery, without the ticking clock of inevitable separation looming over them.

It was a future of days spent with her. And not a single one of them stolen.

"Are you all right?" she asked, her smile belying her nervousness. He knew how much her words had cost her, allowing him to climb into the fortress she had built around her heart. It was a terrifying choice, one he had made himself so long ago. "Say something. Or are you—"

Without a second thought, Thorne seized the front of her dress and pressed his lips to hers. He was rewarded with the sound of her laughter, the brush of her tongue against his, as she kissed him back.

"You're pleased, I take it," she murmured against his lips.

"So very pleased," he replied. Alex was so much more than he deserved. "Come here."

He pulled her close, but she was in control now. Her lips were fierce, her touch insistent. These small movements were nothing short of miraculous: her hand slipping beneath the water to caress his ribs, her fingers pressing firmly against his shoulder. Thorne had always touched Alex with a sense of urgency, as if their time together was as brief and fleeting as a summer rainstorm. It seemed impossible that he could pause to appreciate the texture of her skin. So much of her body had not been given its due.

But Alex, bless her, had her own ideas. "Come out of that bath."

Thorne nipped at her lower lip. "Always bossing me."

"You had best get used to being bossed," she murmured, husky. "In bed and out of it. Now stand."

Thorne did as she asked. As the water cascaded off his body, his wife's blunt appraisal sent a jolt of heat through him that made him instantly hard. Alex's lips curved into a wicked smile. Aye, it was clear she knew the effect she had on him.

Alex grasped the towel beside the bathtub. She dried him off, running her hands across his skin with each stroke of fabric. In Stratfield Saye, he had been captivated by the softness of her hands and fingertips, but writing had transformed her right hand over the years. Thorne couldn't help but admire the changes. Her fingers had grown rough from gripping pens, and the ridges of her fingertips were stained black with ink. Her nails were clipped short. He realised then how few people saw her without gloves. No one but Thorne would ever know the hours she spent bent over a desk, putting her brilliant mind to words on paper.

Her bare hands were a treasure just for him.

Alex tore the towel away, leaving a trail of gooseflesh in its wake. Lips replaced hands, pressed against muscle and sinew – his shoulder, collarbone, throat, and chest. This was a different gift: petal-soft lips, the dart of her tongue caressing his nipple.

A shudder ran like fire through him as she explored his ribcage. She must have felt it – his ragged exhalations, the thundering beat of his heart, and his hard length against the front of her dress. But she didn't stop, didn't pull away – intimacy yielded a power all its own; Thorne thanked God that she would never hesitate to take it for her own.

Suddenly, Alex dropped to her knees and took him in her mouth. The sound that erupted from him was primal, feral, and unrestrained. She wasn't practised, but her eagerness more than made up for it.

God. *God.* He was so close to climax. Too close. If she didn't—

Thorne grasped Alex up and lifted her into his arms. He set her down gently, his fingers already working on the buttons of her dress. "You enjoy seeing me at your mercy," he said with a playful grin.

"I enjoyed having you in my mouth," she replied with a wicked smile, her gaze locked on his.

He fumbled with the buttons, cursing their existence. "I see your taste in literature has come in handy."

She nipped at his jaw. "Would you like me to show you

what I've learned in all the naughty books I've saved from drunk sons?"

Too many buttons. *Damn the buttons*. Thorne took the material in a hard grip and tore. The heavy, damp fabric of her dress fell to the floor.

Alex laughed softly. "I liked that one." Her breathing was fast as he pulled down her petticoat and deftly unlaced her corset.

Thorne's heart raced as he finished undressing her. "I'll buy you a new one," he promised. "A new dress every day if I have to. I want to see everything you've learned, every single depraved thing you've ever read."

Alex's wicked smile made Thorne's breath catch in his throat.

Every inch of her was stunning, from her breasts to the generous flare of her hips. She embodied Thorne's most perverse fantasies, unashamed and confident as she stood before him. Her expression was a challenge, a dare, and Thorne was more than eager to accept it.

He captured her lips with his own, his hands framing her face as he kissed her deeply. It had been so long since he'd had the privilege of touching her, of holding her naked body against his. Thorne's fevered touches tracked down her back, caressing the lush curve of her arse. He felt her moan softly as he pressed his thigh against her wet core.

In an instant, Alex shoved him onto the bed and straddled him, her eyes dark with desire. "Arms up," she commanded.

Thorne gave a slow smile and put his arms over his head. "Bossing me?"

"Always."

"Proposal?"

She leaned down and gave his earlobe a lick. "Me on top."

Oh, he loved the sound of that. "Conditions?"

Her lips trailed down his jawline, leaving a trail of fire in their wake. "You are not to touch me until you beg for it."

Christ, she was going to drive him mad. Nick went for nonchalant: he gave her gorgeous body a frank once-over. "What if I have you begging?" he asked her in a low voice.

Alex seemed both surprised and delighted by his suggestion. She laughed. "Then you may do whatever you like," she said. "Agreed?"

He swallowed a soft groan as she slid her wet heat against him. "Agreed."

She pressed her lips to his pulsing vein, dragging her teeth along his neck. The friction of her hips grinding against him had him on the brink of collapse. Thorne fought the urge to take control, to assert his dominance. His hands tightened in the sheets, a fight against some animal instinct to take her beneath him.

When she finally took him inside of her, Thorne couldn't help but arch his back and let out a sharp cry. *Christ*, he almost begged her. Almost uttered some unintelligible plea to touch her, cup her beautiful breasts, gather her hair in his fist as she plundered his defences. Left him gasping.

But he held back, watching her carefully as she explored herself, discovering what satisfied her. This was new territory for both of them, a lesson in pleasure they were learning together. She moved against him with abandon, her golden hair cascading around her face, her lips parted in ecstasy.

Thorne was transfixed by her loveliness. Every inch of

her was stunning, from the soft curve of her neck to the sway of her breasts.

Thorne grasped the sheets with white-knuckled fists, his desire pulsing through him. He had other ways of making her beg. "Let me touch you," he murmured, his voice a seductive caress. "And I'll show you what it means to be worshipped."

A sound escaped her, somewhere between a gasp and a moan. "Oh, God," she breathed.

Thorne shifted his hips, moving in time with hers. "I'll make you scream my name," he growled, the promise of pleasure dripping from his words. "I'll take you to heights of ecstasy even your most filthy books never dared to describe."

"Nick." She bit her lip, her nails digging into his skin.

Thorne smiled, knowing that he had her exactly where he wanted her. "Tell me what you crave," he urged her, unable to wait any longer. "Look at me."

She obeyed, gazing down at him with eyes blazing with desire. Thorne was more than willing to satiate her every need. He stretched once more, silently conveying his intent. "Command me, Alex," he murmured. "Tell me to take you beneath me, and I'll give it to you. I'll fuck you until you can't stand it any longer."

Her nails scored his flesh. "Do it," she begged, the need in her voice driving him wild. Thorne's hips lifted again, and she let out a guttural moan. "Nick. Please, do it."

Thorne rolled on top of Alex, his body pressing against hers. A ragged laugh escaped his lips, filled with a sense of triumph. She was stunning, a goddess beneath him. She lifted her head and kissed him fiercely, taking control of the moment. Alex was no mere spectator; she knew just how close he'd been to begging and that losing was just as much a thrill as winning.

He quickened his pace, focusing solely on her and what she needed. She arched against him, her fingers digging into his shoulders. Thorne's own climax drew nearer, and then a hoarse cry escaped her lips as she came, her body going limp in his embrace. That was all it took for him to reach his own peak. As he rolled off of her, she smiled.

"I suppose you won," she said.

Thorne let out a chuckle. "I believe we both did."

"Very well. I accept co-victory," she said, sitting up and extending her hand. "Well played, husband."

He shook her hand, barely stifling a grin. *Husband*. She'd called him husband. "Until next time, my dear wife."

The clock chimed, drawing Thorne's attention to the hour. It was the start of prime business hours, and he knew he should make an appearance on the bustling trading floor. If he angled his head just right, he could hear the hum of activity down below.

Alex followed his gaze. "Business calls?"

"Does it call for you?" he inquired.

"I suppose," she began, her voice trailing off. "Well, maybe I'm willing to ignore it. If you are."

His smile faltered as he reached out for her. Physical contact was the only thing that kept him grounded in the moment: this was real; this was happening. "You'll stay here tonight?" he asked her.

"Yes," she replied, her voice soft but resolute. "I'll stay."

26

"*Where the hell is she?*"

The angry voice penetrated Alexandra's peaceful slumber. She stirred slowly, feeling the dull ache in her limbs before something else caught her attention. Nick was wrapped around her, his arm firmly clasping her waist. If she pressed back into him, she could feel the hardness of his body against hers.

The voice came again, cutting through the haze of desire that had settled over her. "*I asked where the hell my sister is.*"

Her eyes flew open.

Oh, Lord. It was James – her eldest brother.

"Nick?" She shook his arm. "Nick, wake up."

"Hmm?" He mumbled something unintelligible before pulling her even closer. His erection pressed against her as he trailed kisses along the back of her neck. "Do you want to be on top this time?" he murmured seductively in her ear.

Oh, God. Alexandra's mind was foggy with lust. *Wait!* James was—

A loud banging echoed through the door. "Nicholas Thorne, get the hell out of that room, you bastard!"

Her husband released her and sat up, his eyes narrowing as he noticed the locked bedroom door. "Excuse me, sweetheart," he said, "I need to go kill someone. Maybe three someones. Starting with my doorman."

Nick leaned in and kissed her, stealing her breath away. "I'll be back soon, once I deal with this idiot," he promised.

Another loud banging. "Thorne! Where the bloody hell is my sister?"

Nick froze, and Alexandra sighed apologetically. "That idiot is James," she said.

"Christ, Kent," a second voice piped up outside the door. "I told you not to charge in like a bloody lunatic."

Alexandra winced. "And that idiot is Richard."

Nick ran a hand through his hair, frustration etched on his face. "Damn," he muttered, slipping on his trousers. He winced as her brother pounded on the door again. "Please, speak to the angry one before he breaks down my door," he said to her.

Alexandra sighed. "James?" she called.

"Alexandra?" James rattled the knob. "Come out of there right this second."

Richard, always the scoundrel, couldn't help but add his own comment. "Unless you need to put clothes on!" She suspected he was enjoying this. Damn him to hell. "In which case, for the love of God, get dressed first."

She could hear James grumbling on the other side of the door, making some incomprehensible noise that sounded like a threat.

"We shall be out in a moment," Alexandra said. Good grief, this was ridiculous. "Meet us in the sitting room upstairs, please. Third door on the right."

She heard muttering and footsteps and then, blissfully, silence. When she turned back to her husband, she found Nick leaning against the bedpost, still holding his shirt. She bit her lip and stared at his naked chest, admiring the beautiful, sculpted lines of muscle. It seemed a shame to cover it up. "The post in the Americas may be slow, but it reaches its destination," she told Nick regretfully. "He was going to come along sooner or later."

Her husband glared at the door. "Was hoping for later."

As Alexandra pushed off the sheets and stood, Nick wrapped an arm around her naked waist, pulling her against his warm body. "Proposal," he whispered, his lips brushing against her cheek. "We ignore the interruption and stay here."

"Counterproposal," Alexandra replied, her voice dripping with desire. "Be nice to my brothers, and let me do the talking. I'll reward you later. In bed. Thoroughly. For hours."

Nick let out a low groan. "You drive a hard bargain," he said, stepping away to put on his shirt. "But very well. I'll be nice."

Alexandra paused at the threshold of the sitting room, taking in the sight before her.

It had been six long months since she'd last seen her brother James, the Earl of Kent. The last time they'd parted ways, he'd been in a mad rush to catch the ship Emma had taken to Boston, leaving without so much as a goodbye. But now, as she looked upon him, Alexandra could see that travel had agreed with her eldest brother.

James was positively glowing with good health and vitality, his typically blond hair now sun-kissed to a shade paler than Richard's. The deep tan he sported indicated a great deal of time spent outdoors, and Alexandra couldn't help but feel a pang of envy at the thought of all the adventures he must have had.

When James finally looked up and saw her, he shot a murderous glare in Nick's direction before holding open his arms in a welcoming embrace. "Come here, you troublesome girl," he said with a resigned sigh.

Alexandra stepped forward eagerly, wrapping her arms around her brother and taking in the scent of the sea that clung to him. "I missed you," she said, her voice full of emotion. "How is Emma? Is she with you?"

He pulled back and shook his head. "She put up a grand argument, but I had to suggest she leave for Roseburn after the journey. She's visibly..." He cleared his throat. "In the family way now."

Alexandra's jaw dropped. Emma, with child! She could hardly fathom why her friend or brother didn't mention it in their letters. "So I am to be an aunt twice over, and *both of you*" – she glared at Richard – "kept it from me?"

Richard settled on the couch, crossing his legs. "Oh, now we're exchanging secrets?" he said with a grin. "How long have you been married again? Four years, was it?"

Fine, she was guilty of secrets.

"It was..." Alexandra hesitated, her mind racing for a suitable explanation. "Complicated."

"Ah, the dreaded 'C' word," James interjected. "Does he," he gestured towards Nick, "need to be present for you to tell it?"

"Would you like me to leave?" Nick asked. Alexandra couldn't quite decipher if he was addressing her or James.

"No, no. Please stay." James flashed a dangerous grin. "It's always useful to have you within arm's reach, just in case I feel like delivering a good punch to your face."

"Oh, Thorne already extended that invitation," Richard interjected cheerfully. "I declined, but I've been reconsidering. I love the idea of a good brawl. Please, Alexandra, tell Kent how you and Thorne became man and wife. I'm positively itching for him to hear it."

For heaven's sake. She loved her brothers, but sometimes she wanted to throw them out of a window. Even James, who was usually the stoic one, seemed to have his brain dribble out of his ears when it came to male posturing.

"I'll not utter another word," she said, "unless I have your solemn vow that you won't lay a finger on Nick. Agreed?"

James huffed, his arms crossed firmly in front of him. A few mumbled syllables escaped his lips, sounding suspiciously like, "I promise," but it could have been, "What piss," for all she knew. She accepted it all the same.

"Understand that I kept this to myself because I wanted to forget the entire ordeal. It was... challenging, given what our father did." She offered Nick an apologetic glance, and he soothed her with a gentle caress. This encouraged her to proceed.

"During my debut season, the former earl learned of my illegitimate status. Seeking revenge on our mother, he sent me to Roseburn and engaged a criminal – no offence, Nick – to pose as a peer of the realm and earn my confidence. He schemed to humiliate me in the most vicious way possible: by tricking me into eloping with this fraud – no offence again – who would subsequently gain control of my trust. And you know the rest now. Nick and I are married. Anyway, would anyone like tea?"

A deafening silence ensued. Alexandra realised too late that she had not done enough to ease James's distress. She had not assured him that Nick, despite causing pain in the past, had earned his redemption. "It was four years ago," she hastened to explain, seeing his face go red. "Father is dead. Things are different now—"

"Move," her brother told Alexandra, his expression a mask of cold fury.

Behind her, she heard her husband whisper very low, "*Damn*."

"No," Alexandra said. "You promised."

James's hands curled into fists. "You made me promise not to hit him," he growled, "so, with immense pleasure, I am going to *murder* him."

Oh, Lord. As her brother stepped forward, Alexandra threw herself in front of Nick. "*James.*"

But her brother wasn't listening. He tried circling her. "Get out of the way, Alexandra."

Even Richard tried reasoning with their sibling. "Kent, this isn't—"

"Shut up, Richard. If you had dealt with this while I was gone, I wouldn't be here." He made some quick move, but Alexandra darted in front of him again. "Choose your second," he snarled.

"Hell," Richard muttered.

"Still trying my best to be nice," Nick told her in a low voice, "but he's making it difficult."

"He's an *idiot*," she hissed back. To James: "You are *not* challenging my husband to a duel! First of all, no one duels anymore because it's illegal. Secondly, no one duels anymore because it's *stupid*."

James's lips tightened. "He has fifteen seconds to change my mind, or I'll return with a pistol and shoot him."

"He doesn't need to change your mind. You're not—"

"I love her," Nick declared.

That got everyone's attention. Alexandra felt her heart skip a beat, and the thorny walls around it began to retract. Though he had uttered those words before, she had always considered them another lie. Even when he claimed they were genuine, the barrier of pain around her heart persisted. It had become her last line of defence, and she could not believe him without undermining its fortifications.

But this time felt different. Last night, Nick had been prepared to let her go and step aside as she pursued the life she desired. He believed she deserved happiness and was willing to sacrifice his own.

This time his words were the truth.

James went still, his eyes intent. "Do you?"

She felt Nick's hand on her again, pressed between her shoulder blades. "Common tale, a confidence artist falling in love with his mark," he said wryly. "Yes, I love her. Always will."

Her brother's expression softened. He and Richard communicated silently, in the way of overprotective siblings, before James gave a small nod. "Fine. But I need one more answer." James regarded Alexandra with some inscrutable expression. "Do *you* want to be married?"

The hand on her back fell away, and she wondered if Nick thought she had changed her mind. But the events of the morning had only strengthened her resolve. "Yes, I do," she replied confidently.

James gave a curt nod. "Good. I'll menace him another time, then." He held out his hand to Nick, and her husband took it. "Welcome to the family. If you break her heart, I'll break your face, etcetera, etcetera. Now I really must go home to my wife." He embraced Alexandra. "Come visit us before she threatens to return to town."

They all said their goodbyes, and James and Richard left the Brimstone.

The silence in the sitting room seemed to stretch. Alexandra suddenly felt shy – an emotion she had not experienced since that summer in Stratfield Saye.

Nick had said he loved her.

He had told *her brothers* he loved her.

As if sensing her apprehension – or, perhaps, her need for some time – Nick gave her an understanding smile. "Work calls," he told her, kissing her cheek. "I'll see you tonight."

Hours later, in her dark bedchamber, Alexandra felt someone pluck the pen from her hand. She realised she'd fallen asleep at her desk after writing into the night.

She would have recognised Nick by his scent anywhere: the sharpness of his soap with a hint of peated whiskey. It had always been thus, even in Stratfield Saye, when he was pretending to be someone else. Then his hands began kneading her weary shoulders.

Magic. His hands were magic.

"Hello," she said with a sigh, turning her head on the desk. "What time is it?"

"Early morning. The sun will be up in a few hours." He started on her shoulder blades. "Been working all day?"

"Yes." She yawned. "I should get back to it."

He made an incoherent noise and kept massaging. "You should sleep," he finally said, taking Alexandra's hand. He brushed his thumb across her fingertips. "You work so hard. I hear you pacing, your pen tapping. Seen how much your stack of papers grows at night. I noticed the callus on this hand where you hold your pen. Ink stains on your fingertips. No gloves?"

"I don't like writing with them. Do you mind the look of my hand?"

"'Course not." He kissed her wrist and resumed rubbing her back. "My wife is determined to destroy a bad man. She's brilliant and talented. Why would I mind that?"

"You always were a charmer, Nicholas Thorne."

She sighed and rested her forehead on the desk as he worked down her spine. She was so tired. She must have fallen asleep because the next thing she knew, Nick had swung her up in his arms. He carried her through the connecting door to his bedchamber and set her on the bed. With deft, silent movements, he removed her clothes, then his own.

When they were both naked, he pulled her under the blankets and settled his arm around her waist. She let herself enjoy him: his scent, his solidity, his warmth. It wasn't an indulgence; it was necessary. *He* was necessary.

"Nick?"

"Hmm?"

"Will you..." She swallowed. "Will you repeat the words? What you said earlier?"

He breathed against her. He was quiet for so long that she wondered if he had fallen asleep. But then he kissed her shoulder and whispered, "I love you."

Contentedness was too close to hope, and Nicholas Thorne knew that hope was dangerous.

He'd watched toffs bet their entire fortunes based on some foolish notion that they'd win the gamble, that luck had blessed them, that their winning streak wasn't a fleeting victory. The more success he had, the more confident a man became in playing the odds.

And the more he lost when that winning streak was over.

A sense of danger settled inside Nick like a stone: he was just another fool on a winning streak, and at any moment, he'd lose everything.

He'd lose *her*.

If Alex noticed his strange moods, she did not indicate it. Over a sennight, they had fallen into a routine of sorts; like Thorne, she worked during the hours after dark. He would spend time relieving toffs of their money, then seeking leads on Whelan. When he returned, it was to find her scratching away at her manuscript. She had an impenetrable focus when she wrote; he could stand at the door for whole minutes without her noticing. When he studied her... he couldn't help but long for the future, but how to have it with her still seemed unfathomable. So much could go wrong.

Whelan was out there. And Thorne's enemy was waiting for the right opportunity.

Now Thorne watched as Alex crouched among Sofia's children in the zoological hall at the International Exhibition. She laughed at something Sofia said, then lifted one of the smaller lads so he could get a better look at the exotic birds. Such an ordinary thing, unremarkable in the grand scheme of the world's moments, but that only made it infinitely precious to Thorne. There was a pleasure in mundanity, for it was a new experience. Their marriage had never existed within the scope of the everyday, the contentment of routine.

And it *was* a comfort: waking up to her, going to bed with her, kissing her, touching her – ordinary moments.

For Thorne, miraculous.

Alex's laughter came again as she took hold of a lass' hand and showed the child how to pet a lizard at the exhibit gently. The hall's mood was boisterous and loud, filled with hundreds of people gawping at animals from far beyond Britain's shores. But Nick and Alex might as well have been the only two people there – that's how attuned he was to her.

"Mr Thorne! Mr Thorne!"

"Oi, my little devils," Thorne said, scooping Dot and Lottie up in each arm as he followed the others through the exhibit. "Anything caught your eye?"

Dot pointed her hand, which had grown pudgy since

Sofia became the orphanage manager. She fed her charges well. "There's them animals, Mr Thorne. I likes the birds."

"Aye, the birds!" Lottie echoed. "They're ever so colourful, Mr Thorne. From the Indies, they are. I've never seen anythin' so beautiful."

"Neither have I, sweetheart," Thorne murmured, watching as Alex smiled at the children. "Neither have I."

He had some wild urge to step forward, take her in his arms, and kiss her senseless in front of everyone. Let them look; let them see he belonged to her. Let the whole damn world know he was hers. She looked up and caught his stare. Thorne was reasonably sure his desire was apparent because Alex flushed and hid a smile. That smile was a gift for him alone.

Dot tugged on Thorne's neckcloth. "Mr Thorne," she whispered in his ear. "I likes the lady."

Thorne grinned. "Do you?"

"Me too!" Lottie said, looping her arms around Thorne's neck. "She gives us pastries. And she don't mind so much when I pick the lock on 'er door."

"Good, because I intend to keep her."

"Do you love her, Mr Thorne?" Dot asked.

Thorne followed as Alex and Sofia took the children through the hall. "Aye, girls," he said. "I love her very much."

Lottie sighed. "That's ever so romantic."

An image struck Thorne – one he had deemed impossible, once – of the children Alex might give him. He would carry them in his arms. Marvel at how much they looked like their ma. And he'd tell them how, after so many years, he adored his wife as much now as on the day they met.

Two real, squirming children interrupted his reverie.

Dot gave a delighted squeak and wriggled to be let down. "Lottie! It's the monkeys! I wanna go see up close!" Thorne released the girls and watched as they ran over to the primate exhibit.

Alex took that moment to approach him, leaving Sofia to watch over her charges. Any onlooker might think her smile polite and ladylike, but Thorne noticed the wicked glint in her eye – an intimate look just for him.

"Thank you for today," she said, slipping her arm through his. Her gloved fingers brushed his palm, and he loathed that layer between them. He wanted to see her ink stains, her callouses, the signs of her work, hidden beneath the soft leather. "As magnificent as your palace is, I was growing tired of staring at my manuscript."

Thorne laughed softly. "One of the maids came to me in a state, said you shooed her away from cleaning again."

Alex made a face. "Morag keeps eyeing my notes in distress."

"They're rather hard to miss, being all over the floor and on every available piece of furniture."

"They're organised!"

"Pfft." He gave a soft laugh. "Looks like a bomb explosion. Even your bed is covered in bits of paper. I don't see how you find anything."

"That bed is where I keep my interview notes, and I know *exactly* where everything is. Which I told Morag at length when she shifted the December interviews closer to the March interviews thinking I wouldn't notice. It ruined my focus for two days."

"I can't pretend to understand any of that, so I won't."

"Good. That means you are learning." She looked smug.

"And anyway, there's no use in clearing off the bed now that I sleep in yours."

Thorne grinned. Now he was imagining her back in his bed, naked and negotiating a new bedroom game. He let his gaze drop down her body and trail up again. Her pink day dress, modest though it was, could not hide her curves. He knew what lay underneath: the dusting of freckles along her thighs, the soft arch of her hips, beautiful breasts, pink nipples. Utter perfection.

She caught his stare and flushed. "You are thinking of wicked things."

"Certainly am. Want me to describe them to you?"

Alex cast a look around them, but they hardly drew notice in the middle of the crowded hall. In a low voice, she said, "Perhaps I do."

"Mr Thorne? Lady Alexandra?" Sofia's voice drew their attention. The manager waited there with an understanding expression on her face. "The children are ready to progress to the India Annexe."

"Go ahead, Mrs Ainsley," Thorne said. "We'll join you in a few moments."

Sofia nodded. "Of course. Come along, children. Adam, darling, stop gawping at the lizard and take my hand."

Nick tugged on Alexandra's hand. "Come with me."

"Where?"

"Anywhere."

Alexandra laughed. People watched them curiously as they passed, perhaps wondering why he sped her through the long hall of the Exhibition Centre in a hurry. After the Queensland Annexe, at a quiet end of the centre, Thorne pulled them through a door and into a small, hidden alcove.

The crowd noise was muffled, filtered through the quiet of the little-used chamber.

Alex's breath caught when he set his hands to the wall on either side of her.

"And what now?" she whispered.

Thorne bent his head and pressed his lips to hers. Alex gave a little groan as she opened her mouth to deepen their kiss. He marvelled at the sound: a confession that she was as much a victim of their desire as he. They had four years to make up. Four years that suddenly felt like a foolish choice he'd made, never to beg for forgiveness.

But, now, he had other things he could do on his knees.

Nick sank to the floor and reached for the bottom of her skirts.

"Nick—" Her next words were cut off with a helpless moan as he pushed up her petticoats. Then he grasped the waistline of her drawers and nudged them down. "If someone sees…"

"They won't."

She jumped when he pressed a kiss to her bare thigh. "What if they hear?"

Thorne lifted his eyes to meet hers. She was a picture of arousal: parted lips, flushed cheeks, hair in disarray. When had that happened? Christ, she looked debauched already. He smiled. "We'd best be quiet, then." He handed her the gathered fabric. "Hold this?"

She took it, murmuring, "You, Nicholas Thorne, are a rogue, a scoundr—"

He leaned forward and flicked his tongue against her quim, and her head thumped against the wall.

"Dear Lord," she whispered.

"Shall I continue?" he asked.

Alex grasped his hair, her gloved hands gripping his scalp. "I never told you to stop."

Thorne gave a soft chuckle and pressed his lips to her once more. Her hips jerked, but he held her fast, running his tongue along the slit of her pussy. Their ragged breathing filled the small alcove. The little noises she made – helpless, her fist pressed to her lips to keep quiet – became directives: she liked his tongue flat against her clitoris; his two fingers inside her, moving in and out at the same pace he knew she loved with his cock. Her hand scraped across his skull, grasping his hair to pull him closer – a silent encouragement to keep going.

Close. Alex was close. He could tell by her shuddering movements, the staccato of her breath.

Ah, there.

She bit her fist to muffle a cry of release. Thorne licked her gently as her tremors ceased, prolonging her pleasure as long as he could. Then, with one final kiss, he slid her drawers in place and stood.

Alex dropped her dress and all but collapsed against the wall. "I think you've killed me," she told him with a laugh.

Thorne brushed her lips with his thumb. "Not a bad way to die, is it?"

"Shall I return the favour?" she asked him.

He shook his head and tucked her hair back into its pins. His efforts were adequate – most onlookers wouldn't notice that she'd been debauched in public. Sofia, however, wouldn't be fooled. "There's only so long Mrs Ainsley can distract the children. But later, in bed?" He gave her a devilish smile. "I'm open to more negotiating."

When Alexandra and Nick walked into the India Annexe, Sofia gave them a knowing look. "See anything interesting?" she asked with a smile.

"A fascinating room," Nick said, casually. "I'd say our exploration there was quite thorough, wouldn't you, Alex?"

Sofia covered her laugh with a gloved hand.

Alexandra flushed and gave Nick a bump with her elbow. "You are *terrible*."

Nick only grinned.

As they strolled through the India Annexe, the children ran between the stalls. They all marvelled at unfamiliar instruments from Calcutta, Bombay, and the Punjab. The art depicted Indian landscapes with rugged cliffs and intricate temples. Alexandra loved the textiles, the chintzes, and floral embroidery that comprised beautiful garments. Paisley patterned shawls, directly from Shāliāt, hung from the stalls in a dizzying array of colours. As they moved to the furniture, Alexandra resisted the urge to touch the beautifully painted vases and chairs carved from rich wood.

"Oh," she breathed as she caught sight of a large writing desk. She looked up at the proprietor and, indicating a wish to inspect it, asked, "May I?"

"Of course, madam," the man said. "Do let me know if I may be of any assistance."

It was made of rosewood, the red colour of it deep and gleaming. Alexandra kneeled and studied the intricate geometric carvings along its legs. Much of the wooden furniture in English homes were simple. This desk had been lovingly designed and engraved from floor to top, where it had a broad surface.

Perfect for writing.

"See something you like?" Nick's husky voice came from behind her.

Alexandra sighed and straightened. "Isn't it lovely?"

Nick studied it with a practised eye and ran his fingertips over the designs. "Good quality wood, unique look to it. If a toff who owed me money had this piece, I'd consider an exchange."

Alexandra raised an eyebrow. "Is that how you evaluate things? Based on whether it's worth taking from a man with a gambling debt?"

"Not all things, but most," he said with a wink. To the seller: "How much?"

"Eighty pounds, sir."

"Tch." Nick clicked his tongue and said in a low voice, "Bit overpriced, sure, but when my wife is stuffing paper in her teacups and covering her bed with interview notes..." He slid his fingers across the drawers, pulling a few open. "And look, hidden compartments for pens, ink, sweets, and—"

"Secrets," she finished.

His eyes met hers. "You remember."

It was strange, how their time at Stratfield Saye could seem both recent and like a distant memory. Compared with their time apart, it had been so brief – not even a whole summer – yet she'd held onto every conversation between them, even when it had brought nothing but hurt.

"I remember," she said softly.

Nick gave a small smile. "Then, if you'll recall, I promised to buy one for you. Besides, you ought to have somewhere to compose your brilliant work in my home. Might as well—" He frowned. "What's that look?"

Alexandra had flinched. Despite their reconciliation – despite a blissful week together – she still had a box of his criticisms. He had written those things and meant her to see them.

He meant her to understand that he considered her station too far above his.

She could not reconcile it with the man in front of her, who casually complimented her essays. Who handed her a pen as if it were a weapon and told her to wield it as she wanted. He had *published* those things.

"You don't like my work," she said flatly.

His brows went up. He looked... bewildered? "The hell I don't," he said in a low voice. "I've read every word. Practically memorised them."

Alexandra drew herself away from him. So he was going to pretend he'd never published those things? Never wrote about how she came and went from the East End as if she were doing something as shallow as changing a dress? Did he not print them to send a message? *Stay away. I have no need of you.*

So she had. For four years.

And she could not pretend it didn't hurt.

"Don't lie to me," she hissed, mortified by the sting of tears in her eyes. She darted a look around, praying no one noticed. "You promised. You *promised* no more lies."

Now he looked alarmed. "Lie? What are you—"

A child's scream echoed through the annexe. Alexandra looked over to find Sofia soothing the sobbing girl – one of her youngest, Mary. Grateful for the interruption, Alexandra hurried over. "What is it? What's happened?"

Sofia made soothing noises and stroked little Mary's hair. "She's left her doll on a bench in the main gallery, beside the fountain."

"I'll go see if it's still there," Alexandra said. "Don't worry, darling. Wait with Mrs Ainsley."

Nick placed a hand on her lower back. "Let me accompany you."

"That's not necessary," Alexandra said, shifting from his touch. She kept her expression neutral, even as his eyes darkened. "I shall return shortly."

She hurried out of the India Annexe and towards the main hall. As she passed the crowds of people gawping at the different displays, she tried to blink back her tears. How embarrassing still to be so upset by Nick's criticisms. It was never *what* he wrote – the words were honest. From another source, she might have used them for improvement.

From Nicholas Spencer, the alias of the man who had lied to her, they were utterly destructive.

You are no longer needed.

"Stop," she told herself. "Stop, stop, stop." It was no use crying in public. She had a doll to find.

As she reached the fountain, Alexandra scanned the benches – *ah, still there*. The cloth doll was frayed, likely of more sentimental than financial value. Relieved to have something to bring back to little Mary, Alexandra picked up the toy.

A hand closed hard around her upper arm, making her drop the doll. She was hauled up against a large male body and felt the sharp prick of a knife in her back.

"Don't scream," the man hissed into her ear. "If you so much as try, I'll shove this blade in, and by the time anyone notices, I'll be gone. Now walk."

Her heart slammed against her ribcage. Alexandra did as the man instructed, walking past crowds of people who wouldn't have noticed if she were in distress. They were so overwhelmed by the exhibition, by the hum of machinery demonstrations, and the exotic artefacts from faraway parts of the world. He was right; he could stab her right here and disappear so fast.

"Would you happen to be Patrick Whelan?" she asked, trying to keep her voice calm.

"No," he said shortly. "But I have blunt waiting for me if I bring you to him."

This confirmed Nick's stories about a man who rarely did his own dirty work. Instead, he employed and manipulated others to commit crimes for him. "You don't have to do this," she murmured. "Whatever he's paid you, I'll double it."

"And have Whelan for an enemy?" he said. "Fuck that."

"Triple."

He shoved her. "Shut up and walk."

If she went with him, Alexandra's chances of survival were slim. She also knew this man expected her to go along in fear. Probably his experience with aristocratic women was limited to seeing them from afar, with their frothy dresses, carefully coifed hair, and chaperones or footmen. This was to her advantage: Alexandra had dealt with dangerous footpads before. She had learned to defend herself; after all, the women in the East End did not have the luxury of safety. She learned from them.

Those lessons would save her, just as they had in her bedchamber, with another man who would have done her harm.

Concentrate, she told herself.

And it became simple: survival. That was all. A basic animal desire to make it from one day to the next. She let the entirety of her mind concentrate on three things: the knife pricking through her dress, the man at her back, the crowd around her. Once she left this building, the last factor would disappear. All the gawping people would slow him down.

Opportunity: take it.

Alexandra took it. She slammed her boot back into his shins, tore out of his grip, and took off, running.

His shout echoed behind her. She ignored the gasps and shocked expressions as she sprinted through the exhibition hall. The man's footsteps were at her heels. Alexandra tried to disregard everything but her task: *survival, remember?* The mind, once cleared of doubts, made uncomplicated decisions. She could not lead him to the children; she'd have to lose him in the street. If he didn't know the area of South Kensington, that would work to her advantage.

Alexandra made for the exit, bursting out onto the street.

When she dared peek over her shoulder, she caught the man's determined gaze. So close. Slowed only by a slight limp she'd caused by her hard kick to his shin. Alexandra darted up the street. The exhibition road was long; she was too visible. Alexandra swung into an alley, but he stayed behind her.

Another alley.

A whistle.

Alexandra nearly careened into the two men who stepped out from behind a building. One was a short, squat man, barely taller than herself. The other was thin and lean, with blond hair escaping from his dirty cap. Their expressions as they advanced were smug. Predatory.

They were hunters who had caught a rabbit in their snare.

The voice behind her sounded amused. "Figured you'd run. I'm not taking any chances with Whelan. He doesn't take too kindly to failure."

"Ye didn't tell me she were a looker, Elijah," Blond said.

"Looker or not, we take her." Alexandra gasped as Elijah seized her arm and shoved her against the wall, pressing the tip of his knife into her cheek. His hard grey eyes glinted as he studied her face. "Whelan said to bring her alive. He has plans for this one." To Alexandra, he said, "Come without a fuss, or I will carve up that pretty face, though."

Three against one. Alexandra didn't like her odds.

Nick, she thought to herself as she got ready to act. She wished she'd kissed him one last time. Had kept her last promise.

I shall return shortly.

Perhaps she wouldn't.

But she would fight to make sure she did.

As Elijah eased the knife away, thinking he had won, she slammed her forehead into his and smacked the blade out of his hand. Elijah shouted in surprise, and she swung her fist into his face. He staggered, colliding with the brick wall of the closest building.

Alexandra dived for the knife. The other men came at her, one grasping her by the hair. A hard strike to her face made her cry out. Stars burst in front of her vision.

Do not lose consciousness, she thought. *Stay awake!*

Her hand closed around the hilt of the blade, and she struck. The blond man swore sharply and shoved Alexandra back to the ground.

"You should have come quietly, bitch," the blond breathed in her ear. "You should've—"

The ugly crack of a fist breaking bones filled the alleyway, and the man screamed. Alexandra blinked to clear her vision, lifting her head as two of her assailants sprinted away in a hurry. *What had scared them?*

A growl came from behind her. Alexandra turned in time to see Nick slam his fist into the blond man's jaw. Blood smeared her abductor's face as he sagged against her husband.

Nick pushed him into the wall. He bared his teeth in a savage grimace quite unfamiliar to her. She had only seen the remnants, once, of this mood: after he'd killed another of Whelan's men. As he touched the tip of his blade to the corner of the man's eye, Nick's expression was one of silent calculation.

"You know who I am?" he asked in a low voice as frigid as the sea in winter. His accent gave it a soothing cadence that made Alexandra shiver. "Your friends knew, which is why they fled like cowards."

The man hesitated, then gave a nod.

"Yet you still came after my wife." Nick's smile was cruel. "How much did Whelan offer for you to do such a stupid thing?" The man hesitated, and Nick's smile disappeared. "*How much.*"

The blond man swallowed. "Two quid."

"Two quid," Nick repeated in a clipped voice. Then he said it again, more softly, as his eyes sought Alexandra's.

He regarded her with a narrowed stare. Alexandra was suddenly aware of how she must have looked. The blood and dirt on her cheeks, her dress torn. Her lip was swollen from where one of her assailants had struck her.

Nick's lip curled in a snarl.

He reared back and jammed his blade into the man's shoulder. The blond's scream was stifled by Nick's hand. "What do you think, Alex?" he asked in that strange voice. "Is your life worth so little?"

The blond gave her a desperate look.

"Nick," Alexandra said as she rose to her feet. "Don't do this."

Her husband's lips tightened into a thin line. "Does he deserve my mercy, then?"

She reached for his shoulder, felt him shudder beneath her hand. "It's not yours to give. It's mine."

Nick's black gaze met hers. That look struck her like a bludgeon. Now she understood the strangeness of his anger, why it seemed different: he was terrified.

For *her*.

Yes, she understood his fear now. Had Nick not come after her – if he had arrived a few minutes later – this man and his friends would have taken her. Like Millie, her contact in St Giles, she would have disappeared without a trace.

But she could not let him bear the burden of another death. Not if she could help it.

She brushed her gloved thumb across his shoulder, and his expression imperceptibly softened. "If you have the police in your pocket, then put them to work," she said.

The quiet between them stretched as he considered her words. Perhaps it was only mere seconds – but it felt minutes long. Then he nodded and pulled out the knife with a sharp jerk. The man's muffled scream made Alexandra wince. He whimpered as Nick lay the blade against his cheek and carved two intersecting lines.

"Every man and woman I own in the city knows this mark," Nick said flatly. "You had best hurry to the police station before one of them sees it. If they do, I'll reward them beyond a mere two quid for your life." With that, he released the man and shoved him hard in the direction of the main street. "Run fast."

The blond man took off, his quick footfalls echoing through the alley.

"Thank you," she said. "For listening to me."

"Don't thank me for that." Nick avoided Alexandra's gaze and took a handkerchief from his pocket to dab the blood on her lip gently. "It's past time to pay Sir Reginald Seymour a visit," he told her.

She winced when he put pressure on the cut. "And I will come."

"No." Nick didn't even hesitate.

"Yes. I know you are worried for me. I also know you mean to go there and make threats. That will not work. Let me use my manuscript."

Her husband did not seem convinced. "Didn't you say you don't have the political influence to accuse him publicly?"

"And you encouraged me to keep writing." She placed her hand over his. "I have an idea. Let me try it before you charge into his home. I may need Mr O'Sullivan to accompany me to a few places."

Nick's hand tightened beneath hers. "I hate your suggestion." Then, with a sigh, he said, "But very well."

She gave a small smile. "Good. Because we're going to need your money."

"Pounds, shillings, and pence," he murmured, pressing a soft kiss to her cheek. "I told you already: everything is yours."

CRO 28 CRO

Days later, in a townhouse in Mayfair, Thorne watched Sir Reginald Seymour enter his dark office. Despite the late hour, servants had taken turns stroking the blazing fire. Thorne and Alex had waited, hidden behind the curtains, until their master returned from White's Club.

Thorne brushed against Alex – a simple touch to feel her solidity. Three days ago, he had almost lost her in that alleyway. Since then, he had thrown himself into work at the Brimstone, leaving her to develop a plan for confronting Sir Reginald. Whatever that plan involved was currently hidden within her leather satchel. She would not budge when he proposed again that he confront Seymour alone.

So here he was, putting her in danger again.

He clenched his teeth and focused on Seymour. Through the slit in the curtain, he saw the other man loosen his cravat and pour himself a snifter of whiskey. Sir Reginald was tall and slim, twice Thorne's age. Another toff who never undertook his own dirty work, who used his position of power for gain. An all-too-familiar tale.

The man sat down at his desk, and Alex stepped out from behind the curtain. "Sir Reginald."

The MP choked on his whiskey. He moved as if to stand, but Thorne got there in a flash. He put a hand on Seymour's thin shoulder and pushed him back down. "Don't think so," he said in a low growl. "Damn well take a seat."

Alex smiled at Thorne, honest admiration in her gaze. Christ, he loved her so damned much. "Sir Reginald, I don't believe you've yet had the pleasure of meeting my husband."

Seymour did not rise to the bait. "I suppose you've brought him here to threaten me."

Alex's expression didn't change. "Of course not. I am perfectly capable of making my own threats. I've come to issue a request."

Seymour shifted beneath Thorne's hand. "And what is that?"

Thorne answered for her. "Pull the contract on her life, Seymour."

The MP reclined in his leather seat. Had Thorne not been touching the other man, his calm façade might have been convincing. But Thorne could feel his tension. "I'm afraid I don't know what you're referring to."

"No? Then let me aid your memory." Alex lifted the satchel and set it on Seymour's desk with a hard thump. "I've learned a *great deal* about the shipping business recently. Imagine my surprise when I discovered the expense of transporting goods from one continent to another. Particularly when they're as distant as, say, Australia. The connections one must have! The capital!" She tilted her head and gave him a cutting smile. "How difficult that must be when MPs earn no salary."

Seymour's expression had gone cold. "I'm the son of the Duke of Wetherby."

"And brother to the Earl of Surrey." Thorne almost let out a surprised laugh when she gave that particular name. The Earl of Surrey was one he knew well. Clever girl. Alex caught his look and gave him a brilliant smile. "You're familiar with the earl, aren't you, darling?"

"I know every name in the Brimstone's books," Thorne said, crossing his arms. "He's settled debts that would have sunk most aristos."

"Oh, I believe they did strain even the duke's flush coffers. And fortunately for Sir Reginald, when I investigate someone, I take copious notes." She opened the satchel and set out paper after paper of sums – not only from the Brimstone, but other businesses. The MP regarded the documents but said nothing. "How much would this leave for a second son's business ventures, I wonder? What do you think, Nick?"

Nick grinned. He could watch her do this all day. "Nothing, I'd wager. Aye, Seymour?"

The MP shoved the papers away. "What of it?" he asked, lifting his shoulders. "It's not unusual to have investors, though I understand women know little of such things."

"Indeed! Investors. Thank you for reminding me." She picked up another paper and flicked it across the desk. "Yes, a dozen or so, and a rather impressive list. You might notice their names are crossed off. I did that as I met with each of them."

Sir Reginald froze. "I beg your—"

"Pardon," she said with a mocking look. "I wasn't finished. They were all under the assumption that your business dealt with shipping supplies and goods, as Australia gives and receives half of its imports and exports. Why, they were *very* interested to know that their investment was put toward illegal human transportation, for the purposes of mining and smuggling opals. I also let them know about the cost involved in transporting the raw gems to Germany for cutting. And how difficult it is getting them there, with the French and Germans at war as recently as last year." She set her hands on the desk and leaned forward, her eyes gleaming. "Imagine their shock when I told them all how their money was being used."

The MP's breath came rapidly. Thorne's, too, but for a different reason: his wife was bloody magnificent.

"Get out of my house," Sir Reginald said, his voice trembling. "Or I will alert the authorities."

Thorne leaned down. "Who do you think owns the authorities?" he asked, flashing his teeth. "I do."

"Now, Nick," his wife said, chastising. "Let's not be rude. We're quite happy to leave, of course. But first, I have one more matter of business to discuss." She reached into the satchel for another sheet and set it down in front of him. "The settling of your debts. To me."

The MP sat straight and stared down at the sheet in alarm. "My – what—"

"You see, once your investors heard that they were being defrauded and unknowingly engaging in illegal trade, they were willing to let me buy up what you owed. So I did." She tapped the paper. "There's the amount, all added up. Quite a sizable sum. But I am willing to consider a trade."

Thorne marvelled at her. He had seen her absorbed in her work and admired how she spoke passionately about politics, but she was in her element now. Like Sir Reginald, he leaned forward to listen to the bargain. To hear what she had worked on for days while he worried over her.

And here she was, saving herself.

Sir Reginald cleared his throat. "Trade?"

Alexandra smiled. "Cancel the contract on my life." But when Sir Reginald almost relaxed, she added, "Then resign your post and leave the country. You will close up your mines and use whatever capital you gained in this trade to pay every single worker a hefty compensation."

The MP shot up from his seat with a snarl, restrained only by Thorne's grip. "That's outrageous!"

"Outrageous?" His wife's smile disappeared. She flipped the satchel shut. "I can't prove that you had my contacts murdered, but I *can* prove you owe me money and that your shipments are fraudulent. Recall that I can take everything you own, right down to the very last button on your coat."

Sir Reginald collapsed in his chair, wild-eyed and a bit stunned. Thorne almost couldn't blame the man – when Alex came here with the intent of destroying this man, she'd performed the task thoroughly. "I... I need time—"

"Call off your assassins and leave, pay your workers, and close the mines, or I will publish every last bit of information I have and financially ruin you. That's my offer. It expires the moment I walk out of that door." Alex picked the satchel up off the desk and moved as if to leave.

"*Wait.*" The MP put up a hand. "All right. *All right.* I" – he clenched his jaw and shot a glare at Thorne – "I accept."

"Good. Then we shall leave your house." She nodded at Thorne and gestured to the door. "Oh, and Sir Reginald?" She gave a small smile. "If I ever see you in England again, or if I hear that you have reneged on our deal, I'll come to collect every last debt you owe. And I won't be so pleasant next time."

Sir Reginald's eyes flashed with fear.

Once they had left the house, Thorne scanned the road. The dark thoroughfare – thank God – was empty. He couldn't restrain himself anymore. He hauled Alex up against the wall of a nearby building and put his mouth to hers.

"I love you," he said, kissing her fiercely. "I love you so much."

Alex let out a breathless laugh. She dropped the satchel and grasped the collar of his jacket to pull him closer. "Why Nicholas Thorne," she murmured against his lips, "do you mean to tell me you find threatening people to be arousing?"

He nipped her lower lip. "I find *you* threatening people to be arousing."

"Mmm." She tilted her head back as he flicked her earlobe with his tongue. "You are perverse."

"I am." He slid his hands behind her. "Very perverse. Utterly hopeless. A complete deviant, mauling his wife on a public street at night because she is just... So. Bloody. Tempting." The last three words were punctuated with kisses down her neck.

At the reminder of where they were, Alex said, "Nick, we shouldn't."

"Right. We shouldn't." He kissed her again anyway.

"You are far too wicked." She put a finger to his lips. "Take me back to the Brimstone."

"And?"

She smiled up at him and looped her arms around his neck. "Show me how tempting you find me."

∽ 29 ∽

Two days later, Thorne received a letter from Sir Reginald Seymour that said, simply:

> *The contract has been cancelled. Check the newspapers.*
> *And call off your wife.*
> *– RS*

Thorne nabbed an issue of *The Times* from the Brimstone's foyer and unfolded it. The top column made him grin: *SEYMOUR STEPS DOWN!* The article expressed bafflement at the MP's sudden plans to resign his post in the House of Commons and retire to America, of all places. What could have precipitated such a mystifying decision? The columnists speculated at business prospects and Seymour's health.

None could have guessed that it was one exceedingly clever woman.

Thorne found her in the sitting room, reading a book at

the bay window that overlooked the street. He paused to admire the way the sun glinted off her golden hair, framing her in a halo of light. Every day, he wanted to walk into a room and find her there – every damn day.

"I have a present for you," he said.

Alex glanced over at him, setting aside her book. Now her smile changed, and this one made his breath catch. This was an intimate look, just for him. "Yes?"

He opened the broadsheet and passed it to her.

"America?" She let out an amused noise. "God help them. Remind me after the little season to make sure he's paid his workers in Australia the compensation we've negotiated, or I'll send someone to threaten him."

"Send someone, or take a holiday with me?"

Alex looked delighted. "Are you saying you want to be my partner in intimidating very bad men?" The bubble of laughter in her voice was its own gift. He had missed it, in the years they were separated.

Thorne leaned down for a kiss. "I'll let you do the intimidating. I'm content to stand back and admire."

"Good answer."

"Come with me." He took Alex's hand and pulled her from the window seat. "I have something else for you."

She followed him into the hallway. "Does it come with more kisses?"

"Maybe." He damn well hoped so.

"Does it involve a bed?"

"No." He gave her a hot look as they came to her bedchamber door. "But it does have a tempting flat surface."

"That sounds very—" She stopped dead when she saw what was inside the room. "Nick," she whispered.

Thorne watched as she approached the desk she'd coveted at the exhibition. Her fingers skated across the surface in a light touch. He had a vision of her, sitting behind it in the years to come, writing away. He'd told her so many lies in Stratfield Saye; this, at least, was one promise he could keep.

"The maids asked if they ought to stack your papers, but I let them know your system made little sense to anyone except you." When she remained quiet, he cleared his throat. She'd seemed strange at the exhibition. Had she changed her mind about liking it? "If you'd like something else, I can—"

Alex lifted her head and met his gaze. "I love you." Thorne froze. It felt strange to hear those words after so long. Had he imagined them? But then she repeated the words: "I love you, Nick."

She strode forward, took his face in her hands, and kissed him hard. Thorne groaned and pulled her closer, wondering how he could be so fortunate. There had been a time when he thought he would never kiss her again, that he'd never hear her say those words. How lucky was he?

"Will you do something with me?" she whispered against his lips.

"Anything." He'd give her anything. Do anything.

Alex walked over to her bed, where she extricated a wooden box from the mountain of notes. She pressed the box into his hands and said, "I want to burn these. With you."

"What are they?" he asked, opening the lid.

"Notes," she said, after a beat of hesitation. "That I gathered about you during my research in the East End.

I had so many questions I was afraid to ask you because I feared being hurt again. And..." She bit her lip. "And your criticisms are in here, as well."

She had looked into him? Thorne's chest tightened at the sudden understanding that she had not been incurious about his past, after all. She had taken notes, in the way her brilliant mind always examined and processed information. She had examined *him*. She had – *wait*. "My what?"

The tender look she had given him turned to impatience. "The reviews, Nick."

What was she talking about? "Reviews? What reviews?"

"The..." She pulled back, scowling. "The reviews. *The. Reviews. Of my work.* You might as well have taken out a full-page advertisement in bold lettering that said, *STAY AWAY, ALEXANDRA*." She tore open the box, plucked a paper out, and slapped it down on the desk. She jabbed her finger at the name. "There. Nicholas Spencer. Unless there is another Nicholas Spencer who has a vested interest in criticising my work."

Nick stared at the articles with unease curdling inside him. Sure, he was a slow reader, but he comprehended well enough from a few short sentences why she had accused him at the exhibition of not liking her work. Why she had flinched at his compliments. While partially constructive, these reviews would have meant something different if she thought they had come from him. These were a commentary on the disparity of their stations. Yes, he did harbour fears about that, but nothing he would have said so publicly. They were his private concerns, things he had only ever confided to O'Sullivan.

"I didn't write these," he said softly.

She sighed and took the paper from him. "Please don't lie to me. I told you already—"

"Alex." His voice was firm. "I never wrote these."

Alexandra stared at him in disbelief. "But… who else would have? Writing these took time and knowledge of my work, as well as of political issues in the East End. Someone who knew about our marriage and the alias you adopted in Hampshire."

Thorne had kept that information strictly limited to his inner circle, to those who helped him take the East End from Whelan. His men needed to know where he got the money, and why he was so racked with guilt that even O'Sullivan had feared for his life—

That lady toff left you a mess after Hampshire. I helped you pick up the pieces last time, remember? Don't make me do it again.

"*Bloody hell*," Nick snarled, seizing the box from the desk. He threw open the door.

"Nick?" Alexandra followed him down the hallway. She put a hand on his arm to try to stop him, but he shook her off. "Nick, what is it?"

Thorne couldn't even get the words out. His anger made his blood run so hot that he saw red. He had told O'Sullivan everything, every fear about his marriage, about how he intended to make it up to her. *Every damn thing*. He barely remembered making it to one of the private gaming rooms. O'Sullivan was there, showing a new dealer how to make a performance out of shuffling the deck.

O'Sullivan looked up as Nick came into the room. He frowned. "What's happened?"

Thorne ignored him and said to the lad, "Get back to work and shut the door." His tone didn't leave any room for argument.

O'Sullivan set the cards on the table. "Problem?"

Thorne smashed his fist into O'Sullivan's face. O'Sullivan stumbled back, hitting the edge of the gaming table. The table rocked, and dice clattered to the floor.

O'Sullivan straightened, his eyes blazing. His jaw was already red from the hit, his lip bleeding and beginning to swell. Tomorrow he'd have a hell of a bruise, but that was less than he deserved. "What the *hell* was that for?"

"You know exactly what that was for," Thorne said, taking another threatening step forward.

"*Nick*." Alex's hand was on his arm. "Don't."

Fine. Thorne threw Alexandra's wooden box of papers into O'Sullivan's chest. The other man caught it. "What is this?"

"Open it," Thorne spat out.

With an exasperated noise, O'Sullivan opened the latch, looked inside, and froze. He shut his eyes. "Thorne." That was it – just the name.

Same as a damned confession.

"Tell me why you wrote those," Nick said, his voice dangerously low. His hands curled into fists. "And I'll consider not breaking your face."

"Nick." Alex's grip on his arm tightened. "It doesn't matter anymore."

"It matters to me. I want him to tell me why." When O'Sullivan didn't answer, Nick snapped, "*Why?*"

"*Because she was asking about you*," O'Sullivan said, wiping the blood from his mouth. "She did her research around Whitechapel and asked about you. And I knew it was only a matter of time before she came back into your life and messed you up again."

"Don't," Thorne said sharply. "Don't you dare pretend this is about her. This is about *you* not trusting aristos after what Sunderland did to you."

O'Sullivan's lips flattened. "This is about you getting a knife to the gut because your mind was on *her*."

"What's he talking about?" Alex asked Thorne softly.

After she'd left him at Roseburn, his obsession with taking power from Whelan consumed him. His enemy was an obstruction, an impediment to a better life. He would go to bed at night and agonise over every moment they spent together, every lie he ever told, until the regret gnawed at him.

But he'd had nothing to give her. What did he have? Money that was hers, power he'd stolen. Dozens of enemies trying to kill him.

So he'd eliminated them.

"You didn't tell her?" At Thorne's silence, O'Sullivan let out a dry laugh. "When he came back from Hampshire, it was as if Thorne was even the same person. He was so obsessed with finding some way of winning over your lofty bloody approval that he barely slept at night. Whelan wasn't the only one looking to grab power, and all it takes is one distraction. So yeah, when you came around asking about him and wrote about the East End, I responded. I wanted you to stay away. Because I didn't want to see you break him."

Alex's touch fell away. Some private grief crossed her expression, and he did not want to see that. Hadn't he hurt her enough?

"Get out," Nick told O'Sullivan quietly. "Grab your things, get out of my club. I'll give you an hour."

For a moment, he wondered if O'Sullivan would argue with him. But the other man gave a nod, set the wooden box of articles on the table, and left.

A heartbeat of silence filled the private game room. When Alex finally spoke, it was to say his name quietly.

"I have work to do," he said to her. "We'll talk later."

∾ 30 ∾

Hours later, Alexandra found Nick alone in a staff room playing a solitary game of billiards.

She watched as he aimed the cue and struck. The coloured balls at the end of the table separated with a *crack*. He lined up another shot, his movements smooth and practised. She wondered how many games he had played in the privacy of this room, with only his thoughts for company. Enough that every shot seemed to take no effort at all.

Alexandra closed the door and leaned against the frame. "So this is billiards," she said. "My brothers described it to me, but I've never seen it played."

Nick didn't look up. "A few officers from India told me about it. Thought it sounded fun, so I commissioned a table. I'll come up to bed in a few hours."

Did he believe he could dismiss her? She almost snorted at the absurdity. He knew her better than that. "I'm not one of your staff to be commanded, Nicholas. I want to know what happened after I left you at Roseburn."

Nick clenched his jaw. "Nothing to tell."

"Mr O'Sullivan seemed to think differently."

He set the cue down on the table with a force that made Alexandra wince. "O'Sullivan's inability to mind his own business is why I sacked him."

"He cares about you," she said, very softly.

"Let me ask you something." His voice was steel scraping over stone. "Did you avoid me because of those reviews? Would you have come to me during those four years if he had never written anything?" At her hesitation, he gave some humourless laugh. "And you want me to forgive him just like that?"

"I never spoke of forgiveness. I pointed out the truth." Nick didn't reply. He toyed with the cue, his fingers fiddling with the wood. "Tell me what happened after Stratfield Saye. You took the East End from Whelan, and then what?"

A sigh left him. "What does it matter?"

Alexandra put her hand on his back. "The scar right here" – she rubbed at his shirt, just over the mark – "I don't recall seeing it four years ago. And a few others." She ran her fingertips down the long line of his torso. She imagined each one, those long thin lines that were not there in Gretna. "What happened to you mattered to Mr O'Sullivan. And it matters to me."

Nick grasped the edge of the billiard table, the line of his shoulders tense. "Not everyone was eager to let me take Whelan's place," he told her. "They told me so at the end of a blade whenever I walked the streets." His face was as still and immovable as stone. "I was tired. The club bled money, and I had long hours until it was in the black. That took two years."

Alexandra didn't want to think of him being attacked while she enjoyed the comfort and safety of St James's. If one assailant had succeeded, she might have become a widow – and she would never have come to know the man she had married. All the years they spent apart seemed so pointless. Why hadn't he come to her?

"Mr O'Sullivan said you kept working to win over my opinion," she said. "Before, I might have wondered if he was wrong. That caring would have required some attempt to visit me and earn my regard. But in all those years, you never came to my door." She dropped her hand from his shoulder. "I want to know why."

"I was there," he said, very softly.

Alexandra froze, sure she had heard him wrong. "Say that again?"

"I showed up a hundred times on your doorstep. Rehearsed a hundred different apologies, a hundred different ways. At first, I left because I had nothing to offer you." He made some bitter noise. "I was a criminal from the streets dodging assassination attempts from men who wanted to challenge me for power, scraping by with my useless life because I had money I stole from you. In what world did I deserve you?" At her silence, he continued, "So I built the club and made it profitable. Reckoned even if I couldn't offer you respectability, then at least I could pay you back every shilling."

Every shilling...? She gaped at him. "That line about pounds, shillings, pence, and properties?"

The look he gave her was tender. "Truth. The club belongs to you. What isn't used to pay wages goes into an account in your name."

The revelation left her with some hollow feeling in her chest. How many times had he stood outside her brother's house, deciding how to word an apology? How many times had she'd been inside, sitting at her desk, torn between hating him and missing him? How many times had the butler come to tell her she had a visitor, and she foolishly wished it was her errant husband?

So many.

And it was never him.

Tears stung her eyes. "You could have told me that," she said. "Or any of the hundred apologies you rehearsed."

"Once I got to your doorstep, they all seemed inadequate."

Alexandra put a hand on his cheek, forcing him to look at her. "Let me hear one."

Nick slid to his knees. He stared up at her, and Alexandra's breath caught. "I'm sorry," he whispered. "And I know that isn't enough. It'll never be enough." He grasped her hand and pressed his lips to her palm. "But I am yours, and I love you. And if you let me, I'll prove it to you every damn day."

She let out a long, slow breath. "You were wrong," she said gently. "That was more than adequate." She smiled at him. "I will demand proof, however."

Nick nipped her fingertips. "Will you?"

"Oh, yes. I've gone without proof for" – Alex glanced at the clock – "approximately eight hours."

"Far too long," he agreed, rising to his feet. "I'll just have to take the rest of the night off and show you again, won't I?"

⌒ 31 ⌒

The open window framed Alex in pale light. Nick stroked her hair – still a mass of tangles from their lovemaking – and she murmured his name in her sleep. *Nick*, she said. *Nick, Nick, Nick*. And he knew, from her soft smile, that she dreamed of good things.

Behind her, the moon peeked through the tenements of the East End. He imagined the weary mothers tucking their children into bed, hoping for a few hours' rest before the factories opened at dawn. He heard the dim shouts and singing of the men and women at their local taverns, enjoying fried oysters and ale – joyful hours between backbreaking work at the docks. He imagined the children in the streets, relying on the kindness of strangers – not always successfully. Sometimes those strangers were looking for another person to break for money.

And one of them still lived.

His wife whispered his name again in her sleep. She would never be safe until he stood over Whelan's corpse. No one would. The weary mothers, the tavern crowds – some of them remembered when Whelan ruled these streets, when they owed protection money that might mean the difference between a full belly or a blade to the gut.

It was time Thorne put an end to it.

As he began pulling on clothes, he imagined them as a suit of armour before walking into his last battle. This time, only one of them would make it out alive.

Thorne picked his weapons, put on his jacket, and bent to kiss his wife. He never wanted to leave her side again. "I love you," he whispered, and he hoped it wasn't for the last time.

Thorne left the club and set off through the streets of Whitechapel. The winding alleyways were redolent with smoke, a hint of meat pie from a nearby tavern. The laughter from across the road did not fit his mood. He felt like a child again, making his way back to his master after a night of work. His pockets then had been laden with coins and pilfered jewellery, things that won no praises from Whelan. They only served to delay another beating.

His breathing quickened as he approached the old tenement where Whelan and his men once resided – where Thorne and O'Sullivan and the other lads had slept in the dark cellar. It was empty now – or it was supposed to be. If people on the streets sought refuge in his former place of torment, he wasn't going to stop them. He'd only bought the building in order to let it rot.

The housing block seemed to loom in the darkness. Nick's building was little different from those beside it, a patchwork of hastily repaired brick that gleamed from a recent downpour, with an arch over the door. Hard to believe this place had haunted his nightmares, that a mere tenement of stone could carve such a permanent corner in his mind. It had reduced him to circling this street for so long, terrified of what he'd find within those dark walls. Fearful of being trapped in the dark again.

Thorne finally understood: this place existed within him. He'd carried it for years, and no amount of distance would ever change that. He could let it rot, let it burn, watch it fall to ash, but he'd still remember every damned creak and rat-infested corner.

And he'd remember the man who put him there.

Thorne went up the steps and through the dark door.

⌒ 32 ⌒

Alexandra woke to an empty bed. The sheets beside her were rumpled but cold. Nick had been gone a while. His warmth had left the room. The noise below stairs indicated the club was still doing brisk business, and the first light of the sun had yet to breach the sky.

Had he changed his mind about taking the night off? Or was he at the billiard table, thinking again about his row with O'Sullivan? She didn't want him to be alone with such doubts.

Alexandra pulled on a wrapper and padded into the hall, where two men were stationed outside the bedchamber door. "Excuse me," she asked the nearest one, who she recognised as Doyle. "But can you tell me where I might find my husband?"

Doyle and the other man exchanged a look. The large man cleared his throat and said, "He's gone, milady."

Gone? "Where?" Another look passed between them, and Alexandra lost patience. "Spit it out."

Doyle swore quietly but answered her. "He wouldn't say, milady. Only that we was to guard the door, and if he didn't return by morning, to take you to O'Sullivan."

Some piercing dread went through her. *Nick, what have you done? Where did you go?* But she already knew the answer: he had gone after Patrick Whelan. And she did not know where, in the labyrinthine streets of the East End, the man was hiding.

But someone else might.

"Where is Mr O'Sullivan?" Her voice was hoarse. At Doyle's hesitation, Alexandra's lips tightened. "You will take me to him. *Now.*"

The journey to O'Sullivan's flat was a blur. Alexandra urged Doyle to hurry, focusing entirely on Nick: where he was, what might be happening. A herd of elephants could have run through Whitechapel, and she wouldn't have noticed.

When Doyle indicated which flat belonged to O'Sullivan, Alexandra threw open the door of the building and raced up the uneven stone steps to the second floor. The door was shut, with no light or noise from within. God, she hoped he was home.

Alexandra gave three firm, no-nonsense raps. "Mr O'Sullivan?"

A sleepy groan answered. Alexandra's heart flipped in relief. "Mr O'Sullivan, it's Alexandra. Please open the door; it's urgent."

Another groan, a foul curse, then some rustling. The door opened to reveal a scowling O'Sullivan, wearing only a pair of trousers and a loose lawn shirt. If the smell of spirits and a pair of bloodshot eyes was any indication, he was recovering from an evening of carousing. His gold hair stuck up in uneven tufts, which he smoothed down in irritation, knocking his spectacles askew. O'Sullivan looked like a disgruntled angel.

He pushed his spectacles up his nose with a sigh. "What?" Before she could get a word in, he looked past her and straightened, all concern now. "Don't tell me you walked through Whitechapel in the middle of the night by yourself."

"Doyle accompanied me." Alexandra didn't have time for this. "I need you to tell me where it was Whelan kept you and Nick. The cellar he spoke of. I only know it was in the Old Nichol."

O'Sullivan stiffened, and something haunted flickered over his face. But a moment later, it was gone. "Where is Thorne?" he asked her, very softly.

"He's missing," Alexandra said. "I think he's gone... to that place. If Whelan is tracking his movements, he'll follow."

O'Sullivan shut his eyes. "Damn. Two seconds." He backed into his room and emerged a moment later with a jacket on. Alexandra followed him down to the street, where Doyle was still waiting on the pavement. "Accompany her back to the club, Doyle," said O'Sullivan, "I've business in the Green."

Alexandra stopped him. "Absolutely not. I won't sit in the Brimstone while—"

"What do you think Thorne will do if something happens to you?" O'Sullivan shook his head. "No. I can't take you with me."

Alexandra gave him her steeliest look, the one she gave any ruffian who might be eyeing her pockets with interest. "Mr O'Sullivan." Her voice was firm. "I love him every bit as much as you do. Imagine how you would feel if I ordered *you* to return to the club and wait."

"Oof." Doyle clicked his tongue. "She's gotta good point there, boss."

O'Sullivan tilted his head back and let out a long breath. "Hell. That she does."

33

Going down into the cellar made Thorne feel like a child again.

The stench hit him first. It was the musty odour of old stones, water, and enclosed space. The second? He couldn't tell if it were real, or another waking nightmare: the piss and shit that emanated from one corner of the room, the sweat of a dozen bodies in a space that got tighter and tighter as they grew. They had all huddled in the darkness for warmth and protection from the rats.

But the rats came, perhaps attracted by the scent of a boy who perished from cold or hunger. They came, and their noises would pierce the black.

More memories erupted: the frigid winters; being kicked awake by a hard boot; broken bones and bloodied fingers when he didn't do a job right.

The tread of boots on the stone steps drew Thorne's attention.

Patrick Whelan stood silhouetted in the doorway, holding

a lantern in his hand. Another memory came fast: Thorne was twelve years old, waiting for this man to come down into the dark, hoping for another opportunity that would earn him scraps for a job well done.

God, he'd worked so damn hard for the pathetic bites of food he'd been given. So damn hard for any praise at all.

Now that Thorne's eyes had adjusted to the lantern light, he could see his former tormentor more clearly. Whelan had aged a great deal since Thorne stuck a knife in his gut on the new London Bridge and tossed him into the Thames. His face was heavily lined, and his hair had greyed all the way through. Whelan was once a mountain of a man – not as large as O'Sullivan, but formidable. Terrifying. Now he was as thin as an opium addict. But while his body had lost its musculature, his eyes were still as sharp and cunning as ever – cold, dead eyes. Devoid of warmth and emotion, for the man was capable of neither.

"I was wonderin' when you'd show up," Whelan said. "You learned a lot from me in these walls, Nicky-boy."

"I suppose I did," Thorne replied.

A strange calm settled over Thorne. Yes, he had learned a lot from this man. He had learned about survival. He learned how to lie awake at night and plan how he'd gain power. He remembered every shrewd skill necessary to take it, whether at the end of a blade or in the houses of Parliament. And now he was the master of the East End.

And every damned street in it.

"I reckon you owe me a debt for that," Whelan continued. "And for the money I lost when you pulled Seymour's contract. I promised my men a share of the blunt."

Thorne gave a small smile. "Is *that* what you think?

That I owe you money for the assassination contract on my wife?" He gave a sharp laugh. "How far you've fallen, to be beholden to other men."

Whelan straightened, his lips flattening. "Yeah, you got grand, haven't you, lad? I reckon you could use remindin' of where you come from."

"I know where I came from," Thorne said, very softly. "I've never let myself forget."

"That right?" Whelan's eyes glittered in the lantern light. "Seems to me you've forgotten. Almost got a toff's accent now. Wearin' those fancy clothes, playin' lord with your lady, you seem little different from a nob. You and I both know that you'll never be more than the lad I picked from the gutters, who'd whore himself out for a bite of bread and kill a man for a coin."

Some dim flicker of shame went through Thorne, chased away by his memories of Alex. Alex, kneeling beside the bath, asking him to go on that journey with her in the future. Alex, tracing his scars and hearing the story of each one. Alex, granting him forgiveness, a gift he had never allowed himself to hope for. She knew his darkest secrets, that life he had kept hidden from her in Stratfield Saye. Thorne understood now that truth held some power, for it was an offering: *Here is everything I have done, and everything I've learned. Will you take me as I am?*

And Alex had taken him, past and all.

"Never say you're jealous," Thorne said with a laugh.

"*Jealous?*" Whelan snarled, moving closer to Thorne. "Yeah, you've changed, Nicky-boy, if you think I'm jealous of a pretend nob. Your wife's softened you up, ain't she? You're thinkin' you're respectable now?"

"What does it matter?" Thorne suddenly felt impatient. "Seymour pulled the contract. She's nothing more to do with us."

"She's everything to do with us!" Whelan hissed. He lashed out with his fist, slamming it against Thorne's jaw. Thorne stepped back but showed nothing; no pain, no fear. He had grown used to Whelan's brutality years ago; it had left marks on him. Whelan grasped the front of Thorne's shirt. "You came back four years ago with enough blunt to ruin me and thought I wouldn't find out where you got it? You have my best men slaughtered and think I won't notice?"

Thorne licked the blood from his lip. "After what you did to O'Sullivan and me and the rest of the lads, it was fair play."

"I fed you, sheltered you—"

"Forced us to steal for you, murder for you, whore ourselves out, and sleep in this dark cell at night. Aye, fine father figure you are."

Whelan pulled a pistol out of his dirty coat and pointed it at Thorne. A sliver of fear went through Nick, but he tamped it down. This would end. Tonight, this would end.

"Don' care," Whelan hissed. "You owe me a debt, Nicky. And if you don' pay up, I'll collect it tonight. And tomorrow, I'll take the rest from your wife."

Thorne went cold, his entire focus on the gleaming barrel of the pistol as he edged a hand inside his jacket. "End it, then. Shoot me."

Whelan cocked the pistol and aimed.

34

A gunshot rang out through the streets of the Old Nichol. "Oh, no," Alexandra whispered, as she and O'Sullivan raced for the door of the tenement.

Her heart was in her throat, her thoughts replaying that awful sound and wondering what it meant – dreading what it meant. Beside her, O'Sullivan was gasping as they pushed their way into the old, empty tenement. He hurried through another opening and down a stone staircase.

Alexandra followed, terrified of what she'd find – and then sobbed with relief when she saw Nick. He held a bloody knife in a firm grip as he stood over a crumpled figure on the ground. The man who must have been Whelan had a pistol in his limp hand.

The sight of it sent a jolt through Alexandra. How close had she been to losing Nick? If he had been less handy with a blade... if he had been a bit slower, a bit more tired...

She could barely fathom losing him.

Nick turned to her and O'Sullivan with a displeased look.

"O'Sullivan, what the hell are you doing here? I thought I told you—"

"Oh, do shut up, Nick," Alexandra said and grasped his shirt to haul him in for a kiss.

With a soft groan, Nick slid his arms around Alexandra's waist. Only then did she notice that he trembled, that his calm demeanour was a façade. His hands grasped at her hips, fingertips digging into the fabric of her dress. Yes, perhaps he had sensed how close he'd come to losing tonight. She returned his desperate touch with her own. It gave her reassurance: he was warm. The solid pressure of his hands on her back was real. His lips were on hers. This was no dream.

He was alive. *He was alive.*

A throat cleared beside them. With a soft noise, Nick pulled back to scowl at O'Sullivan. "You brought her. Here."

O'Sullivan rolled his eyes. "You know your wife, yes? As if I could stop her."

"In fact" – Alexandra smiled brilliantly – "you could say *I* brought *Mr O'Sullivan.*"

Nick sighed. "Of course you did."

O'Sullivan kneeled next to Patrick Whelan's body, his eyes sharp as he absorbed the sight of the dead man's features. Some unreadable expression crossed his face. "I wish I'd been here to see it," he murmured.

Nick released Alex to clasp O'Sullivan's shoulder. The two remained side by side, staring at their tormentor in the place they had grown up in so long ago. Alexandra could never truly comprehend what they had experienced in the cellar, all those years before. All she could do was be there for Nick when the nightmares came again – and she knew they would. They always would.

"I'm sorry," Nick said to O'Sullivan.

"Don't be," O'Sullivan said, rising to his feet. "I've two bullets in a pistol I'm saving. Neither of them is for Whelan." Then, very softly, "I'm sorry for trying to keep her from you."

"Don't do it again."

"I won't." O'Sullivan gave a small smile. "Men like us don't often get second chances with women like that. I'm glad you punched me in the face for it." With that, he started up the stairs. "Night, boss. Lady Alexandra."

When they were alone, Alexandra studied the dark cellar. This had been where he'd slept once, where he'd lived. Where he'd survived. In the dim light of the lantern, she could see the haunted look in his eyes. No, killing his old tormentor would not heal the scars beneath his skin. She knew that. They would always be part of the man she loved.

"Are you all right?" she whispered.

"No." He grasped her hand and pressed his lips to her palm. "But I think I will be."

"Good." She threaded her fingers through his. "Then come home with me, and I'll give you better memories that take place in the dark."

EPILOGUE

ANCONA, ITALY

Two months later

"Nick. Wake up, or you'll miss it." Alex pressed her lips to his cheek. "It's moonrise."

Thorne eased his eyes open to find his wife leaning over him with a soft smile on her face. Behind her, the sky was the deep blue of twilight, but the air was still as warm as daytime. Hours ago, they had walked the cliffs near Ancona's port and come to a halt in a spot that overlooked the Adriatic Sea. They had polished off a bottle of Italian wine, and when his wife kissed him, her lips were as sweet as the *moscato blanco*.

How had he ended up here? As he stared up at his wife, he marvelled at how his life had shifted. Thorne never had the opportunity to relax, to share the burden of his responsibilities. After killing Whelan, he'd wanted to give Alex that future she'd longed for, the ship that took them to distant places.

After all, they'd never had a honeymoon.

O'Sullivan had taken over duties at the club in Thorne's

absence. The business appeared to be running smoothly; the factotum had even hired a proper bookkeeper. It was strange to wake up without the weight of his obligations. To see this woman every day and wonder at the gift she had given him: a lifetime with her.

Her expression softened. "What are you thinking?"

Thorne smiled and shook his head. "Just admiring you."

She had lines in the corners of her eyes from laughing. Thorne traced them with his fingertips, amazed that he would get to watch them deepen with time. That, though they had spent years apart, they would spend years more together.

"Admire me in a moment." Alex pulled away and gestured at the seascape. "Look. It's just as beautiful as the guidebook's description."

Thorne sat up and stared at the sight with her. The full moon rose over the sea, its light spilling across the calm water below. The palate of colours was an artist's dream: gold and blue, purple and orange, each colour set in a vibrant gradient of shades he did not know the names of. The waves sighed against the rocks, filling the night with the breathing rhythm of the sea.

Alex sighed and rested her head against his shoulder. "'I do not remember ever being so enchanted by any view as that now presented to us,'" she recited from the passage she had memorised in the guidebook, in a voice that was as calm and beautiful as the tide. "'I know not whether daylight would rob it of any portion of its beauty and soothing influence; I can only speak of it as it impressed me then – so calm, so pure, so still.'"

"Perhaps you'll write a memoir of our travels," Thorne

said. "*An Englishwoman's Adventures at Sea, with an Irish Husband and a Writing Desk in Tow.*"

He had never seen the sea before they set off in the steamer weeks ago. Had never travelled beyond the sprawl of London before he met her. Three weeks ago, they had been in Paris. A week ago, in Cadiz. Within the next fortnight, they would find their way to Venice, and wherever she wanted, after that. He had purchased a portable writing desk for her, that neatly folded into a trunk. The trunk itself had hidden compartments.

After all, his wife still needed a place for pens, ink, sweets, and secrets.

Alex laughed. "A memoir of our travels would cause moral outrage. Two parts travel, one part erotic tale."

"One part? You issuing a challenge?"

Her smile turned wicked. "Maybe."

"Good," he said, leaning forward to kiss her. "Because it ought to be at least two parts erotic."

Later, as they lay naked on the blanket, Alexandra dropped a kiss on Nick's shoulder. His skin was warm, and he tasted of salt from the sea. His soft moan gratified her, for she had spent these last few weeks learning him. Memorising the texture of his skin beneath her lips, the sounds he made when she touched him. These were lessons she hoped to carry through the years of their marriage, when they had settled into their lives. When they fitted beside each other like two stones that had scraped together long enough to sand their rough edges.

"After Venice," she said quietly, "I want to return to

Stratfield Saye. Anne wrote that she and Richard will be staying at Roseburn with James and Emma until their babies are born."

Nick's fingertips brushed her neck. "All right."

Alexandra lifted her head so she could stare down at him. His black gaze glittered in the darkness, full of stars so like the sky above them. "Will you come with me?"

"Leave the club in the extended care of O'Sullivan?" He made a face, then gave a long sigh. "I'll come."

"Good, because there's something I've been thinking..."

"Oh ho!" Nick grinned. "My wife's been thinking. Dangerous words, those. Very well, let's hear it."

Alexandra grazed his cheek with her fingertips, her expression suddenly serious. "Marry me."

Nick gave a little frown, his smile fading. "If you're wondering whether our marriage lines are legitimate—"

"I know they're legitimate. Years ago, I visited the parish in Gretna. I saw the register. This would not be a legal ceremony. I want to say the vows to you in front of my family and a priest. I want to repeat them knowing everything that you are and that I love you beyond measure. I want to marry *you*, Nicholas Thorne. Will you say the vows with me?"

Nick rolled her beneath him, his lips coming together with hers in a fierce kiss. He tasted like the sweet wine from earlier, and he smelled like the ocean. As he gathered her against him, he whispered, "I love you."

"Is that a yes?"

"Yes. God, yes."

Laughing, she kissed him again and kept him in her embrace until the sun came up over the sea.

AUTHOR'S NOTE

The guidebook that Alexandra recites to Thorne is from The Englishwoman in Italy by Mrs G. Gretton.

An assortment of different sources helped my descriptions of the East End, but those of the Old Nichol in Bethnal Green were significantly aided by Sarah Wise's *The Blackest Streets: The Life and Death of a Victorian Slum.*

During my research for this book, I learned quite a bit about opals and opal mining. There were a few decades in the early 1800s when opals were considered bad luck. However, Queen Victoria loved opals and helped bring them back into fashion among the wealthy. It certainly helped that massive opal deposits had been discovered in Australia during her reign.

I would be remiss if I did not mention the human cost of the British Empire's colonialism. Under a persistent British military presence, Australia had a corrupt government and was subject to unfair taxes (particularly the miners).

Their labour was exploited by a rich ruling class, and white colonists grotesquely treated indigenous Australians.

Though I dramatised the smuggling of opals for this book, the labour involved in opal mining did not require much in the way of fictionalisation. It was – and still is – a dangerous profession that requires climbing down a ladder into a narrow hole that goes fifteen metres into the earth. Many of these mines are located in the Outback, which is very hot and isolated. One of the ways people survive is by living in below-ground residences due to the extreme temperatures.

If this is a subject that interests you, I recommend *A History of South Australian Opal, 1840–2005* by Len Cram.

All my best,
Katrina

ACKNOWLEDGEMENTS

As always, thank you to my husband, who always gets me through every manuscript, and to my dearest friend Tess Sharpe for tolerating my messages at all hours.

I am immensely grateful to my agent Danny Baror for being such a champion of this series. And my editor, Rosie de Courcy, whose notes are always a delight to read and whose emails are the best part of my day. The rest of the team at Head of Zeus/Bloomsbury, including Bianca Gillam, Charlotte Hayes-Clemens, and everyone I haven't met but who work tirelessly behind the scenes – thank you all so much.

Also, the girls in the Trifecta, who all had a good laugh when I told them how long it took me to write the few lines of Alexandra's Ode To Nick's Arse (the answer is embarrassing) – I may be a writer, but I am not a poet!

And to my readers – I couldn't have written this without your tremendous support and love.

ABOUT THE AUTHOR

KATRINA KENDRICK is the romance pen name for *Sunday Times* bestselling science fiction and fantasy author Elizabeth May. She is Californian by birth and Scottish by choice, and holds a Ph.D. from the University of St Andrews. She currently resides on an eighteenth-century farm in the Scottish countryside with her husband, three cats, and a lively hive of honey bees that live in the wall of her old farmhouse.

www.katrinakendrick.com